FOREWORD

In the Fall of 1966 I went to the University of Wisconsin, only to find that Columbia had accepted me off its waiting list. I had then to choose between the schools. My impression at the time was that the choice would affect things far beyond my comprehension, that I could not really know what the choosing meant.

Two Springs later I sat-in in a Columbia building, with no object in mind but to end the war and stop the university's expansion. But then a friend on *The Harvard Crimson* asked me to write up the Rebellion for them, and I did; and *New York Magazine* saw my story and bought it; and Random House saw it in *New York*, and asked me to write a book; and I was a writer and appeared on television, and a girl saw me on television and called me up, wanted to meet me, and now we are married. And things go on.

Is it any wonder I love to hitchhike, to stand on the macadam waiting list and see who has been wending the way toward me many years to let me in and take me and leave me somewhere with his memory? And all the time the roads are already there, waiting.

I get the idea, sometimes strongly, sometimes not, that I am involved in purposes not strictly my own. I understand that a lot of other people feel the same way, and since some of them are writers, there is a movement in literature which expresses this idea. And things go on.

JAMES S. KUNEN
*by phone from
New York City,
May Day, 1971*

OTHER DELL PUBLICATIONS
OF CONTEMPORARY FICTION

inn●vative fictio↵

STORIES
FOR THE
SEVENTIES

EDITED AND WITH AN INTRODUCTION BY

JEROME KLINKOWITZ

AND

JOHN SOMER

A LAUREL ORIGINAL

Published by
Dell Publishing Co., Inc.
750 Third Avenue
New York, New York 10017

ACKNOWLEDGMENTS

"Autobiography" by JOHN BARTH: From *Lost in the Funhouse* by John Barth, copyright © 1968 by John Barth. Reprinted by permission of Doubleday & Company, Inc.

"Porcupines at the University" by DONALD BARTHELME: Reprinted by permission of Donald Barthelme c/o International Famous Agency. Copyright © 1970 The New Yorker Magazine, Inc.

"Robert Kennedy Saved from Drowning" by DONALD BARTHELME: Reprinted with the permission of Farrar, Straus & Giroux, Inc. from *Unspeakable Practices, Unnatural Acts* by Donald Barthelme, copyright © 1968 by Donald Barthelme.

"Views of My Father Weeping" by DONALD BARTHELME: Reprinted with the permission of Farrar, Straus & Giroux, Inc. from *City Life* by Donald Barthelme, copyright © 1969, 1970 by Donald Barthelme.

"Prologue to Grider Creek," "Sea, Sea Rider," "The Shipping of Trout Fishing in America Shorty to Nelson Algren," and "The Cleveland Wrecking Yard" by RICHARD BRAUTIGAN: From *Trout Fishing in America* by Richard Brautigan. Copyright © 1967 by Richard Brautigan. A Seymour Lawrence book/Delacorte Press. Reprinted by permission of the publisher.

"The Babysitter" by ROBERT COOVER: From the book *Pricksongs & Descants* by Robert Coover. Copyright © 1969 by Robert Coover. Published by E. P. Dutton & Co., Inc., and reprinted with their permission.

"Mr. Blue" by ROBERT CREELEY: "Mr. Blue" is reprinted by permission of Charles Scribner's Sons from *The*

and Other Stories by Ronald Sukenick. Reprinted by permission of the publisher, The Dial Press.

"The Hyannis Port Story" by KURT VONNEGUT, JR.: Copyright © 1968 by Kurt Vonnegut, Jr. From *Welcome to the Monkey House* by Kurt Vonnegut, Jr. A Seymour Lawrence book/Delacorte Press. Reprinted by permission of the publisher.

Laurel ® TM 674623, Dell Publishing Co., Inc.

ISBN: 0-440-34011-X

Printed in the United States of America
First printing—August 1972
Second printing—July 1973
Third printing—August 1975
Fourth printing—July 1977

I listened to the Phantom by Ontario's shore,
I heard the voice arising demanding bards,
By them all native and grand, by them alone
    can these States be fused into the compact
    organism of a Nation.

To hold men together by paper and seal or by
    compulsion is no account,
That only holds men together which aggregates
    all in a living principle, as the hold of the
    limbs of the body or the fibres of plants.

Of all races and eras these States with veins
    full of poetical stuff most need poets, and
    are to have the greatest, and use them the
    greatest,
Their Presidents shall not be their common
    referee so much as their poets shall.

WALT WHITMAN—"By Blue Ontario's Shore"

We can't put it together.
It is together.
        The Whole Earth Catalogue

CONTENTS

PREFACE

Henry James had no more than dignified fiction as an art before it entered its most vigorous period of growth. Its most daring innovators in the novel, Zola, Proust, Conrad, Joyce, Faulkner, accelerated beyond their public, and it is only now, more than a half-century later, that we finally appreciate their accomplishments. Still the innovators forge ahead into new realms of thought and form, spurred on by post-Einsteinian physics, new respect for primitive sensibilities, and the floundering of a decadent social structure groping for new forms. This time, however, the innovators are attacking the short story, long a stable genre, and have startled its traditional readers.

Because readers are confounded by the new, offended by the abstruse, and frightened by the unfamiliar, they need time, or a perspective from which to view innovations, to absorb and appreciate them. When fiction first began its rapid growth, critics could only wait and see, depend on time to help them evaluate the proliferation of new techniques. But with hindsight, we can see that time is not the only measuring stick. An open mind and in-depth exposure to the unfamiliar robs it of its strangeness and reveals its underlying order. *Innovative Fiction* does not pretend to provide the reader with an open mind (although it may contribute to it), but it can provide a systematic and orderly immersion into the startling world of the contemporary short story. It can take the reader by the hand and guide him from the more conventional innovations, through the tortuous paths of straining imaginations into the vibrant center of the intuition, and awaken him there to the literary tensions of his own age.

Innovative Fiction: Stories for the Seventies represents the range of the new short story by including sixteen of its most respected innovators. Its twenty-three stories represent the finest work by these writers, some of them in depth. Also, we have arranged the stories so that their readers are initiated rather than alienated. Our selection serves two purposes: first, by moving from the familiar to the unfamiliar, we create a sense of orderly immersion into new and strange forms; second, we chose familiar stories that articulate, as well as respond to, modern problems, so the technical innovations in the unfamiliar stories are justified and explained before a reader experiences them.

We wish to thank Elaine Klinkowitz and Connie Somer, all of the authors, editors, and agents who cooperated in granting permissions, and especially Richard Huett of Dell Publishing Co., without whom this book would not have been possible; we also express our gratitude to Marco Polo, Galileo Galilei, Bertrand Russell, and Albert Einstein, without whom this book would not have been necessary.

J. K.
J. S.

innovative fiction

INNOVATIVE SHORT FICTION:
"VILE AND IMAGINATIVE THINGS"

Fiction constitutes a way of looking at the world. Therefore I will begin by considering how the world looks in what I think we may now begin to call the contemporary post-realistic novel. Realistic fiction presupposed chronological time as the medium of a plotted narrative, an irreducible individual psyche as the subject of its characterization, and, above all, the ultimate, concrete reality of things as the object and rationale of its description. In the world of post realism, however, all of these absolutes have become absolutely problematic.

The contemporary writer—the writer who is acutely in touch with the life of which he is part—is forced to start from scratch: Reality doesn't exist, time doesn't exist, personality doesn't exist. God was the omniscient author, but he died; now no one knows the plot, and since our reality lacks the sanction of a creator, there's no guarantee as to the authenticity of the received version. Time is reduced to presence, the content of a series of discontinuous moments. Time is no longer purposive, and so there is no destiny, only chance. Reality is, simply, our experience, and objectivity is, of course, an illusion. Personality, after passing through a phase of awkward self-consciousness, has become, quite minimally, a mere locus for our experience. In view of these annihilations, it should be no surprise that literature, also, does not exist—how could it? There is only reading and writing, which are things we do, like eating and making love, to pass the time, ways of maintaining a considered boredom in face of the abyss.

Not to mention a series of overwhelming social dislocations.

What you have just read is a statement of the problem the modern writer faces, but it is also the opening to Ronald Sukenick's novella *The Death of the Novel*,[1] and thus what is a philosophical statement of the problem is conversely a technical reaction to it. Sukenick has written, and we are reading. But are we reading "Literature"? According to the introduction of *The Death of the Novel*, no. It claims literature does not exist in the contemporary world because the reality of our world does not exist. Therefore fiction or literature, which "constitutes a way of looking at the world," cannot exist because there is no world to look at. And yet he writes, and we read, page after page. Why? He says there is no reality, no time, no personality, no God, and even, heaven forbid, no plot. And yet there is something compelling in the way he writes that forces us to read. Is this compulsion "like eating and making love," merely a way "to pass the time," a way "of maintaining a considered boredom in the face of the abyss? If it is, it is therefore essential to life. If existence has truly slipped out of artistic reach, literature will of course have to be something more than a way of "looking at the world." In uncertain times, perhaps literature can perform a more primal act. Perhaps it can create a world with a built-in perspective. It can, if literature were in its purest form an epistemological act. This sounds like an innovative idea, and it would be in any society other than those primitive ones that are constantly in the act of creating their world day by day. But to contemporary man, creation must be the very essence of literature, like eating and making love, if literary art is to be of use.

Ours is an exciting time because we share with primitive man the notion that unless we do something, life as a meaningful experience will die. In stories by Ronald Sukenick and other new short fictionists, this writing and reading of it is one of the things we do, not to ward off boredom,

but death itself, one of the things we do to create tomorrow
so we may step into the future with confidence that it will
be there. As Sukenick has indicated, radical changes have
swept away our comfortable understanding of life, and left
us with an existence sometimes chaotic, most times insipid-
ly unimaginative and dull. But reading and writing, as epistemological act, is essential to man because it restores his
dignity, places him at the center from which all reality issues, and makes it possible and necessary for him once
again, like primitive man, to experience a rite of initiation.
Such a possibility could not have arrived at a more urgent
time, when annihilation, by nuclear fission or eroded ecology, may be just around the corner. We must undergo some
initiation, mature some way quickly, or the promise of
creatio continue will be lost.

Unfortunately, however, we differ from primitive man in
one important way. His initiation rite was an integral, organic part of his epistemological relationship with his
world, because his world was defined by what he could see
with his eyes. His world was small, encircled by the horizon. If he was a hunter, he immersed himself in the animal
world, created totems, found his identity and origins in this
world, lost his ego, his self-centeredness there, and finally
experienced an initiation into a mature relationship with his
world. The same was true for the plant gatherer and the
star gazer. But contemporary man with his optical instruments lives in a world microscopically small and telescop-
ically huge. He is consciously aware of a world so vast that
his intuition cannot absorb it, a world so intangible that he
is afraid to immerse himself in it. Primitive man lived in a
three-dimensional world; contemporary man lives poised
on a fourth-dimensional world and is unable to enter it.

Our rapidly shrinking world needs an apocalyptical initiation to unite it. The old myths were limited by both their
inclusiveness and their exclusiveness. They harmonized
what they encompassed, but at the expense of what they
excluded. Today our horizons extend around the Earth,
through it, and on into Einstein's time-space continuum. If
our historical circumstances were not so desperate, perhaps
we could live for a century in the unsettling state of uncer-
tainty while our intellects continue their frightening explo-
rations of the intangible and feed our ravenous intuitions

the information they need to solve the problem while we sleep. Possibly, when our intuitions have absorbed the vastness of the universe, they will allay the fears of our intellects, and we may slowly immerse ourselves into the fourth dimension and experience there the ultimate initiation. In that moment the entire Earth would be as one tribe. Reality, time, personality, God, and even plot would be revitalized and harmony would reign. Of course, we have no assurance that such a miracle will ever occur, no assurance that man is even capable of boldly and consciously stepping into the fourth dimension, even after centuries of evolution.

Such a cosmic initiation seems clear enough when illustrated by simple metaphors. According to Einstein, gravity and inertia on the cosmic scale balance one another so that bodies in space do not pull and tug, but fall through space in a balanced relationship.[2] For man to enter the fourth dimension he would have to learn literally to fall through space free of the Earth's tug in a harmonious relationship to it. This physical initiation may be impossible to achieve for two reasons. In the first place, such small creatures as human beings would either have to grow to enormous size in order to generate enough inertia to offset the pull of Earth's gravity, or they would have to position themselves far enough away from the Earth to exist in harmony with it. Secondly and more fundamentally, man has been conditioned through a million years of evolution and experience to accept gravity as a normal state. It is therefore unlikely that a few centuries could undo such extensive conditioning and eliminate man's one sure instinct—his fear of falling. Consequently, it seems impossible both physically and emotionally for man to experience a cosmic initiation, the initiation that is inherent in the world vision man rationally has defined for himself. But it is equally impossible for man to live in our world where there is no rite of initiation without destroying himself. In these circumstances the old comfortable notion of time is our enemy, not our friend.

Thus our literature may be even more important to us than eating and lovemaking. Through the epistemological act of reading and writing, we create a world that our intuition can comprehend. We do not have to listen to Einstein. In fact, we do not have the time to listen to him, to try to accommodate ourselves to his vision of reality. We must forge a vision that we Earth-bound creatures can comprehend and surrender to, a vision that we can immerse ourselves in, a vision that will absorb our greed, hate, and fear of one another, a vision that will disarm us. What is a rite of initiation if not the absorption, the annihilation of the ego in a vision of the world that the ego has created? That is really what all our reading and writing is about. These acts are experiments in creating a world that will allow all men to serve one another. The novel has long been busy with this problem. Zola, James, Proust, Joyce, Faulkner, worked at it. Now in France Robbe-Grillet is writing and reading, creating a phenomenological world that can absorb man. In the United States, Kurt Vonnegut, Jr. has created a vision which shows man how to live with his schizophrenic nature. Poetry also has been concerned with this issue. The innovative work of Yeats, Eliot, Cummings, and Stevens testifies to that. The short story, however, has until recently ignored the problem. Yet within the last decade it has not only confronted man's greatest challenge by undergoing the corresponding shift in emphasis and technique, but, as a genre, has moved to the fore of the avant-garde. Because the short story was a conventional form for so long, readers have been doubly dismayed by such radical innovation in a genre they thought was stable. The battle, fought first between the "novel of selection" and the "novel of saturation" and then between the innovative poetry of symbolism and the lingering, reactionary lyrics of the Georgians in England or the sentimental idealists in America, has now moved into the realm of the story. Our most impressive new fictionists—Donald Barthelme, Robert Coover, LeRoi Jones, Jorge Luis Borges—are preeminently writers of short stories. Bizarrely experimental pieces by Barthelme, Borges, and W. S. Merwin outnumber the conventional "New Yorker" stories of such writers as O'Hara, Updike, and Cheever, even in the pages of *The New Yorker* itself. The principles of "selection" developed in the dialogue between Henry James and H. G. Wells and apparently fully tested in such American novels as *The Great Gatsby* and *The Sound and the Fury* have in recent stories been pushed to radically new limits of epistemology. Beckett left his characters waiting for Godot; the new story

writers, responding to the altered structures of experience,
leave their readers, in terms of Faulkner's novel, quite literally waiting for Dilsey. Conflicts are not conventionally re-
solved, nor are expectations conventionally satisfied, and
few of their pictures are at the end so pleasingly unpuzzled
as readers of conventional stories have come to expect.

The explanation for this recent obsession with new forms
may be sought on different levels. The world has radically
changed, and the artistic ethos must be expected to change
with it. But more simply (and perhaps, for the artist, more
authentically), readers and writers have become bored with
the old conventions. After the violent, wrenching alienation
following the World Wars, the new writers found that life
had settled down into something banal, insipid, and dull.
Donald Barthelme is the most vehement: " 'The per-capita
production of trash in this country is up from 2.75 pounds
per day in 1920 to 4.5 pounds per day in 1965 . . . and . . .
may very well soon reach a point where it's 100 percent.' "[3] His solution as a writer is to place himself " 'on
the leading edge . . . of the trash phenomenon,' "[4] paying
particular attention to language when it might be "fill,"
"blanketing," or *"dreck,"* and then somehow recycling or
reviving it for human use. Ronald Sukenick again states the
problem in a more scholarly fashion, this time in his study
of Wallace Stevens: "Adequate adjustment to the present
can only be achieved through ever fresh perception of it,
and this is the effort of [Stevens'] poetry."[5] Fresh perception is the stuff of Sukenick's and especially Barthelme's
stories. The latter revitalizes tired forms by toying with
imaginative content: the insipid talk of engineers is re-
charged when Barthelme shows them boasting, " 'We have
rots, blights, and rusts capable of attacking [the enemy's]
alphabet.' "[6] and further developing " 'realtime online
computer-controlled wish evaporation' "[7] in order to meet
" 'the rising expectations of the world's peoples, which are
as you know rising entirely too fast.' "[8] He seizes the
phraseological structures of such technocrats and deftly in-
serts his own absurdity, and suddenly the form itself is
more interesting. Watching the Ed Sullivan Show, his nar-
rator becomes bored with an Ed Ames song which is "submemorable." He quickly substitutes, as the medium itself
might, "Something memorable: early on Sunday morning a

pornographic exhibition appeared mysteriously for eight minutes on television station KPLM, Palm Springs, California. A naked man and woman did vile and imaginative things to each other for that length of time, then disappeared into the history of electricity. Unfortunately, the exhibition wasn't on a network. What we really want in this world, we can't have."[8]

Barthelme, through the imagination, recovers specific experiences for the life of art, and hence for the life of man. Richard Brautigan's aim is more cosmic, rescuing the entire world from banality. Critic John Clayton has termed Brautigan's method "the politics of imagination"[9]; every page speaks in images, such as dust looking "like the light from a Coleman lantern," or the smell of Lysol in a hotel lobby sitting "like another guest on the stuffed furniture, reading a copy of the *Chronicle*, the Sports Section." Perception, for Brautigan, is a constant act of comparison. A ukulele seems "pulled like a plow through the intestine"; more lyrically, "The water bugs were so small I practically had to lay my vision like a drowned orange on the mud puddle." His very title, *Trout Fishing in America*, is pushed to imaginative limits: it takes shape as a life experience, a hotel, or a paraplegic wino crated and shipped to Nelson Algren in Chicago. The trout stream is finally sold in foot lengths at the Cleveland Wrecking Yard. Clayton observes, "The view I'm offered at the Cleveland Wrecking Yard's window is one of bitterness and deadening brick. But Brautigan lets me out of dealing directly with that desperate reality (and I want to be let out); he snatches me up inside his *process of imagination*—the magazines eroding like the Grand Canyon, the magical perception of the patients' complaints. I am given imaginative magic as a liberation from decay."[10] Dull, insipid reality is revitalized. As Sukenick suggests, "This vivid sense of reality is produced by the imagination and captured in some metaphor or description."[11] Such is the motive for metaphor, and the making of it can be a story's entire substance. In Robert Coover's "The Elevator" his hero constructs an elaborate fantasy of plunging to his death; however, at the last minute he neatly steps out of his imaginative structure, allowing it to move on without him (and the elevator car to plunge down the shaft empty).[12] LeRoi Jones constructs "A Chase (Alighieri's Dream)" with multiple images: running through ghetto streets, engaging in a sexual encounter, scoring a touchdown after a broken field run.[13] But the reader is not invited to see sex and football as metaphors for the chase, nor vice versa. Instead, Jones offers one suprarational, poetic kaleidoscope, with no tenor to the metaphor at all. It is all vehicle.

Viewing such imaginative structures, the critic might suppose that the short fictionists have simply caught up with their counterparts of up to a century before, who borrowed the lyrical and imaginative properties of poetry to write what Ralph Freedman has termed "the lyrical novel." Some of the most impressive writers of the new story—Robert Creeley, LeRoi Jones, Richard Brautigan, W. S. Merwin—are also poets of the first rank, and Ronald Sukenick, whose novel *Up* and collection of stories are among the most experimentally dense in the genre, began his career as an academic critic of Wordsworth, Stevens, and the French Symbolists. The lyrical novel, however, is predominantly an ideal form, substituting the subjective for the objective and reducing the world, as Freedman says, "to a *lyrical point of view,* the equivalent of the poet's 'I': the lyrical self."[14] The new story, however, is not so prone to subjective perceptions. Sukenick reminds us that Stevens' intention was not to change reality but to have a "favorable rapport"—or simply how to live with it.[15] "The Mind orders reality," he goes on to say, "not by imposing ideas on it but by discovering significant relations with it,"[16] We know that Wordsworth, making accommodations to a time wracked by revolution, did not, after all, materially change the English landscape. Sukenick describes the function of innovation: "When, through the imagination, the ego manages to reconcile reality with its own needs, the formerly insipid landscape is infused with the ego's emotion [.] and reality, since it now seems intensely relevant to the ego, suddenly seems more real."[17]

As we said before, the world, both of ideas and of facts, has changed so radically that man needs a new initiation. The new story forms, bizarrely experimental and outspokenly hostile to previous conventions, are the artistic expression of this rite. Critics have unintentionally discounted the new stories' validity by habitually describing them in negative terms. Seen as "anti-stories," exercises as if in parody against the traditional elements of plot, subject, development, and meaning, the fiction of such writers as Barthelme and Coover hardly seems a positive expression in man's continuing relationship with the world. But the new story exists in its own right, and, far from being simply a satiric echo of earlier forms, it speaks for a new order of existence—and a necessarily new perception of that existence. Young artists have in the last decade done other things besides write stories: most notably, they have explored new life styles, adopted different cultural values, and experimented with such perception-altering drugs as peyote, mescaline, and LSD. The "acid test" becomes the initiation into this new world, and Tom Wolfe, studying Ken Kesey and his followers, describes its function: "In ordinary perception, the senses send an overwhelming flood of information to the brain, which the brain then filters down in a trickle it can manage for the purpose of survival in a highly competitive world. Man has become so rational, so utilitarian that the trickle became most pale and thin. It is efficient for mere survival, but it screens out the most wondrous part of man's potential experience without his even knowing it. *We're shut off from our own world.*"[18] Rational man can no longer handle impulses from an increasingly irrational world. To try to do so, as William Barrett has shown, makes him hopelessly alienated from his very life.[19] The new story writers argue further that if man so estranges himself, he imaginatively dies. When new experiences resist conventional forms, man can either go with the experience or cling to the more comfortable although irrelevant notions of time and space. Robert Creeley argues for the former:

> The story has no time finally. Or it hasn't here. Its shape, if form can so be thought of, is a sphere, an egg of obdurate kind. The only possible reason for its existence is that it has, in itself, the fact of reality and the pressure. There, in short, is its form—no matter how random and broken that will seem. The old assumptions of beginning and end—those very neat assertions—have fallen away completely in a place

> where the only actuality is life, the only end (never
> realized) death, and the only value, what love one can
> manage.[20]

The world is new, and its experiences must be known by
a new epistemology. Story writers experiment with new
systems, coming to know the irrational or relativistic
through something other than the older rational forms.
Bernard Malamud, a mainstream writer of traditional
Jewish-American stories, can revitalize the tired situation of
a shabby and smelly Jewish grandfather living-in with his
children by casting him as a talking bird, "The Jewbird."[21]
In the process we learn things about life that we might have
missed in the old forms. Robert Coover takes a simple,
middle-class suburban story of a babysitter and writes it in
the form of television-channel-switching: fragments come
at us from all directions, defying plot or progress, but the
development offered is more insightful to the psychic nature of the experience[22] (many of John Hawkes' stories use
similar techniques). As Conrad Knickerbocker has noted
of Hughes Rudd's story "Miss Euayla is the Sweetest
Thang!,"[23] "Rudd demonstrates how ordinary aspirations
have transcended the absurd to reach, at last, the purely
stupid. Lafond T. Cunningham, the hero, is a would-be
Texas radio personality who describes himself as no taller
than a shotgun, just as Truman Capote once did. In a few
pages, Lafond stumbles through the entire range of Southern irrelevancies, capped by the explosion of a mail-order
diamond ring. In ways beyond the scope of traditional fiction, Rudd's distortion of regional posturing reveals the
emptiness behind the false fronts of our social landscape."[24]
In his two most famous stories, "Robert Kennedy Saved
from Drowning" and "Views of My Father Weeping,"
Donald Barthelme details what the old epistemology cannot
achieve, and what the new forms can. The first story, with
its random assemblage of notes, seems experimental, although in its method it is a conventional way of knowing.
Gathering together various accounts of Kennedy, the story
tries to understand the man, to put down on paper the
meaning of his life. But the reports are ambiguous, the de-
scriptions vague, and the words of Kennedy himself
cloaked in filling, blanketing, and *dreck*. The result is an in-

tentional series of bad snapshots, far from the "key shot" that Karsh of Ottawa was more successful in capturing of Hemingway and Churchill.[25] "Views of My Father Weeping," instead of collecting reporters' notes, studies the knowing process itself. The hero ponders:

> Yet it is possible that it is not my father who sits there in the center of the bed weeping. It may be someone else, the mailman, the man who delivers the groceries, an insurance salesman or the tax collector, who knows. However, I must say, it resembles my father. The resemblance is very strong. He is not smiling through his tears but frowning through them. I remember once we were out on the range shooting peccadillos (result of a meeting, on the plains of the West, of the collared peccary and the nine-banded armadillo). My father shot and missed. He wept. This weeping resembles that weeping.[26]

Although the father's murderer is never discovered, and the son, in the act of learning, often fails, still the process of knowledge has been made clear. Process is the story itself, and by means of it the father's presence has been sustained and studied more effectively than the conventional epistemology of "Robert Kennedy Saved from Drowning" would allow. The father is not understood rationally, nor is his memory recounted in a linear mode. Instead, we know him in a suprarational, emotional complex: the process by which he is known to his son.

Rightly initiated into the new world, man can respond coherently, knowing the world and himself and being able to structure the two in a proper relationship. In a cosmos no longer anthropocentric, a universe no longer directed by Reason according to Newtonian principles of order, man's self holds a position which is all the more precarious if he tries to live according to the forms of a different existence. Because of this danger, and because of the writing produced by such displaced imaginations, John Hawkes undertook "The Voice Project," the task of which was "to encourage the non-fiction writing student to discover himself as the center of a writing process which results in a personal or identifiable prose, rather than in 'machine' or 'voiceless' prose."[27] The reorganization of values in the twentieth century has displaced man from his traditional notion of self. To regain any notion of the self at all, new writers of short fiction have placed themselves at the fore of movements to understand and artistically interpret the Einsteinian, relativistic, fourth-dimensional world, and the quality of man's life in it. Fiction, a way of looking at the world, is also, as art, man's statement of a favorable rapport with it. The artist of Thomas Glynn's story "Except for the Sickness I'm Quite Healthy Now. You Can Believe That" establishes this rapport in his expanding painting, which enables man to imaginatively experience the initiation rite of Einstein's fourth dimension:

> Some people are good at falling, and some not. I'll show this in my picture. My picture takes place in an elevator shaft. Everybody crowding in at the top, falling in the middle. There is no landing. Nobody ever lands. There will be arms and legs and dog heads twirling past elevator cables, some people will slide, holding onto the greased cables with bloody hands and a look of automated horror. Others will ignore the cables and fall like Buddhists burning in Saigon, arrow sure. The grabbers will reach out, twirl, shiver, and fall like animated cartwheels in a firecracker carnival. Everyone will fall in my picture. Heads of state, models, safe-crackers, highway patrolmen. I'm considering other things falling. Alarm clocks and forks and crutches.[28]

Having disavowed the outmoded conventions of an earlier, three-dimensional world, writers such as Barthelme, Coover, and Glynn have struck beyond the limits of comfortable, decorous existence into the imaginatively strange and vile. Anything else is submemorable, and, in terms of the universe, physically dead. Man seeks life. After making a morass of modern life by delaying facing it with the meaningful forms of understanding, everyone, as Glynn understands, "wants to fall in my painting." Misfits, derelicts, and bums flock to his studio; placed in the new form, initiated into the fourth dimension, they live.

NOTES

[1]*The Death of the Novel and Other Stories* (New York: Dial, 1969), p. 41.

[2]Guy Murchie, *The Music of the Spheres* (Cambridge: Houghton Mifflin, 1961), p. 571.

[3]Donald Barthelme, *Snow White* (New York: Atheneum, 1967), p. 97.

[4]*op. cit.,* pp. 97–98.

[5]*Wallace Stevens: Musing the Obscure* (New York: New York University Press, 1967), p. 3.

[6]"Report," *Unspeakable Practices, Unnatural Acts* (New York: Farrar, Straus & Giroux, 1968), p. 56.

[7]*op. cit.,* p. 54.

[8]"And Now Let's Hear It for the Ed Sullivan Show," *Esquire,* 71 (April, 1969), 56.

[9]"Richard Brautigan: The Politics of Woodstock," *New American Review,* #11 (1971), p. 56.

[10]*op. cit.,* p. 57.

[11]*Wallace Stevens, op. cit.,* p. 14.

[12]*Pricksongs & Descants,* (New York: Dutton, 1969), pp. 125–37.

[13]*Tales* (New York: Grove Press, 1967), pp. 1–4.

[14]*The Lyrical Novel* (Princeton: Princeton University Press, 1963), p. 8.

[15]*Wallace Stevens, op. cit.,* p. 3.

[16]*Wallace Stevens, op. cit.,* p. 12.

[17]*Wallace Stevens, op. cit.,* pp. 14-15.

[18]*The Electric Kool-Aid Acid Test* (New York: Bantam, 1969), p. 40.

[19]*Irrational Man* (New York: Doubleday Anchor, 1962).

[20]"Preface," *The Gold Diggers* (New York: Scribners, 1965), p. 7.

[21]*Idiots First* (New York; Dell, 1966), pp. 94–105.

[22]*Pricksongs & Descants, op. cit.,* pp. 206-39.

[23]*Paris Review,* #26 (Summer–Fall, 1961), pp. 13–27.

[24]"Humor with a Moral Sting," collected in *The World of Black Humor,* ed. Douglas M. Davis (New York: Dutton, 1966), pp. 304–05.

[25]*Unspeakable Practices, op. cit.,* pp. 39–40.

[26]*City Life* (New York: Farrar, Straus & Giroux, 1970), pp. 3–4.

[27]"The Voice Project: An Idea for Innovation in the Teaching of Writing," collected in *Writers as Teachers/ Teachers as Writers*, ed. Jonathan Baumbach (New York: Holt, Rinehart & Winston, 1970), pp. 89–90.

[28]*Paris Review*, #42 (Winter–Spring, 1968), p. 82.

inn●vative fiction

THE HYANNIS PORT STORY

KURT VONNEGUT, JR.

The farthest away from home I ever sold a storm window was in Hyannis Port, Massachusetts, practically in the front yard of President Kennedy's summer home. My field of operation is usually within about twenty-five miles of my home, which is in North Crawford, New Hampshire.

The Hyannis Port thing happened because somebody misunderstood something I said, and thought I was an ardent Goldwater Republican. Actually, I hadn't made up my mind one way or the other about Goldwater.

What happened was this: The program chairman of the North Crawford Lions Club was a Goldwater man, and he had this college boy named Robert Taft Rumfoord come talk to a meeting one day about the Democratic mess in Washington and Hyannis Port. The boy was national president of some kind of student organization that was trying to get the country back to what he called First Principles. One of the First Principles, I remember, was getting rid of the income tax. You should have heard the applause.

I got a funny feeling that the boy didn't care much more about politics than I did. He had circles under his eyes, and he looked as though he'd just as soon be somewhere else. He would say strong things, but they came out sounding like music on a kazoo. The only time he got really interesting was when he told about being in sailboat races and golf and tennis matches with different Kennedys and their friends. He said that there was a lot of propaganda around about what a fine golfer Bobby Kennedy was, whereas

Bobby actually couldn't golf for sour apples. He said Pierre Salinger was one of the worst golfers in the world, and didn't care for sailing or tennis at all.

Robert Taft Rumfoord's parents were there to hear him. They had come all the way from Hyannis Port. They were both very proud of him—or at least the father was. The father had on white flannel trousers and white shoes, even though there was snow on the ground, and a double-breasted blue coat with brass buttons. The boy introduced him as *Commodore* William Rumfoord. The Commodore was a short man with very shaggy eyebrows, and pale blue eyes. He looked like a gruff, friendly teddy-bear, and so did his son. I found out later, from a Secret Service man, that the Kennedys sometimes called the Rumfoords *"the Pooh people,"* on account of they were so much like the bear in the children's book *Winnie the Pooh*.

The Commodore's wife wasn't a Pooh person, though. She was thin and quick, and maybe two inches taller than the Commodore. Bears have a way of looking as though they're pretty much satisfied with everything. The Commodore's lady didn't have that look. I could tell she was jumpy about a lot of things.

After the boy was through pouring fire and brimstone on the Kennedys, with his father applauding everything he said, Hay Boyden, the building mover, stood up. He was a Kennedy Democrat, and he said some terrible things to the boy. The only one I remember is the first thing he said: "Son, if you keep blowing off steam like this during your Boy Scout days, you aren't going to have an ounce of pressure left when you're old enough to vote." It got worse from there on.

The boy didn't get mad. He just got embarrassed, and answered back with some more kazoo music. It was the Commodore who really cared. He turned the color of tomato juice. He stood up and he argued back, did it pretty well, even though his wife was pulling at the bottom of his brass-buttoned coat the whole time. She was trying to get him to stop raising such an uproar, but the Commodore loved the uproar.

The meeting broke up with practically everybody embarrassed, and I went over to Hay Boyden to talk to him about something that didn't have anything to do with Kennedy *or*

Goldwater. It was about a bathtub enclosure I sold him. He had insisted on installing it himself, saving himself about seven dollars and a half. Only it leaked, and his dining-room ceiling fell down, and Hay claimed that was the fault of the merchandise and not the installation. Hay had some poison left in his system from his argument with the boy, so he used it up on me. I answered him back with the truth, and walked away from him, and Commodore Rumfoord grabbed my hand and shook it. He thought I'd been defending his boy and Barry Goldwater.

"What business you in?" he asked me.

I told him, and, the next thing I knew, I had an order for storm windows all around on a four-story house in Hyannis Port. The Commodore called that big old house a cottage.

"You're a Commodore in the Navy?" I asked him.

"No," he said. "My father, however, was Secretary of the Navy under William Howard Taft. That's my full name: Commodore William Howard Taft Rumfoord."

"You're in the Coast Guard?" I said.

"You mean the *Kennedy Private Fleet?*" he said.

"Pardon me?" I said.

"That's what they ought to call the Coast Guard these days," he said. "Its sole mission seems to be to protect Kennedys while they water-ski behind high-powered stink-pots."

"You're *not* in the Coast Guard?" I said. I couldn't imagine what was left.

"I was Commodore of the Hyannis Port Yacht Club in 1946," he said.

He didn't smile, and neither did I, and neither did his wife, whose name was Clarice. But Clarice *did* give a little sigh that sounded like the whistle on a freight train far, far away on a wet morning.

I didn't know what the trouble was at the time, but Clarice was sighing because the Commodore hadn't held any job of any description since 1946. Since then, he'd made a full-time career of raging about whoever was President of the United States, including Eisenhower.

Especially Eisenhower.

So I went down to Hyannis Port in my truck to measure

the Commodore's windows late in June. His driveway was on Irving Avenue. So was the Kennedys' driveway. And President Kennedy and I hit Cape Cod on the very same day.

Traffic to Hyannis Port was backed up through three villages. There were license plates from every state in the Republic. The line was moving about four miles an hour. I was passed by several groups of fifty-mile hikers. My radiator came to a boil four times.

I was feeling pretty sorry for myself, because I was just an ordinary citizen, and had to get stuck in lines like that. But then I recognized the man in the limousine up ahead of me. It was Adlai Stevenson. He wasn't moving any faster than I was, and his radiator was boiling, too.

One place there, we got stuck so long that Mr. Stevenson and I got out and walked around a little. I took the opportunity to ask him how the United Nations were getting along. He told me they were getting along about as well as could be expected. That wasn't anything I didn't already know.

When I finally got to Hyannis Port, I found out Irving Avenue was blocked off by police and Secret Service men. Adlai Stevenson got to go down it, but I didn't. The police made me get back into line with the tourists, who were being shunted down a street one block over from Irving Avenue.

The next thing I knew I was in Hyannis going past the *Presidential Motor Inn,* the *First Family Waffle Shop,* the *PT-109 Cocktail Lounge,* and a miniature golf course called the *New Frontier.*

I went into the waffle shop, and I called up the Rumfoords to find out how an ordinary storm-window salesman was supposed to get down Irving Avenue without dying in a hail of lead. It was the butler I talked to. He took down my license number, and found out how tall I was and what color my eyes were and all. He said he would tell the Secret Service, and they would let me by next time.

It was late in the afternoon, and I'd missed lunch, so I decided to have a waffle. All the different kinds of waffles were named after Kennedys and their friends and relatives. A waffle with strawberries and cream was a *Jackie.* A waffle with a scoop of ice cream was a *Caroline*. They even had a waffle named *Arthur Schlesinger, Jr.*

I had a thing called a *Teddy*—and a cup of *Joe*.

I got through next time, went right down Irving Avenue behind the Defense Minister of Pakistan. Except for us, that street was as quiet as a stretch of the Sahara Desert.

There wasn't anything to see at all on the President's side, except for a new, peeled-cedar fence about eight feet high and two hundred feet long, with a gate in it. The Rumfoord cottage faced the gate from across the street. It was the biggest house, and one of the oldest, in the village. It was stucco. It had towers and balconies, and a veranda that ran around all four sides.

On a second-floor balcony was a huge portrait of Barry Goldwater. It had bicycle reflectors in the pupils of its eyes. Those eyes stared right through the Kennedy gate. There were floodlights all around it, so I could tell it was lit up at night. And the floodlights were rigged with blinkers.

A man who sells storm windows can never be really sure about what class he belongs to, especially if he installs the windows, too. So I was prepared to keep out from under foot, and go about my business, measuring the windows. But the Commodore welcomed me like a guest of great importance. He invited me to cocktails and dinner, and to spend the night. He said I could start measuring the next day.

So we had martinis out on the veranda. Only we didn't sit on the most pleasant side, which looked out on the Yacht Club dock and the harbor. We sat on the side that looked out on all the poor tourists being shunted off toward Hyannis. The Commodore liked to talk about all those fools out there.

"Look at them!" he said. "They wanted glamour, and now they realize they're not going to get it. They actually expected to be invited to play touch football with Eunice and Frank Sinatra and the Secretary of Health and Welfare. Glamour is what they voted for, and look at 'em now. They don't even get to look at a Kennedy chimney up above the trees. All the glamour they'll get out of this administration is an overpriced waffle named *Caroline*."

A helicopter went over, very low, and it landed somewhere inside the Kennedy fence. Clarice said she wondered who it was.

"Pope John the Sixth," said the Commodore.

The butler, whose name was John, came out with a big bowl. I thought it was peanuts or popcorn, but it turned out to be Goldwater buttons. The Commodore had John take the bowl out to the street, and offer buttons to the people in cars. A lot of people took them. Those people were disappointed. They were sore.

Some fifty-mile hikers, who'd actually hiked sixty-seven miles, all the way from Boston, asked if they could please lie down on the Rumfoord lawn for a while. They were burned up, too. They thought it was the duty of the President, or at least the Attorney General, to thank them for walking so far. The Commodore said they could not only lie down, but he would give them lemonade, if they would put on Goldwater buttons. They were glad to.

"Commodore," I said, "where's that nice boy of yours, the one who talked to us up in New Hampshire."

"The one who talked to you is the only one I've got," he said.

"He certainly poured it on," I said.

"Chip off the old block," he said.

Clarice gave that faraway freight-whistle sigh of hers again.

"The boy went swimming just before you got here," said the Commodore. "He should be back at any time, unless he's been decapitated by a member of the Irish Mafia on water skis."

We went around to the water side of the veranda to see if we could catch sight of young Robert Taft Rumfoord in swimming. There was a Coast Guard cutter out there, shooing tourists in motorboats away from the Kennedy beach. There was a sight-seeing boat crammed with people gawking in our direction. The barker on the boat had a very loud loudspeaker, and we could hear practically everything he said.

"*The white boat there is the* Honey Fitz, *the President's personal yacht*," said the barker. "*Next to it is the* Marlin, *which belongs to the President's father, Joseph C. Kenne-*

dy, former Ambassador to the Court of St. James."

"The President's stinkpot, and the President's father's stinkpot," said the Commodore. He called all motorboats stinkpots. "This is a harbor that should be devoted exclusively to sail."

There was a chart of the harbor on the veranda wall. I studied it, and found a *Rumfoord Point,* a *Rumfoord Rock,* and a *Rumfoord Shoal.* The Commodore told me his family had been in Hyannis Port since 1884.

"There doesn't seem to be anything named after the Kennedys," I said.

"Why *should* there be?" he said. "They only got here day before yesterday."

"Day before yesterday?" I said.

And he asked me, "What would *you* call nineteen-twenty-one?"

"No, sir," the barker said to one of his passengers, *"that is not the President's house. Everybody asks that. That great big ugly stucco house, folks, that's the Rumfoord Cottage. I agree with you, it's too big to be called a* cottage, *but you know how rich people are."*

"Demoralized and bankrupt by confiscatory taxation," said the Commodore. "You know," he said, "it isn't as though Kennedy was the first President we ever had in Hyannis Port. Taft, Harding, Coolidge, and Hoover were all guests of my father in this very house. Kennedy is simply the first President who's seen fit to turn the place into an eastern enclave of *Disneyland."*

"No mam," said the barker, *"I don't know where the Rumfoords get their money, but they don't have to work at all, I know that. They just sit on that porch there, and drink martinis, and let the old mazooma roll in."*

The Commodore blew up. He said he was going to sue the owners of the sight-seeing boat for a blue million. His wife tried to calm him down, but he made me come into his study with him while he called up his lawyers.

"You're a witness," he said.

But his telephone rang before he could call his lawyers. The person who was calling him was a Secret Service Agent named Raymond Boyle. I found out later that Boyle was known around the Kennedy household as the *Rum-*

foord Specialist or the *Ambassador to Rumfoordiana.*
Whenever anything came up that had to do with the Rumfoords, Boyle had to handle it.

The Commodore told me to go upstairs and listen in on
the extension in the hall. "This will give you an idea of how
arrogant civil servants have become these days," he said.

So I went upstairs.

"The Secret Service is one of the least secret services I've
ever come in contact with," the Commodore was saying
when I picked up the phone. "I've seen drum and bugle
corps that were less obtrusive. Did I ever tell you about the
time Calvin Coolidge, who was also a President, as it happened, went fishing for scup with my father and me off the
end of the Yacht Club dock?"

"Yessir, you have, many times," said Boyle. "It's a good
story, and I want to hear it again sometime. But right now
I'm calling about your son."

The Commodore went right ahead with the story anyway. "President Coolidge," he said, "insisted on baiting his
own hook, and the combined Atlantic and Pacific Fleets
were not anchored offshore, and the sky was not black with
airplanes, and brigades of Secret Service Agents were not
trampling the neighbors' flowerbeds to purée."

"Sir—" said Boyle patiently, "your son Robert was apprehended in the act of boarding the President's father's
boat, the *Marlin*."

"Back in the days of Coolidge, there *were* no stinkpots
like that in this village, dribbling petroleum products,
belching fumes, killing the fish, turning the beaches a
gummy black."

"Commodore Rumfoord, sir," said Boyle, "did you hear
what I just said about your son?"

"Of course," said the Commodore. "You said Robert, a
member of the Hyannis Port Yacht Club, was caught
touching a vessel belonging to another member of the club.
This may seem a very terrible crime to a landlubber like
yourself; but it has long been a custom of the sea, Mr.
Boyle, that a swimmer, momentarily fatigued, may, upon
coming to a vessel not his own, grasp that vessel and rest,
without fear of being fired upon by the Coast Guard, or of
having his fingers smashed by members of the Secret Serv-

ice, or, as I prefer to call them, the *Kennedy Palace Dragoons.*"

"There has been no shooting, and no smashing, sir," said Boyle. "There has also been no evidence of swimmer's fatigue. Your Robert went up the anchor line of the *Marlin* like a chimpanzee. He *swarmed* up that rope, Commodore. I believe that's the proper nautical term. And I remind you, as I tried to remind him, that persons moving, uninvited, unannounced, with such speed and purposefulness within the vicinity of a President are, as a matter of time-honored policy, to be turned back at all costs—to be turned back, if need be, *violently.*"

"Was it a Kennedy who gave the order that the boarder be repelled?" the Commodore wanted to know.

"There was no Kennedy on board, sir."

"The stinkpot was unoccupied?"

"Adlai Stevenson and Walter Reuther and one of my men were on board, sir," said Boyle. "They were all below, until they heard Robert's feet hit the deck."

"Stevenson and Reuther?" said the Commodore. "That's the last time I let my son go swimming without a dagger in his teeth. I hope he was opening the seacocks when beaten insensible by truncheons."

"Very funny, sir," said Boyle, his voice developing a slight cutting edge.

"You're sure it was my Robert?" said the Commodore.

"Who else but your Robert wears a Goldwater button on his swimming trunks?" asked Boyle.

"You object to his political views?" the Commodore demanded.

"I mention the button as a means of identification. Your son's politics do not interest the Secret Service. For your information, I have spent seven years protecting the life of a Republican, and three protecting the life of a Democrat," said Boyle.

"For your information, Mr. Boyle," said the Commodore, "Dwight David Eisenhower was *not* a Republican."

"Whatever he was, I protected him," said Boyle. "He may have been a Zoroastrian, for all I know. And whatever the next President is going to be, I'll protect him, too. I also protect the lives of persons like your son from the consequences of excessive informality where the Presidential presence is concerned." Now Boyle's voice really started to cut. It sounded like a bandsaw working on galvanized tin. "I tell you, officially and absolutely unsmilingly now, your son is to cease and desist from using Kennedy boats as love nests."

That got through to the Commodore, bothered him. "Love nests?" he said.

"Your Robert has been meeting a girl on boats all over the harbor," said Boyle. "He arranged to meet her today on the *Marlin*. He was sure it would be vacant. Adlai Stevenson and Walter Reuther were a shock."

The Commodore was quiet for a few seconds, and then he said, "Mr. Boyle, I resent your implications. If I ever hear of your implying such a thing about my son to anyone else, you had better put your pistol and shoulder holster in your wife's name, because I'll sue you for everything you've got. My Robert has never gone with a girl he wasn't proud to introduce to his mother and me, and he never will."

"You're going to meet this one any minute now," said Boyle. "Robert is on his way home with her."

The Commodore wasn't tough at all now. He was uneasy and humble when he said, "Would you mind telling me her name?"

"Kennedy, sir," said Boyle. "*Sheila* Kennedy, fresh over from Ireland, a fourth cousin of the President of the United States."

Robert Taft Rumfoord came in with the girl right after that, and announced they were engaged to be married.

Supper that night in the Rumfoord cottage was sad and beautiful and happy and strange. There were Robert and his girl, and me, and the Commodore and his lady.

That girl was so intelligent, so warm, and so beautiful that she broke my heart every time I looked at her. That was why supper was so peculiar. The girl was so desirable, and the love between her and Robert was so sweet and clean, that nobody could think of anything but silly little things to say. We mainly ate in silence.

The Commodore brought up the subject of politics just

once. He said to Robert, "Well—uh—will you still be making speeches around the country, or—uh—"

"I think I'll get out of politics entirely for a while," said
Robert.

The Commodore said something that none of us could
understand, because the words sort of choked him.

"Sir?" said Robert.

"I said," said the Commodore, " 'I would think you
would.' "

I looked at the Commodore's lady, at Clarice. All the
lines had gone out of her face. She looked young and beautiful, too. She was completely relaxed for the first time in
God-knows-how-many years.

One of the things I said that supper was was *sad*. The
sad part was how empty and quiet it left the Commodore.

The two lovers went for a moonlight sail. The Commodore and his lady and I had brandy on the veranda, on the
water side. The sun was down. The tourist traffic had pe-
tered out. The fifty-mile hikers who had asked to rest on
the lawn that afternoon were still all there, sound asleep,
except for one boy who played a guitar. He played it slowly. Sometimes it seemed like a minute between the time he
would pluck a string and the time he would pluck one
again.

John, the butler, came out and asked the Commodore if
it was time to turn on Senator Goldwater's floodlights yet.

"I think we'll just leave him off tonight, John," said the
Commodore.

"Yes, sir," said John.

"I'm still *for* him, John," said the Commodore. "Don't
anybody misunderstand me. I just think we ought to give
him a rest tonight."

"Yes, sir," said John, and he left.

It was dark on the veranda, so I couldn't see the Commodore's face very well. The darkness, and the brandy, and
the slow guitar let him start telling the truth about himself
without feeling much pain.

"Let's give the Senator from Arizona a rest," he said.
"Everybody knows who *he* is. The question is: Who am I?"

"A lovable man," said Clarice in the dark.

"With Goldwater's floodlights turned off, and with my son engaged to marry a Kennedy, what am I but what the man on the sight-seeing boat said I was: A man who sits on this porch, drinking martinis, and letting the old mazooma roll in."

"You're an intelligent, charming, well-educated man, and you're still quite young," said Clarice.

"I've got to find some kind of work," he said.

"We'll both be so much happier," she said. "I would love you, no matter what. But I can tell you now, darling—it's awfully hard for a woman to *admire* a man who actually doesn't do anything."

We were dazzled by the headlights of two cars coming out of the Kennedy's driveway. The cars stopped right in front of the Rumfoord Cottage. Whoever was in them seemed to be giving the place a good looking-over.

The Commodore went to that side of the veranda, to find out what was going on. And I heard the voice of the President of the United States coming from the car in front.

"Commodore Rumfoord," said the President, "may I ask what is wrong with your Goldwater sign?"

"Nothing, Mr. President," said the Commodore respectfully.

"Then why isn't it on?" asked the President.

"I just didn't feel like turning it on tonight, sir," said the Commodore.

"I have Mr. Khrushchev's son-in-law with me," said the President. "He would very much enjoy seeing it."

"Yes, sir," said the Commodore. He was right by the switch. He turned it on. The whole neighborhood was bathed in flashing light.

"Thank you," said the President. "And *leave* it on, would you please?"

"Sir?" said the Commodore.

The cars started to pull away slowly. "That way," said the President, "I can find my way home."

MISS EUAYLA IS THE SWEETEST THANG!

HUGHES RUDD

The first day Miss Euayla came into the China Nook, my style just hit her right in the eye. I was dusting off some armadillo baskets when she came in the door and I thought, Lafond T. Cunningham, that's your life mate. Yes, sir. I dropped those baskets and came skipping around the counter and right up to her.

"You sweet *thang!*" I hollered, and went right up on my toes and kissed her on the cheek. You wouldn't believe it, but that's the way I am, impulsive, just impulsive to a fault.

Well, Miss Euayla just stood there a while, looking down at me, neither of us moving an inch, but I could see the feathers in her hat trembling and I just waited her out until finally she just *had* to say something.

"Well," she said. "You sure think you're somebody, don't you."

"That's right," I said, quick as a wink, right back at her. "My name's Lafond T. Cunningham and I'm no bigger than a shotgun."

Well, we just both broke out to laughing until we couldn't see where we were and finally Miss Euayla staggered over and sat down on a wireback chair, whooping and choking until I thought she'd never recover, and I sort of tottered out the door onto the sidewalk, bent over backwards and holding on to my head with both hands, and then I tottered back into the China Nook, my face as red as a dime bandanna. I was screaming like an Indian full of turpentine. We just hit it off right from the start, and all because of my style.

That's just what Rabe Thompson *doesn't* have, of course: my style. I don't care what they say about how good looking he is, and what if he is six feet tall? He's just a big lump of nothing if you ask me and he got mighty worried as soon as he found out I was seeing Miss Euayla. Thought he *knew* something. Went around telling people I was after Miss Euayla's farm, can you imagine that? Me? Working in the China Nook with a perfectly assured future career ahead of me at that time and don't know a plow from a prunehook. I tried to tell him that the night he hid in my car and tried to scare me silly.

Miss Euayla and me'd been out to the Hickory Rib, sitting in a booth drinking ammonia cokes and playing nickels in the music vendor and that's absolutely all, and about ten o'clock I drove her up into the front yard and parked my '33 Chevie under that big chinaberry tree. We got right out of the car and went in the house and she fixed me a big glass of Kool-Aid, it was hotter than a blister that night, and I came right out of the house and down the steps and bumped into the Chevie before I even saw it. They have darker nights in McClellan county than anywhere in the world, I guess. Well, I got in the car and before I could even step on the starter I feel somebody's breath on the back of my neck and a voice says, "Now I got you!" and without even thinking I let out a holler and started kicking my feet on the floorboards. I like to broke my ankle on the brake pedal, if you want to know the truth. I have very delicate bones.

Well, as soon as I started hollering I heard Miss Euayla start hollering in the house and here she came busting through the screen door and down the steps in the dark like a boxcar of loose roller skates being unloaded.

"Lafond!" she hollered, and ran right into the side of the car. "Damn!" she said, "are you all right?" and right then she sort of grunted and I heard a man's voice say, "Ain't this a fine way to behave? Ain't it?" and it was the same voice that had been talking to me in the car. That scared me so bad I started kicking my feet on the floorboards again so I missed some of what they said, but it was Rabe

Thompson hiding out there, waiting and trying to catch us. He and Miss Euayla scuffled around in the dark, both of them cussing and yelling, and Rabe Thompson making out what a skunk I was.

"All he wants is your farm!" he yelled, and Miss Euayla yelled back, "You're a liar! You're a liar!"

It was terrible, the way they kept it up. I rolled up all the windows and locked the doors and nearly suffocated. Every once in a while I'd lean down and holler through the little doors that open up by your feet on those '33 Chevies, but they didn't pay any attention. They'd known each other all their lives, you know. It's a very unhealthy situation, the way people live out in the country, and when they get mad it seems like there isn't anything they won't say to each other, just for spite. Now, growing up in Fort Worth like I did, it's an altogether different thing. You don't have all kinds of people keeping track of you all the time in the city. In Fort Worth it's just plain old "Live and let live." Powder river, let 'er buck, that's the word up there. But of course it's not that way down in McClellan county.

That's one reason why, although Miss Euayla was taken with me right from the minute she saw me in the China Nook, she couldn't quite make me out. I just had a different air than anything she was used to, of course, and she couldn't understand why I was working in the China Nook instead of up in Fort Worth in one of the big department stores.

"Why, look here," I told her one night out at the Hickory Rib, "I'm going to *be* somebody. I'll probably own that old China Nook by next Christmas, armadillo baskets and all."

Miss Euayla took a sip of her dope and just looked at me for a minute.

"How come you couldn't own one of them big stores in Fort Worth by Christmas?" she said after a while.

"That's a different thing and you know it," I told her. "Have another beef sandwich. Sometimes I think you people down here in McClellan county don't understand anything at all."

She just ate her beef sandwich and kept looking at me. Miss Euayla has the worst staring habit of any woman I ever met in my life, and that's a fact. It took me a long time to figure out she was giving me love looks instead of just looking straight through me.

But I'm telling you the honest truth, that night when Rabe Thompson hid in the car just about took ten years off my life. The next day in the China Nook my hands were shaking so bad that I knocked over a whole display of little ceramic Bibles we had piled up there for Easter gifts. They were the cutest things: they had slots in the side where the pages were so you could put money in there and save it up for Sunday school, I suppose. Anyway, Miss Clara, she owns the China Nook, you know, Miss Clara like to died when I knocked them over. I must have busted fifteen of those little Bibles all on account of that Rabe Thompson, and I told Miss Clara so.

"Ha," she said, looking at me with those little beady eyes of hers, just like a weasel looking at a crippled hen. "You better look out, Lafond T.," she said. "That Rabe Thompson's daddy has just about all the money in McClellan county and what he don't have he knows how to lay his hands on it mighty quick," she said. Miss Clara's grammar is just awful. "On top of that," she said, all beady eyes, "they've both of 'em got about the worst tempers in Texas. Why, I can recall when Rabe's daddy was courting his mother," she said, and let off a great string of stories about all the awful things that Mr. Thompson did to boys that were trying to court his future bride at the same time he was. But I just didn't faze, no, sir.

"The pen is mightier than the sword, Miss Clara," I told her, just as chipper as you please. "Might don't always make right, you know. Nowadays a young fellow's got to have brains," I said. "B,r,a,i,n,s."

"Um, hm," Miss Clara said. "Now you sweep up them Bibles."

Honestly! I felt like telling her, Why, no, Miss Clara, I thought I'd just run the Hoover over those little busted up Bibles. Miss Clara, however, is what you might call obtuse. She has absolutely no sense of humor whatever.

Now that was probably very largely responsible for my getting to feel so blue right along in there. I got to thinking that persons that don't have any sense of humor, especially women, live forever, you know; they're the most stubborn

things about going off to their just reward that ever was.
That's just a plain fact and everybody knows it. Well, here
I was, embarked on a dead-end career, when I stopped to
think about it.

"It's a burden," Miss Euayla said when I told her about
it, but I could see she didn't really understand what I was
talking about. The fact of the matter is that Miss Euayla is
just the sweetest thing you ever saw for a big girl, but she's
pretty short on humor. I guess having her daddy leave her
all that money and having to worry about all that cotton
makes her that way.

"Yes," I told her, "it is a burden," but I thought, you
don't even know what a burden is, you sweet, rich thang,
you. "Here I come all the way down to McClellan county
from Fort Worth," I told her, "looking for my dear Uncle
Dell, and he's flown off somewhere and the first career I
pick out for myself, right there in the China Nook, is a big,
fat dead-end."

"I declare," Miss Euayla said, taking a big bite of beef
sandwich. It's a fact, you have to stoke that girl like an
ocean liner.

It was the plain truth about my Uncle Dell. I had a letter
from him telling me to come on down and join up with him
in something good, and when I got to McClellan county all
I could find out was that he'd run off somewhere in a 1929
Pierce Arrow touring sedan. Bright red. Everybody said he
went to California, but he wouldn't wait for me, oh, no.
Selfish, just plain selfish.

"How'm I ever going to get ahead?" I said. "I'll have to
cast about for a new career."

Miss Euayla polished off her sandwich and looked at me.

"How about Rabe's daddy's compress," she said. "Maybe
he'd give you a job."

Well, I laughed so hard I like to fell out of the booth.

"Me?" I said. "Lafond T. Cunningham stalking around a
cotton compress, breathing all that fuzz and listening to all
that racket?"

"You're afraid of Rabe," Miss Euayla said, looking
around in that puzzled fashion that means she wants another beef sandwich.

"Oh, no you don't!" I hollered. "You're not going to pin

that label on a Cunningham!" I told her, but she waved her
hand at the waitress.

"You've no call to be afraid of Rabe," she said, looking
at me again.

"Oh, no?" I said. "Not that I am, mind you, but if I
don't have any call to be afraid of him, what you come
running out of the house that way that night? When he hid
in the car and tried to scare me into my grave, I mean."

"That was different," she said. "It was dark. It ain't dark
around a compress."

Well, I just wanted to scream, or hit her over the head
with that little pile of sandwich plates she had stacked in
front of her.

"*Isn't* dark," I said. "Not *ain't*."

"All right," she said.

I could see I wasn't going to make Miss Euayla understand economics in a hurry, and I wasn't *about* to go to
work in a cotton compress, and certainly not in one where
Rabe Thompson could get hold of me. Like I say, I have
very delicate bones, it's a part of the Cunningham style,
and a cotton compress is like all hell's broken loose in an
insane asylum. Noise? That's where they invented noise. I
have no doubt that three or four people get killed each and
every day in Texas cotton compresses. I decided maybe I'd
go on the radio.

That's one nice thing you can say for the radio, it's clean
work, and if you don't like the noise you can put on some
of those headphone things and just look interested without
even turning the thing on while you sit right in the studio
where they're making the racket. I've seen them do that in
the movies, you know. It's sort of like being deaf and turning down the volume on your hearing aid: that's why so
many deaf people have such sweet smiles, my Uncle Dell
always said, and I believe it.

Well, I called up Miss Clara on the telephone next
morning and told her I had a sick headache and was going
to stay in bed all day with wet teabags on my eyes. There
was just a humming kind of silence for a while, and then
she hung up. The rudest old party you ever ran across.

I put on my checkered suit and my black and white perforateds and strutted right on down to the radio station,
carrying my guitar in a yellow pillow slip. I've had that box

for years: it was left to me, but some jealous person or other stole the case a long while ago. I'm not going to name any names, you understand: whoever did it knows he did it, and I don't think the entire city of Fort Worth is big enough to hold his guilty conscience. Envy is a terrible thing.

But anyway. In the radio station there was this dangerous-looking blonde behind the counter and she let me right on in to see Mr. Big himself. When I opened the door to his office I had the pillow slip off the guitar and folded up and stuck in my pocket, and I went right into my act.

"Yes, sir!" I said, skipping through the door. "I'm the biggest little singer west of the Sabine river!" and with that I lit right into the opening of "I Want to Live Fast, Love Hard, Die Young and Leave a Beautiful Memory."

Well, that man was stunned. He just sat there behind his desk looking at me, and his mouth got open wider and wider until you could have driven a team of mules through his dentures and right out again and I don't think he'd have known a thing.

Of course I hadn't been getting much exercise in the China Nook and I was breathing pretty hard when I hit the last chord. I pulled the pillow slip out of my pocket and dabbed at my face with it, at the same time giving him a stylish little bow, with the guitar flung off to one side in my left hand and my left foot out and pointed. Style! If there's one thing I know about, it's style.

"How do you like that for a starter?" I said, puffing a little, and the man closed his mouth.

"If you'd just wait in the outer office," he said, still sitting there looking at me.

"Certainly!" I cried. "Make it easy on yourself!" and I did a quick off-to-Buffalo back out where the blonde was and sat down on a bench to get my breath. The air in McClellan county is as heavy as lead: you'd think you were in Death Valley all the time.

They had a radio going in there and a man was talking about the biggest discovery in the scientific world since the atom bomb, he said. I wasn't paying too much attention, but I began to make out that he was talking about Hollywood Synthetic Diamond Rings. You could send off for them, like something out of the Ivor Johnson catalogue, and they were absolutely guaranteed. Well, I surely was surprised. I started to listen pretty hard but I heard Mr. Big's voice, talking in his office over the telephone and it sounded urgent, like on Dragnet.

"He's crazy as a bedbug," I heard him say. "You better get somebody down here right away." There was a little pause and he said, "Sure, he's dangerous! You ought to see him! He looks like a June bug peeking out from behind a chrysanthemum when he starts to waving that yellow pillow case around!"

Well, I had to admit it, he was talking about me! I've never been so shocked in my life, nor so insulted. I just marched right out of there and went back to my room and sat right down and wrote off a letter to the Hollywood Synthetic Diamond people and then went down to the post office and stuck a four ninety five money order in it and mailed it. I was sick and tired of fooling around. If you ask me a person can stand just so much. The Lord helps those who helps themselves, you know, you can't just stand around hoping to get a leg up on somebody else's bootstraps, or whatever it is.

After I mailed off the letter I went back to my rooming house and changed my clothes and went out back and polished up that '33 Chevie until it squeaked when you looked at it. The finish had a shine like a raven's wing in the sunlight: a lot of the black was a little worn off in places and looked sort of bluish-black and green. Just beautiful. But of course that's just about the hardest work a man can do. I had to go upstairs and lay down for a while with a magazine. If you want a good workout, go down to McClellan county and polish a '33 Chevie some afternoon. I was too tuckered to talk.

But it passed off after I'd had my lie-down, of course. I got up and telephoned Miss Euayla.

"I'm going to have some mighty big news before long for you," I told her, in spite of the fact I wasn't too certain yet myself what it was going to be.

"What are you going to do," she said after a minute, sounding so faint and far away and distracted I could tell she was hungry and looking around her living room for something to eat. "You going to work in the compress?"

"You just stop that," I said. "Fortune might turn my way at any time, Miss Smarty. You'll see."

"All right," she mumbled with her mouth full, and hung up.

Some people just don't know destiny when it walks up and hits them in the face.

But I made it a little plainer next day. Miss Euayla came in the China Nook looking for a wedding present for some one of her cotton-headed cousins out in the country, and I fired my arrow.

"I'm going to be looking for a wedding present myself one of these days," I told her. "For my bride."

Miss Euayla looked at me, then back at the ceramic frog flower holder she was weighing in her hand.

"You can't ever tell," I said. "One of these days!"

"I think I'll send them this," Miss Euayla said, handing me the frog.

"You ought to give a party for that barefooted cousin of yours," I told her as I wrapped up the frog in a big wad of pink tissue paper. "A big engagement party of some kind."

"Mm," Miss Euayla said, blinking at me. "That's what Rabe thinks, too."

"Oh, does he!" I hollered. "Well, maybe he's got some ulterior motive or other. Me, I just like to see folks have a good time. There's little enough that's jolly in this old world."

"Mm, hm," Miss Euayla said. "That's what Rabe thinks."

"Well, then, go on and give your old party!" I said, hopping up and down a little. I was so put out I was furious, but anyway she was going to have the party and as soon as she left the China Nook I could see that was all that mattered. I have too much pride, I guess I know that as well as anybody does, and temperament, too, it just seems to go with talent.

Miss Euayla even put it in the paper about the party. She sent out little bids to it, all printed up, inviting the bearer to be present at the Fish Pond, which is the ridiculous name they have in McClellan county for that splintered old shack they call a country club. They don't even have a pond. There's nothing out there but an old stagnant ox-bow lake, and if you don't look out you can step right through the clubhouse floor and fall in the water. Society!

Well, anyway, the great day dawned, as they say in the classics. I had my plot all ready, but I was nearly taken off in a fit, waiting for the Hollywood diamond people to come through. I didn't get the package until 3 p.m., I'll have you know, and if I hadn't been right there when the postman came up the front porch steps I probably never would have gotten it. That landlandy of mine was the nosiest old blister you ever saw. I just ran right by her with that package and right on up the stairs, with her hollering down at the foot, "What's that you got, Lafond? You sent off for something through the mail?"

"That's for me to know and you to find out!" I hollered back, just sassed her good, and went into my room and opened the package.

It just plain took your breath away. That Hollywood diamond was as big around as a bottle cap. I held the ring over by the window in the light and it just snapped and sparkled, just sat right up and looked you in the eye. It wasn't even cracked, after coming all the way from Hollywood, which I guess is about as far from McClellan county as a person could get without a passport. Just beautiful! I gave that diamond a good burst with some patented window cleaner I kept in there for my dresser mirror and rubbed it on my sleeve and my, heavens! you could hardly stand to look at it.

It took me the rest of the afternoon to get dressed. My checkered suit hadn't even hardly got rumpled at the radio station so I wore that and a new pink shirt I'd been saving to go off with Uncle Dell in, if he ever showed up. And my perforateds, of course: even after my radio audition they were still in A number one shape, I'm that careful of myself, you know.

So, there I was. When I came downstairs the landlady, Miss Vandy, came out to devil me some more about that package but when she saw me she was just speechless. She stared at me for a good minute without saying a thing.

"Take a good look," I told her. "You're looking at a young man on the threshold," I said. "How do you like my cravat?"

Miss Vandy swallowed a couple of times and nodded.

"You're just a picture, Lafond," she said. "Just a picture."

"That's vanadium green," I said, shaking my cravat at her.

"A beautiful necktie," she said. "Just beautiful. Are you off to a wedding?"

"No, Miss Nosey!" I said, "nor to a hanging, either!" and with that I skipped out the screen door, flip! flap! "I'll tell you when it's wedding time!" I hollered back over my shoulder.

Everybody in the world was out at the Fish Pond. Cars, you never saw so many cars, and Japanese lanterns strung up and down the veranda. There was a crowd at the water doing a lot of yelling and swearing, because of course somebody had already driven off the bank in the dark. That happens at least once every time there's a party out there. I just hoped it was Rabe Thompson, with his mouth full of live catfish.

I parked that '33 Chevie and even at night it had a shine on it from the lanterns up on the veranda. There was not a thing in the world about the car to be ashamed of. I closed the door gently just to hear the sound: I had the insides of the doors sprayed with asphalt up in Fort Worth. There's a place up there that does things like that and the man who runs it told me that's what they do on all those big new cars in Detroit. It's quite the thing, he said, and it surely gives the door a nice tone when it shuts: expensive.

I tiptoed up to the veranda, trying to keep my perforateds from getting absolutely soaked by the dew, because they either have dew in McClellan county at night or frost. It's always one or the other and of course all that moisture just plays hob with two-tone shoes. I finally got up to the door, bent over and gave my footgear a quick flick with my handkerchief and then flew into the ballroom, skipping for all I was worth.

"Where's that lucky couple!" I hollered, skipping through that great roil of people like a fresh breeze. I could see Miss Euayla's hat sticking up away over yonder in the corner where they keep the nickelodeon so I just bent my course in that direction and pretty soon I busted out of the dancers right in front of her.

She had one of those little canvas sacks in her hand that you use to take the money to the bank in, and she was fishing nickels out of it and stuffing them into the music box. They never seem to be able to put the vendor on automatic down there, somebody has to stand there and feed it, and usually it's the hostess. Just no savoir faire in the whole county. That's French.

"My dear madame," I said, giving her that deep bow of mine, foot pointed, arm flung out to one side, the whole works. "You *are* the sweetest *thang*," I said, "and you are mine tonight!"

"Hello, Lafond," Miss Euayla said, looking up from that grubby sackful of nickels. She looked at me, just taking me in for a minute. "Where'd you get that necktie?" she said finally.

"This is a cravat," I told her. "When you pay two and a half for a necktie, it's a cravat. Vanadium green," I told her. "That's a mineral color."

"Mm, hm," she said. "It looks more like a vegetable color. Kind of spinach."

"Just rave on, my girl," I told her, haughty as could be. "Just enjoy yourself. You are looking at a man of the world, that's all, if you only had sense enough to see it. Fortune has finally smiled."

"Mm, hm," Miss Euayla said. "What'd you do, get another job?"

"Job!" I cried. "You are looking at a Cunningham of independent means. I just got the word today."

"Word?" Miss Euayla looked at that sack of nickels, then back at me. I could tell I had her curiosity up or she'd have gone on fishing out nickels.

"About my Uncle Dell," I said. "That poor, rich man. He's had a terrible accident in that big red Pierce Arrow of his, out in Hollywood. Ran into some big movie star or other and killed them both outright. I forget the other fellow's name."

"For heaven's sake," she said.

"Just awful," I said, "and now he's left me so much money I don't know what to do with it. Probably be even more cash later. I'm going to sue that other fellow's estate, of course."

"Is that a fact," Miss Euayla said, looking at me.

Well, it could have been, you know. The important thing in this life is to think big, if you want to be big. Of course I knew the time would have to come when I'd be bound to explain a few things to Miss Euayla, but that would be after we were welded together in the sanctity of marriage.

"Just rich as a black marketeer," I told her. "And look here what I got you today," and I hauled that big sparkler out of my pocket and slipped it on her finger before you could say scat.

"What on earth," Miss Euayla said, while I shoved and pushed on that ring until we both of us like to fell crash into the juke box. The ring was too little to go on her ring finger, I finally saw that after huffing and puffing around for a while, so I put it on her little finger, but it wouldn't go there, either. Honestly! You can't trust anybody at all, not even the diamond trust. I shoved it back on her ring finger but it stuck out there on the first joint, just wouldn't go past that first knuckle.

While all that was going on Miss Euayla forgot to keep stuffing that music box with nickels and it was good and quiet when I stepped back from her and made my announcement.

"There!" I said, flinging out my arms like I was on a stage. "You are bound to Lafond T. Cunningham for life, you big sweet thang, you!" but there was a kind of a roar behind my back.

I looked around and here came Rabe Thompson, roaring like a wounded mastodon, all covered with mud from trying to get some fool's car out of the water, just dripping and squishing across the dance floor like a creature from out of the wet past.

"No, you ain't!" he trumpeted at Miss Euayla. "You ain't bound to nobody but me!" and he commenced to fumbling in his pockets with those muddy hams of his until he finally dredged out a little blue box no bigger than a carbuncle and snapped it open in front of Miss Euayla's face.

Well, it was just laughable. There was a little bitty old ring in there, sort of gold colored with a stone in it about the size of the head on a kitchen match.

"Now, look at that!" I said, striking a pose with my

hands on my hips. "Did you ever see such a piker? Just you take a good big fat look at that ring *I* just slipped on that girl's finger!" I told him, and he did.

"I ain't going to stand for it!" he roared in that big undignified voice of his, and he grabbed my ring off Miss Euayla's fingertip and hurled it, just hurled it, down on the floor.

Now, a lot of people wouldn't believe this, but it's just the kind of luck I had up there in McClellan county all the time. That diamond ring just exploded when it hit the floor, just flew into a million pieces and scattered all over. We all just stood there for a second, and then Rabe Thompson let out a great bellow.

"That ain't no diamond ring!" he shouted at Miss Euayla. "He's trying to take advantage of you just like I said he would! He's after your cotton!" and he made a grab for me, but I slipped away just as nimble as you please and went running for the door. Just before I took off I noticed the strangest thing: Miss Euayla had a big fat grin on her face and I don't believe she was paying any attention at all. Isn't that the most peculiar thing you ever heard of in your entire life?

But I didn't have time to think about it, I just made for the door, with Rabe Thompson right after me.

"You're a liar!" I told him over my shoulder. We went through that door like the locomotive and the coal car on the Bluebonnet Special, both of us yelling for all we were worth. I don't recall hearing Miss Euayla's voice at all.

It was quite a chase, just like something in the first part of a Doug Fairbanks picture, with me playing Doug Fairbanks, of course. Up hill, down dale, hither and thither, you might say, just screaming through the night.

Well, I finally shook him on the edge of town and doubled back out to the Fish Pond and got my car. I didn't even bother to go back to my rooming house to pick up my things. There's no telling what an animal type like Rabe Thompson might do, you know: just watch him any afternoon in the week, swaggering around down on the square in his Daddy's pickup truck. No, sir, I just headed straight south and here I am.

I've been here in Galveston two weeks now, with this *very* pleasant job handing out bathing suits in Murdoch's

Swimming Pavilion, and any day now I'm going to contact Miss Euayla for the good news. She doesn't know my exact whereabouts, you understand, or of course she'd have gotten in touch already. I just know she's going to tell me she's run that Rabe Thompson off for good and that she wants me to hop right back up there, quick as a wink. Absence makes the heart grow fonder, you know, and my style just shows off even better this way, at this point in time, sort of aloof and withdrawn down here on the edge of this dirty old Gulf of Mexico, just sending off an occasional little love note up there to McClellan county. And there's no two ways about it, most of those cotton-heads up there never even heard of the Gulf of Mexico, much less ever saw it, and I just leave it to you to guess how glamorous that old Galveston postmark will look to Miss Euayla. Just one of those little things, but you add them all up and you've got style, and that's just me, Lafond T. Cunningham.

PROLOGUE TO GRIDER CREEK

RICHARD BRAUTIGAN

Mooresville, Indiana, is the town that John Dillinger came from, and the town has a John Dillinger Museum. You can go in and look around.

Some towns are known as the peach capital of America or the cherry capital or the oyster capital, and there's always a festival and the photograph of a pretty girl in a bathing suit.

Mooresville, Indiana, is the John Dillinger capital of America.

Recently a man moved there with his wife, and he discovered hundreds of rats in his basement. They were huge, slow-moving, child-eyed rats.

When his wife had to visit some of her relatives for a few days, the man went out and bought a .38 revolver and a lot of ammunition. Then he went down to the basement where the rats were, and he started shooting them. It didn't bother the rats at all. They acted as if it were a movie and started eating their dead companions for popcorn.

The man walked over to a rat that was busy eating a friend and placed the pistol against the rat's head. The rat did not move and continued eating away. When the hammer clicked back, the rat paused between bites and looked out of the corner of its eye. First at the pistol and then at the man. It was a kind of friendly look as if to say, "When my mother was young she sang like Deanna Durbin."

The man pulled the trigger.

He had no sense of humor.

There's always a single feature, a double feature and an eternal feature playing at the Great Theater in Mooresville, Indiana: the John Dillinger capital of America.

SEA, SEA RIDER

RICHARD BRAUTIGAN

The man who owned the bookstore was not magic. He was not a three-legged crow on the dandelion side of the mountain.

He was, of course, a Jew, a retired merchant seaman who had been torpedoed in the North Atlantic and floated there day after day until death did not want him. He had a young wife, a heart attack, a Volkswagen and a home in Marin County. He liked the works of George Orwell, Richard Aldington and Edmund Wilson.

He learned about life at sixteen, first from Dostoevsky and then from the whores of New Orleans.

The bookstore was a parking lot for used graveyards. Thousands of graveyards were parked in rows like cars. Most of the books were out of print, and no one wanted to read them any more and the people who had read the books had died or forgotten about them, but through the organic process of music the books had become virgins again. They wore their ancient copyrights like new maidenheads.

I went to the bookstore in the afternoons after I got off work, during that terrible year of 1959.

He had a kitchen in the back of the store and he brewed cups of thick Turkish coffee in a copper pan. I drank coffee and read old books and waited for the year to end. He had a small room above the kitchen.

It looked down on the bookstore and had Chinese screens in front of it. The room contained a couch, a glass

cabinet with Chinese things in it and a table and three chairs.
There was a tiny bathroom fastened like a watch fob to the
room.

I was sitting on a stool in the bookstore one afternoon
reading a book that was in the shape of a chalice. The book
had clear pages like gin, and the first page in the book
read:

Billy
the Kid
born
November 23,
1859
in
New York
City

The owner of the bookstore came up to me, and put his
arm on my shoulder and said, "Would you like to get
laid?" His voice was very kind.

"No," I said.

"You're wrong," he said, and then without saying anything else, he went out in front of the bookstore, and
stopped a pair of total strangers, a man and a woman. He
talked to them for a few moments. I couldn't hear what he
was saying. He pointed at me in the bookstore. The woman
nodded her head and then the man nodded his head.

They came into the bookstore.

I was embarrassed. I could not leave the bookstore because they were entering by the only door, so I decided to
go upstairs and go to the toilet. I got up abruptly and
walked to the back of the bookstore and went upstairs to
the bathroom, and they followed after me.

I could hear them on the stairs.

I waited for a long time in the bathroom and they waited
an equally long time in the other room. They never spoke.
When I came out of the bathroom, the woman was lying
naked on the couch, and the man was sitting in a chair with
his hat on his lap.

"Don't worry about him," the girl said. "These things
make no difference to him. He's rich. He has 3,859 Rolls
Royces." The girl was very pretty and her body was like a

clear mountain river of skin and muscle flowing over rocks
of bone and hidden nerves.

"Come to me," she said. "And come inside me for we
are Aquarius and I love you."

I looked at the man sitting in the chair. He was not smiling and he did not look sad.

I took off my shoes and all my clothes. The man did not
say a word.

The girl's body moved ever so slightly from side to side.

There was nothing else I could do for my body was like
birds sitting on a telephone wire strung out down the
world, clouds tossing the wires carefully.

I laid the girl.

It was like the eternal 59th second when it becomes a
minute and then looks kind of sheepish.

"Good," the girl said, and kissed me on the face.

The man sat there without speaking or moving or sending out any emotion into the room. I guess he *was* rich and
owned 3,859 Rolls Royces.

Afterwards the girl got dressed and she and the man left.
They walked down the stairs and on their way out, I heard
him say his first words.

"Would you like to go to Ernie's for dinner?"

"I don't know," the girl said. "It's a little early to think
about dinner."

Then I heard the door close and they were gone. I got
dressed and went downstairs. The flesh about my body felt
soft and relaxed like an experiment in functional background music.

The owner of the bookstore was sitting at his desk behind the counter. "I'll tell you what happened up there," he
said, in a beautiful anti-three-legged-crow voice, in an anti-
dandelion side of the mountain voice.

"What?" I said.

"You fought in the Spanish Civil War. You were a
young Communist from Cleveland, Ohio. She was a painter. A New York Jew who was sightseeing in the Spanish
Civil War as if it were the Mardi Gras in New Orleans
being acted out by Greek statues.

"She was drawing a picture of a dead anarchist when
you met her. She asked you to stand beside the anarchist
and act as if you had killed him. You slapped her across

the face and said something that would be embarrassing for me to repeat.

"You both fell very much in love.

"Once while you were at the front she read *Anatomy of Melancholy* and did 349 drawings of a lemon.

"Your love for each other was mostly spiritual. Neither one of you performed like millionaires in bed.

"When Barcelona fell, you and she flew to England, and then took a ship back to New York. Your love for each other remained in Spain. It was only a war love. You loved only yourselves, loving each other in Spain during the war. On the Atlantic you were different toward each other and became every day more and more like people lost from each other.

"Every wave on the Atlantic was like a dead seagull dragging its driftwood artillery from horizon to horizon.

"When the ship bumped up against America, you departed without saying anything and never saw each other again. The last I heard of you, you were still living in Philadelphia."

"That's what you think happened up there?" I said.

"Partly," he said. "Yes, that's part of it."

He took out his pipe and filled it with tobacco and lit it.

"Do you want me to tell you what else happened up there?" he said.

"Go ahead."

"You crossed the border into Mexico," he said. "You rode your horse into a small town. The people knew who you were and they were afraid of you. They knew you had killed many men with that gun you wore at your side. The town itself was so small that it didn't have a priest.

"When the rurales saw you, they left the town. Tough as they were, they did not want to have anything to do with you. The rurales left.

"You became the most powerful man in town.

"You were seduced by a thirteen-year-old girl, and you and she lived together in an adobe hut, and practically all you did was make love.

"She was slender and had long dark hair. You made love standing, sitting, lying on the dirt floor with pigs and chickens around you. The walls, the floor and even the roof of the hut were coated with your sperm and her come.

"You slept on the floor at night and used your sperm for a pillow and her come for a blanket.

"The people in the town were so afraid of you that they could do nothing.

"After a while she started going around town without any clothes on, and the people of the town said that it was not a good thing, and when you started going around without any clothes, and when both of you began making love on the back of your horse in the middle of the zócalo, the people of the town became so afraid that they abandoned the town. It's been abandoned ever since.

"People won't live there.

"Neither of you lived to be twenty-one. It was not necessary.

"See, I do know what happened upstairs," he said. He smiled at me kindly. His eyes were like the shoelaces of a harpsichord.

I thought about what happened upstairs.

"You know what I say is the truth," he said. "For you saw it with your own eyes and traveled it with your own body. Finish the book you were reading before you were interrupted. I'm glad you got laid."

Once resumed, the pages of the book began to speed up and turn faster and faster until they were spinning like wheels in the sea.

THE SHIPPING OF
TROUT FISHING IN AMERICA
SHORTY TO NELSON ALGREN

RICHARD BRAUTIGAN

Trout Fishing in America Shorty appeared suddenly last autumn in San Francisco, staggering around in a magnificent chrome-plated steel wheelchair.

He was a legless, screaming middle-aged wino.

He descended upon North Beach like a chapter from the Old Testament. He was the reason birds migrate in the autumn. They have to. He was the cold turning of the earth; the bad wind that blows off sugar.

He would stop children on the street and say to them, "I ain't got no legs. The trout chopped my legs off in Fort Lauderdale. You kids got legs. The trout didn't chop your legs off. Wheel me into that store over there."

The kids, frightened and embarrassed, would wheel Trout Fishing in America Shorty into the store. It would always be a store that sold sweet wine, and he would buy a bottle of wine and then he'd have the kids wheel him back onto the street, and he would open the wine and start drinking there on the street just like he was Winston Churchill.

After a while the children would run and hide when they saw Trout Fishing in America Shorty coming.

"I pushed him last week,"

"I pushed him yesterday,"

"Quick, let's hide behind these garbage cans."

And they would hide behind the garbage cans while Trout Fishing in America Shorty staggered by in his wheelchair. The kids would hold their breath until he was gone.

Trout Fishing in America Shorty used to go down to *L'Italia*, the Italian newspaper in North Beach at Stockton and Green Streets. Old Italians gather in front of the newspaper in the afternoon and just stand there, leaning up against the building, talking and dying in the sun.

Trout Fishing in America Shorty used to wheel into the middle of them as if they were a bunch of pigeons, bottle of wine in hand, and begin shouting obscenities in fake Italian.

Tra-la-la-la-la-la-la-Spa-ghet-tiii!

I remember Trout Fishing in America Shorty passed out in Washington Square, right in front of the Benjamin Franklin statue. He had fallen face first out of his wheelchair and just lay there without moving.

Snoring loudly.

Above him were the metal works of Benjamin Franklin like a clock, hat in hand.

Trout Fishing in America Shorty lay there below, his face spread out like a fan in the grass.

A friend and I got to talking about Trout Fishing in America Shorty one afternoon. We decided the best thing to do with him was to pack him in a big shipping crate with a couple of cases of sweet wine and send him to Nelson Algren.

Nelson Algren is always writing about Railroad Shorty, a hero of the *Neon Wilderness* (the reason for "The Face on the Barroom Floor") and the destroyer of Dove Linkhorn in *A Walk on the Wild Side*.

We thought that Nelson Algren would make the perfect custodian for Trout Fishing in America Shorty. Maybe a museum might be started. Trout Fishing in America Shorty could be the first piece in an important collection.

We would nail him up in a packing crate with a big label on it.

Contents:
Trout Fishing in America Shorty

Occupation:
Wino

Address:
C/O Nelson Algren
Chicago

And there would be stickers all over the crate, saying:
"GLASS/HANDLE WITH CARE/SPECIAL HAN-
DLING/GLASS/DON'T SPILL/THIS SIDE UP/HAN-
DLE THIS WINO LIKE HE WAS AN ANGEL"

And Trout Fishing in America Shorty, grumbling, puking and cursing in his crate would travel across America,
from San Francisco to Chicago.

And Trout Fishing in America Shorty, wondering what
it was all about, would travel on, shouting, "Where in the
hell am I? I can't see to open this bottle! Who turned out
the lights? Fuck this motel! I have to take a piss! Where's
my key?"

It was a good idea.

A few days after we made our plans for Trout Fishing in
America Shorty, a heavy rain was pouring down upon San
Francisco. The rain turned the streets inward, like drowned
lungs, upon themselves and I was hurrying to work, meeting swollen gutters at the intersections.

I saw Trout Fishing in America Shorty passed out in the
front window of a Filipino laundromat. He was sitting in
his wheelchair with closed eyes staring out the window.

There was a tranquil expression on his face. He almost
looked human. He had probably fallen asleep while he was
having his brains washed in one of the machines.

Weeks passed and we never got around to shipping
Trout Fishing in America Shorty away to Nelson Algren.
We kept putting it off. One thing and another. Then we lost
our golden opportunity because Trout Fishing in America
Shorty disappeared a little while after that.

They probably swept him up one morning and put him
in jail to punish him, the evil fart, or they put him in a nut-
house to dry him out a little.

Maybe Trout Fishing in America Shorty just pedaled
down to San Jose in his wheelchair, rattling along the freeway at a quarter of a mile an hour.

I don't know what happened to him. But if he comes
back to San Francisco someday and dies, I have an idea.

Trout Fishing in America Shorty should be buried right beside the Benjamin Franklin statue in Washington Square. We should anchor his wheelchair to a huge gray stone and write upon the stone:

> Trout Fishing in America Shorty
>   20¢ Wash
>   10¢ Dry
>   Forever

THE CLEVELAND WRECKING YARD

RICHARD BRAUTIGAN

Until recently my knowledge about the Cleveland Wrecking Yard had come from a couple of friends who'd bought things there. One of them bought a huge window: the frame, glass and everything for just a few dollars. It was a fine-looking window.

Then he chopped a hole in the side of his house up on Potrero Hill and put the window in. Now he has a panoramic view of the San Francisco County Hospital.

He can practically look right down into the wards and see old magazines eroded like the Grand Canyon from endless readings. He can practically hear the patients thinking about breakfast: *I hate milk*, and thinking about dinner: *I hate peas*, and then he can watch the hospital slowly drown at night, hopelessly entangled in huge bunches of brick seaweed.

He bought that window at the Cleveland Wrecking Yard.

My other friend bought an iron roof at the Cleveland Wrecking Yard and took the roof down to Big Sur in an old station wagon and then he carried the iron roof on his back up the side of a mountain. He carried up half the roof on his back. It was no picnic. Then he bought a mule, George, from Pleasanton. George carried up the other half of the roof.

The mule didn't like what was happening at all. He lost a lot of weight because of the ticks, and the smell of the wildcats up on the plateau made him too nervous to graze there. My friend said jokingly that George had lost around two hundred pounds. The good wine country around Pleasanton in the Livermore Valley probably had looked a lot better to George than the wild side of the Santa Lucia Mountains.

My friend's place was a shack right beside a huge fireplace where there had once been a great mansion during the 1920s, built by a famous movie actor. The mansion was built before there was even a road down at Big Sur. The mansion had been brought over the mountains on the backs of mules, strung out like ants, bringing visions of the good life to the poison oak, the ticks, and the salmon.

The mansion was on a promontory, high over the Pacific. Money could see farther in the 1920s, and one could look out and see whales and the Hawaiian Islands and the Kuomintang in China.

The mansion burned down years ago.

The actor died.

His mules were made into soap.

His mistresses became bird nests of wrinkles.

Now only the fireplace remains as a sort of Carthaginian homage to Hollywood.

I was down there a few weeks ago to see my friend's roof. I wouldn't have passed up the chance for a million dollars, as they say. The roof looked like a colander to me. If that roof and the rain were running against each other at Bay Meadows, I'd bet on the rain and plan to spend my winnings at the World's Fair in Seattle.

My own experience with the Cleveland Wrecking Yard began two days ago when I heard about a used trout stream they had on sale out at the Yard. So I caught the Number 15 bus on Columbus Avenue and went out there for the first time.

There were two Negro boys sitting behind me on the bus. They were talking about Chubby Checker and the Twist. They thought that Chubby Checker was only fifteen years old because he didn't have a mustache. Then they talked about some other guy who did the twist forty-four hours in a row until he saw George Washington crossing the Delaware.

"Man, that's what I call twisting," one of the kids said.

"I don't think I could twist no forty-four hours in a

row," the other kid said. "That's a lot of twisting."

I got off the bus right next to an abandoned Time Gaso-
line filling station and an abandoned fifty-cent self-service
car wash. There was a long field on one side of the filling
station. The field had once been covered with a housing
project during the war, put there for the shipyard workers.

On the other side of the Time filling station was the
Cleveland Wrecking Yard. I walked down there to have a
look at the used trout stream. The Cleveland Wrecking
Yard has a very long front window filled with signs and
merchandise.

There was a sign in the window advertising a laundry
marking machine for $65.00. The original cost of the ma-
chine was $175.00. Quite a saving.

There was another sign advertising new and used two
and three ton hoists. I wondered how many hoists it would
take to move a trout stream.

There was another sign that said:

THE FAMILY GIFT CENTER,
GIFT SUGGESTIONS FOR THE ENTIRE FAMILY

The window was filled with hundreds of items for the entire family. *Daddy, do you know what I want for Christmas? What, son? A bathroom. Mommy, do you know what
I want for Christmas? What, Patricia? Some roofing mate-
rial.*

There were jungle hammocks in the window for distant
relatives and dollar-ten-cent gallons of earth-brown enamel
paint for other loved ones.

There was also a big sign that said:

USED TROUT STREAM FOR SALE.
MUST BE SEEN TO BE APPRECIATED.

I went inside and looked at some ship's lanterns that were
for sale next to the door. Then a salesman came up to me
and said in a pleasant voice, "Can I help you?"

"Yes," I said. "I'm curious about the trout stream you
have for sale. Can you tell me something about it? How
are you selling it?"

"We're selling it by the foot length. You can buy as little

as you want or you can buy all we've got left. A man came in here this morning and bought 563 feet. He's going to give it to his niece for a birthday present," the salesman said.

"We're selling the waterfalls separately of course, and the trees and birds, flowers, grass and ferns we're also selling extra. The insects we're giving away free with a minimum purchase of ten feet of stream."

"How much are you selling the stream for?" I asked.

"Six dollars and fifty cents a foot," he said. "That's for the first hundred feet. After that it's five dollars a foot."

"How much are the birds?" I asked.

"Thirty-five cents apiece," he said. "But of course they're used. We can't guarantee anything."

"How wide is the stream?" I asked. "You said you were selling it by the length, didn't you?"

"Yes," he said. "We're selling it by the length. Its width runs between five and eleven feet. You don't have to pay anything extra for width. It's not a big stream, but it's very pleasant."

"What kinds of animals do you have?" I asked.

"We only have three deer left," he said.

"Oh . . . What about flowers?"

"By the dozen," he said.

"Is the stream clear?" I asked.

"Sir," the salesman said. "I wouldn't want you to think that we would ever sell a murky trout stream here. We always make sure they're running crystal clear before we even think about moving them."

"Where did the stream come from?" I asked.

"Colorado," he said. "We moved it with loving care. We've never damaged a trout stream yet. We treat them all as if they were china."

"You're probably asked this all the time, but how's fishing in the stream?" I asked.

"Very good," he said. "Mostly German browns, but there are a few rainbows."

"What do the trout cost?" I asked.

"They come with the stream," he said. "Of course it's all luck. You never know how many you're going to get or how big they are. But the fishing's very good, you might say it's excellent. Both bait and dry fly," he said smiling.

"Where's the stream at?" I asked. "I'd like to take a look at it."

"It's around in back," he said. "You go straight through that door and then turn right until you're outside. It's stacked in lengths. You can't miss it. The waterfalls are upstairs in the used plumbing department."

"What about the animals?"

"Well, what's left of the animals are straight back from the stream. You'll see a bunch of our trucks parked on a road by the railroad tracks. Turn right on the road and follow it down past the piles of lumber. The animal shed's right at the end of the lot."

"Thanks," I said. "I think I'll look at the waterfalls first. You don't have to come with me. Just tell me how to get there and I'll find my own way."

"All right," he said. "Go up those stairs. You'll see a bunch of doors and windows, turn left and you'll find the used plumbing department. Here's my card if you need any help."

"Okay," I said. "You've been a great help already. Thanks a lot. I'll take a look around."

"Good luck," he said.

I went upstairs and there were thousands of doors there. I'd never seen so many doors before in my life. You could have built an entire city out of those doors. Doorstown. And there were enough windows up there to build a little suburb entirely out of windows. Windowville.

I turned left and went back and saw the faint glow of pearl-colored light. The light got stronger and stronger as I went farther back, and then I was in the used plumbing department, surrounded by hundreds of toilets.

The toilets were stacked on shelves. They were stacked five toilets high. There was a skylight above the toilets that made them glow like the Great Taboo Pearl of the South Sea movies.

Stacked over against the wall were the waterfalls. There were about a dozen of them, ranging from a drop of a few feet to a drop of ten or fifteen feet.

There was one waterfall that was over sixty feet long. There were tags on the pieces of the big falls describing the correct order for putting the falls back together again.

The waterfalls all had price tags on them. They were

more expensive than the stream. The waterfalls were selling
for $19.00 a foot.

I went into another room where there were piles of
sweet-smelling lumber, glowing a soft yellow from a different color skylight above the lumber. In the shadows at
the edge of the room under the sloping roof of the building
were many sinks and urinals covered with dust, and there
was also another waterfall about seventeen feet long, lying
there in two lengths and already beginning to gather dust.

I had seen all I wanted of the waterfalls, and now I was
very curious about the trout stream, so I followed the salesman's directions and ended up outside the building.

O I had never in my life seen anything like that trout
stream. It was stacked in piles of various lengths: ten, fifteen, twenty feet, etc. There was one pile of hundred-foot
lengths. There was also a box of scraps. The scraps were in
odd sizes ranging from six inches to a couple of feet.

There was a loudspeaker on the side of the building and
soft music was coming out. It was a cloudy day and sea-
gulls were circling high overhead.

Behind the stream were big bundles of trees and bushes.
They were covered with sheets of patched canvas. You
could see the tops and roots sticking out the ends of the
bundles.

I went up close and looked at the lengths of stream. I
could see some trout in them. I saw one good fish. I saw
some crawdads crawling around the rocks at the bottom.

It looked like a fine stream. I put my hand in the water.
It was cold and felt good.

I decided to go around to the side and look at the
animals. I saw where the trucks were parked beside the
railroad tracks. I followed the road down past the piles of
lumber, back to the shed where the animals were.

The salesman had been right. They were practically out
of animals. About the only thing they had left in any abun-
dance were mice. There were hundreds of mice.

Beside the shed was a huge wire birdcage, maybe fifty
feet high, filled with many kinds of birds. The top of the
cage had a piece of canvas over it, so the birds wouldn't
get wet when it rained. There were woodpeckers and wild
canaries and sparrows.

On my way back to where the trout stream was piled, I found the insects. They were inside a prefabricated steel building that was selling for eighty cents a square foot. There was a sign over the door. It said:

INSECTS

THE JEWBIRD

BERNARD MALAMUD

The window was open so the skinny bird flew in. Flappity-
flap with its frazzled black wings. That's how it goes. It's
open, you're in. Closed, you're out and that's your fate.
The bird wearily flapped through the open kitchen window
of Harry Cohen's top-floor apartment on First Avenue
near the lower East River. On a rod on the wall hung an
escaped canary cage, its door wide open, but this black-
type longbeaked bird—its ruffled head and small dull eyes,
crossed a little, making it look like a dissipated crow—
landed if not smack on Cohen's thick lamb chop, at least
on the table, close by. The frozen foods salesman was sitting at supper with his wife and young son on a hot August
evening a year ago. Cohen, a heavy man with hairy chest
and beefy shorts; Edie, in skinny yellow shorts and red
halter; and their ten-year-old Morris (after her father)—
Maurie, they called him, a nice kid though not overly
bright—were all in the city after two weeks out, because
Cohen's mother was dying. They had been enjoying Kings-
ton, New York, but drove back when Mama got sick in
her flat in the Bronx.

"Right on the table," said Cohen, putting down his beer
glass and swatting at the bird. "Son of a bitch."

"Harry, take care with your language," Edie said, looking at Maurie, who watched every move.

The bird cawed hoarsely and with a flap of its bedraggled wings—feathers tufted this way and that—rose heavily

to the top of the open kitchen door, where it perched staring down.

"Gevalt, a pogrom!"

"It's a talking bird," said Edie in astonishment.

"In Jewish," said Maurie.

"Wise guy," muttered Cohen. He gnawed on his chop, then put down the bone. "So if you can talk, say what's your business. What do you want here?"

"If you can't spare a lamb chop," said the bird, "I'll settle for a piece of herring with a crust of bread. You can't live on your nerve forever."

"This ain't a restaurant," Cohen replied. "All I'm asking is what brings you to this address?"

"The window was open," the bird sighed; adding after a moment, "I'm running. I'm flying but I'm also running."

"From whom?" asked Edie with interest.

"Anti-Semeets."

"Anti-Semites?" they all said.

"That's from who."

"What kind of anti-Semites bother a bird?" Edie asked.

"Any kind," said the bird, "also including eagles, vultures, and hawks. And once in a while some crows will take your eyes out."

"But aren't you a crow?"

"Me? I'm a Jewbird."

Cohen laughed heartily. "What do you mean by that?"

The bird began dovening. He prayed without Book or tallith, but with passion. Edie bowed her head though not Cohen. And Maurie rocked back and forth with the prayer, looking up with one wide-open eye.

When the prayer was done Cohen remarked, "No hat, no phylacteries?"

"I'm an old radical."

"You're sure you're not some kind of a ghost or dybbuk?"

"Not a dybbuk," answered the bird, "though one of my relatives had such an experience once. It's all over now, thanks God. They freed her from a former lover, a crazy jealous man. She's now the mother of two wonderful children."

"Birds?" Cohen asked slyly.

"Why not?"

"What kind of birds?"

"Like me. Jewbirds."

Cohen tipped back in his chair and guffawed. "That's a big laugh. I've heard of a Jewfish but not a Jewbird."

"We're once removed." The bird rested on one skinny leg, then on the other. "Please, could you spare maybe a piece of herring with a small crust of bread?"

Edie got up from the table.

"What are you doing?" Cohen asked her.

"I'll clear the dishes."

Cohen turned to the bird. "So what's your name, if you don't mind saying?"

"Call me Schwartz."

"He might be an old Jew changed into a bird by somebody," said Edie, removing a plate.

"Are you?" asked Harry, lighting a cigar.

"Who knows?" answered Schwartz. "Does God tell us everything?"

Maurie got up on his chair. "What kind of herring?" he asked the bird in excitement.

"Get down, Maurie, or you'll fall," ordered Cohen.

"If you haven't got matjes, I'll take schmaltz," said Schwartz.

"All we have is marinated, with slices of onion—in a jar," said Edie.

"If you'll open for me the jar I'll eat marinated. Do you have also, if you don't mind, a piece of rye bread—the spitz?"

Edie thought she had.

"Feed him out on the balcony," Cohen said. He spoke to the bird. "After that take off."

Schwartz closed both bird eyes. "I'm tired and it's a long way."

"Which direction are you headed, north or south?"

Schwartz, barely lifting his wings, shrugged.

"You don't know where you're going?"

"Where there's charity I'll go."

"Let him stay, papa," said Maurie. "He's only a bird."

"So stay the night," Cohen said, "but no longer."

In the morning Cohen ordered the bird out of the house but Maurie cried, so Schwartz stayed for a while. Maurie was still on vacation from school and his friends were away. He was lonely and Edie enjoyed the fun he had, playing with the bird.

"He's no trouble at all," she told Cohen, "and besides his appetite is very small."

"What'll you do when he makes dirty?"

"He flies across the street in a tree when he makes dirty, and if nobody passes below, who notices?"

"So all right," said Cohen, "but I'm dead set against it. I warn you he ain't gonna stay here long."

"What have you got against the poor bird?"

"Poor bird, my ass. He's a foxy bastard. He thinks he's a Jew."

"What difference does it make what he thinks?"

"A Jewbird, what a chuzpah. One false move and he's out on his drumsticks."

At Cohen's insistence Schwartz lived out on the balcony in a new wooden birdhouse Edie had bought him.

"With many thanks," said Schwartz, "though I would rather have a human roof over my head. You know how it is at my age. I like the warm, the windows, the smell of cooking. I would also be glad to see once in a while the *Jewish Morning Journal* and have now and then a schnapps because it helps my breathing, thanks God. But whatever you give me, you won't hear complaints."

However, when Cohen brought home a bird feeder full of dried corn, Schwartz said, "Impossible."

Cohen was annoyed. "What's the matter, crosseyes, is your life getting too good for you? Are you forgetting what it means to be migratory? I'll bet a helluva lot of crows you happen to be acquainted with, Jews or otherwise, would give their eyeteeth to eat this corn."

Schwartz did not answer. What can you say to a grubber yung?

"Not for my digestion," he later explained to Edie. "Cramps. Herring is better even if it makes you thirsty. At least rainwater don't cost anything." He laughed sadly in breathy caws.

And herring, thanks to Edie, who knew where to shop, was what Schwartz got, with an occasional piece of potato pancake, and even a bit of soupmeat when Cohen wasn't looking.

When school began in September, before Cohen would once again suggest giving the bird the boot, Edie prevailed on him to wait a little while until Maurie adjusted.

"To deprive him right now might hurt his school work, and you know what trouble we had last year."

"So okay, but sooner or later the bird goes. That I promise you."

Schwartz, though nobody had asked him, took on full responsibility for Maurie's performance in school. In return for favors granted, when he was let in for an hour or two at night, he spent most of his time overseeing the boy's lessons. He sat on top of the dresser near Maurie's desk as he laboriously wrote out his homework. Maurie was a restless type and Schwartz gently kept him to his studies. He also listened to him practice his screechy violin, taking a a few minutes off now and then to rest his ears in the bathroom. And they afterwards played dominoes. The boy was an indifferent checker player and it was impossible to teach him chess. When he was sick, Schwartz read him comic books though he personally disliked them. But Maurie's work improved in school and even his violin teacher admitted his playing was better. Edie gave Schwartz credit for these improvements though the bird poohpoohed them.

Yet he was proud there was nothing lower than C minuses on Maurie's report card, and on Edie's insistence celebrated with a little schnapps.

"If he keeps up like this," Cohen said, "I'll get him in an Ivy League college for sure."

"Oh I hope so," sighed Edie.

But Schwartz shook his head. "He's a good boy—you don't have to worry. He won't be a shicker or a wifebeater, God forbid, but a scholar he'll never be, if you know what I mean, although maybe a good mechanic. It's no disgrace in these times."

"If I were you," Cohen said, angered, "I'd keep my big snoot out of other people's private business."

"Harry, please," said Edie.

"My goddamn patience is wearing out. That crosseyes butts into everything."

Though he wasn't exactly a welcome guest in the house, Schwartz gained a few ounces although he did not improve in appearance. He looked bedraggled as ever, his feathers unkempt, as though he had just flown out of a snowstorm. He spent, he admitted, little time taking care of himself. Too much to think about. "Also outside plumbing," he told Edie. Still there was more glow to his eyes so that though Cohen went on calling him crosseyes he said it less emphatically.

Liking his situation, Schwartz tried tactfully to stay out of Cohen's way, but one night when Edie was at the movies and Maurie was taking a hot shower, the frozen foods salesman began a quarrel with the bird.

"For Christ sake, why don't you wash yourself sometimes? Why must you always stink like a dead fish?"

"Mr. Cohen, if you'll pardon me, if somebody eats garlic he will smell from garlic. I eat herring three times a day. Feed me flowers and I will smell like flowers."

"Who's obligated to feed you anything at all? You're lucky to get herring."

"Excuse me, I'm not complaining," said the bird. "You're complaining."

"What's more," said Cohen, "even from out on the balcony I can hear you snoring away like a pig. It keeps me awake at night."

"Snoring," said Schwartz, "isn't a crime, thanks God."

"All in all you are a goddamn pest and free loader. Next thing you'll want to sleep in bed next to my wife."

"Mr. Cohen," said Schwartz, "on this rest assured. A bird is a bird."

"So you say, but how do I know you're a bird and not some kind of a goddamn devil?"

"If I was a devil you would know already. And I don't mean because of your son's good marks."

"Shut up, you bastard bird," shouted Cohen.

"Grubber yung," cawed Schwartz, rising to the tips of his talons, his long wings outstretched.

Cohen was about to lunge for the bird's scrawny neck but Maurie came out of the bathroom, and for the rest of the evening until Schwartz's bedtime on the balcony, there was pretended peace.

But the quarrel had deeply disturbed Schwartz and he slept badly. His snoring woke him, and awake, he was fearful of what would become of him. Wanting to stay out of

Cohen's way, he kept to the birdhouse as much as possible. Cramped by it, he paced back and forth on the balcony ledge, or sat on the birdhouse roof, staring into space. In the evenings, while overseeing Maurie's lessons, he often fell asleep. Awakening, he nervously hopped around exploring the four corners of the room. He spent much time in Maurie's closet, and carefully examined his bureau drawers when they were left open. And once when he found a large paper bag on the floor, Schwartz poked his way into it to investigate what the possibilities were. The boy was amused to see the bird in the paper bag.

"He wants to build a nest," he said to his mother.

Edie, sensing Schwartz's unhappiness, spoke to him quietly.

"Maybe if you did some of the things my husband wants you, you would get along better with him."

"Give me a for instance," Schwartz said.

"Like take a bath, for instance."

"I'm too old for baths," said the bird. "My feathers fall out without baths."

"He says you have a bad smell."

"Everybody smells. Some people smell because of their thoughts or because who they are. My bad smell comes from the food I eat. What does his come from?"

"I better not ask him or it might make him mad," said Edie.

In late November Schwartz froze on the balcony in the fog and cold, and especially on rainy days he woke with stiff joints and could barely move his wings. Already he felt twinges of rheumatism. He would have liked to spend more time in the warm house, particularly when Maurie was in school and Cohen at work. But though Edie was goodhearted and might have sneaked him in in the morning, just to thaw out, he was afraid to ask her. In the meantime Cohen, who had been reading articles about the migration of birds, came out on the balcony one night after work when Edie was in the kitchen preparing pot roast, and peeking into the birdhouse, warned Schwartz to be on his way soon if he knew what was good for him. "Time to hit the flyways."

"Mr. Cohen, why do you hate me so much?" asked the bird. "What did I do to you?"

"Because you're an A-number-one trouble maker, that's why. What's more, whoever heard of a Jewbird? Now scat or it's open war."

But Schwartz stubbornly refused to depart so Cohen embarked on a campaign of harassing him, meanwhile hiding it from Edie and Maurie. Maurie hated violence and Cohen didn't want to leave a bad impression. He thought maybe if he played dirty tricks on the bird he would fly off without being physically kicked out. The vacation was over, let him make his easy living off the fat of somebody else's land. Cohen worried about the effect of the bird's departure on Maurie's schooling but decided to take the chance, first, because the boy now seemed to have the knack of studying—give the black bird-bastard credit—and second, because Schwartz was driving him bats by being there always, even in his dreams.

The frozen foods salesman began his campaign against the bird by mixing watery cat food with the herring slices in Schwartz's dish. He also blew up and popped numerous paper bags outside the birdhouse as the bird slept, and when he had got Schwartz good and nervous, though not enough to leave, he brought a full-grown cat into the house, supposedly a gift for little Maurie, who had always wanted a pussy. The cat never stopped springing up at Schwartz whenever he saw him, one day managing to claw out several of his tailfeathers. And even at lesson time, when the cat was usually excluded from Maurie's room, though somehow or other he quickly found his way in at the end of the lesson, Schwartz was desperately fearful of his life and flew from pinnacle to pinnacle—light fixture to clothes-tree to door-top—in order to elude the beast's wet jaws.

Once when the bird complained to Edie how hazardous his existence was, she said, "Be patient, Mr. Schwartz. When the cat gets to know you better he won't try to catch you any more."

"When he stops trying we will both be in Paradise," Schwartz answered. "Do me a favor and get rid of him. He makes my whole life worry. I'm losing feathers like a tree loses leaves."

"I'm awfully sorry but Maurie likes the pussy and sleeps with it."

What could Schwartz do? He worried but came to no decision, being afraid to leave. So he ate the herring gar-
nished with cat food, tried hard not to hear the paper bags
bursting like firecrackers outside the birdhouse at night,
and lived terror-stricken closer to the ceiling than the floor,
as the cat, his tail flicking, endlessly watched him.

Weeks went by. Then on the day after Cohen's mother
had died in her flat in the Bronx, when Maurie came home
with a zero on an arithmetic test, Cohen, enraged, waited
until Edie had taken the boy to his violin lesson, then open-
ly attacked the bird. He chased him with a broom on the
balcony and Schwartz frantically flew back and forth, finally escaping into his birdhouse. Cohen triumphantly
reached in, and grabbing both skinny legs, dragged the bird
out, cawing loudly, his wings wildly beating. He whirled
the bird around and around his head. But Schwartz, as he
moved in circles, managed to swoop down and catch Cohen's nose in his beak, and hung on for dear life. Cohen
cried out in great pain, punched the bird with his fist, and
tugging at its legs with all his might, pulled his nose free.
Again he swung the yawking Schwartz around until the
bird grew dizzy, then with a furious heave, flung him into
the night. Schwartz sank like stone into the street. Cohen
then tossed the birdhouse and feeder after him, listening at
the ledge until they crashed on the sidewalk below. For a
full hour, broom in hand, his heart palpitating and nose
throbbing with pain, Cohen waited for Schwartz to return
but the broken-hearted bird didn't.

That's the end of that dirty bastard, the salesman
thought and went in. Edie and Maurie had come home.

"Look," said Cohen, pointing to his bloody nose swollen
three times its normal size, "what that sonofabitchy bird
did. It's a permanent scar."

"Where is he now?" Edie asked, frightened.

"I threw him out and he flew away. Good riddance."

Nobody said no, though Edie touched a handkerchief to
her eyes and Maurie rapidly tried the nine times table and
found he knew approximately half.

In the spring when the winter's snow had melted, the
boy, moved by a memory, wandered in the neighborhood,
looking for Schwartz. He found a dead black bird in a

small lot near the river, his two wings broken, neck twisted, and both bird-eyes plucked clean.

"Who did it to you, Mr. Schwartz?" Maurie wept.

"Anti-Semeets," Edie said later.

PECAN TREE

JAMES GILES

Dusk-blackness enveloping him, midnight only moments away and Ben Hickerson, carrying an axe, drifting through the haze. The fence floating placidly by him as he walks, and then the tree, with the branches hanging over the fence, dropping pecans on the invisible ground, across the fence . . . across the fence . . .

I told H.C. iffen he didn't cut them branches. I told him. I ain't ashamed. He should a known what I'd do.

The axe swinging through the air. Bark flying. Night air chilling him but the sweat beginning to burst out all over his body then salty wetness in his eyes and mouth. The salt bitter.

"You can't cut down that thar tree. That thar tree belonged to ole H.C. You can't cut down that thar tree." The voice was that of a small boy whom he had chased out of his yard only last week.

Should have seen him, how long has he been thar in the dark watching with them little ugly eyes that glow like that? How long? Maybe he seen or heard the other.

"You go on home afore I take this axe to you. You go on home."

"I know."

"What you know?"

"I know about before."

"Before. What you mean 'before'?"

"I mean I know about in thar."

The house, does he know about the house, he'll tell ev-

eryone and then they'll come. Hell, so he tells them, they'll know anyway, and they'll know when Ben Hickerson talks he means what he says, so what if they know, I warned him, didn't I tell him iffen he didn't cut off them branches . . .

"Get out!" The axe swinging wildly in the direction of the small figure and the scream coming from the smallboy voice and then the boy running.

"Get him! Hurry! Afore he gets me!" the boy yelling frantically at no one, at anyone.

Guess they'll know, but what iffen they do, didn't I warn him and not only him. Yesterday I sat right there and I says to all five of them, 'he lets that damn pecan tree dump its damn branches and pecans on my side of the fence and I tell him to cut off them goddam branches and he won't pay no attention to me and iffen he don't do something about them branches I'm a-goin' to shoot the ole bastard,' and George butts in, 'Ben you ain't goin' to shoot nobody, them branches ain't a hurtin' you,' and they laugh like they always laugh and I says again, 'Iffen he don't cut off them branches I'm a-goin' to shoot him,' and that damn fool Salty speaks up, 'Now Ben if you would jest speak to him,' and I says to the ole fool and he is the goddamdest ole fool in all this county except for H.C. 'I did talk to him . . .'

Blood running into his mouth from where the bark flew up and cut him over the eye. The blood mixing with the salt from the sweat in his mouth and tasting sweet.

I talked to ole H.C. jest a few hours ago, I sat right thar in that house at his table and I told him to cut off them branches, and he gives that fool grin he always had since I knowed him as a boy and we would go swimmin' and while he was swimmin' he would grin, I never saw him when he wasn't grinnin' 'cept when Louisa, his wife, died then he didn't grin . . .

"Thar it's done." The tree falling and the dust coming up and pervading his nostrils. His hands bloody and raw from swinging the axe and his entire body filled with rawness and soreness.

If he would a only done what I told him but no when I warn him he only grins and says, 'Now Ben you don't mean that,' and I says, 'Yes,' and he says, 'Even you ain't that mean Ben sides I couldn't cut them branches off I love that ole tree, that tree's been here ever since I had this

*place, I love it, it's like me old but still here,' and he goes
on talkin' foolishness like that until I warn him again and
then he says 'But Ben I couldn't cut them branches off . . .'*

Walking back and past the fence and into his yard and
sitting down on the porch and laying the axe by him on the
ground. Concrete porch steps cold this late at night.

*If he only would a done it but I knew he wouldn't so I
went back and went in my house and got the gun and loaded it with the shells I been keepin' in the drawer jest in case
he wouldn't, and then I go back and he's still sittin' thar,
and he looks so funny when he sees me with the gun. First
he grins and then he doesn't grin like when Louisa died,
and I says, 'Are you goin' to?' and he says, 'No Ben now
put . . .'' and that's all he can get out cause afore I know
I've shot him, it was kinda funny he was talkin' and then
there was jest blood all over his what-was-face, and he fell
and the blood spreading all over the room even to my
shoes, they's still some on there, and so I leave and come
back over here and put up the gun and get the axe . . .*

"He's over thar. He's over thar." The smallboy voice
yelling, and the disciplined murmur of the crowdvoice
coming toward him.

Ole Ben looked up at the sound of the voices.

*Well I guess they're comin' now. They'll know. They'll
know I mean it when I talk. And didn't I warn him . . .*

Five months later, *The Travis City, Texas Daily Herald*
ran the following news feature:

> A jury last week sentenced Ben Hickerson to a two-
> year suspended sentence for the murder of H.C.
> Webb. The jury explained the leniency of the sentence
> on the basis that Hickerson had been defending his
> personal property at the time of the killing. . . .

A HARVEST

GLENN MEETER

"We shall come rejoicing, bringing in the sheaves."

Ah, spring is in the air, and the blood leaps to the high-way's call. Fields from Kansas to the Panhandle lie white unto the harvest, and north from Dakota to Athabaska's smoking muskeg the acres of green blades glitter, potentially gold. Each time the earth turns around the sun spreads eighteen hours of light at your feet like a rose and silver rug. In a dozen ports of entry comrades and customers wait, scanning the sky which bulges profitably blue, and pray your safe arrival. Grain prices climb with the arc of the sun, the great plain labors with bread for the world, and your harvesters wait for you, greased, gassed, insured. Come along!

If you hesitate I can understand. You, like myself, are no tiller of soil, no giant in the earth, no warrior, pioneer, entrepreneur, no Hemingway hero either (bullfighter, expatriate soldier, wounded fisher for trout), but more of an Updike sort of fellow, a dealer in certain abstractions, propositions, positions, promotions, situations . . . An expert. Our offices maintain forever a temperate, shady, though well-lighted, climate. We do work that is also done by women. How to suspend disbelief in a job that follows the seasons, rises with the dawn, engages heavy machines against the earth? And how to imagine ourselves part of such a thick-fingered family as this, where wives get up in darkness to bake bread for their men, make their break-

fasts, clean their boots, and then deferentially wake them,
obeisance in the touch of their hands?

"Hank—"

A genuflection in the dark doorway; on his bed the god
stirs, phlegmatic.

"Coffee's ready—Hank?"

Imagine only a marriage. One female child in this tribe
of farmers and mowers, escaping the usual fate of exposure
to the elements, was allowed to grow up and go to the city:
there you married her, partly from that romantic streak
that makes you sometimes mention that your grandfather
lived "on the land." And so here you are on the prairie, en
route to metropolitan in-service expense-paid and tax-de-
ductible conference, convention, symposium, or workshop,
breathing the once-a-year air, getting your hair cut for a
dollar and a quarter, and storing the mind with second-
hand rural delights.

You are no harvester. You feel that, though their smiles
around the groaning board concede that freeways are as
worthy an opponent as nature; you feel it in the pallor of
your fingers on rough-textured slices which they cut from
thick, legendary loaves and butter with the high-priced
spread, loyal to their guild. You are no harvester but you
agree to a harvest of sorts: you will drive with an older
brother (he leaves his farm to a sixteen-year-old son) seven
hundred grassy miles south, so that he can replace the
youngest brother on a combine crew. This youngest brother, now swinging a John Deere across Oklahoma like Alley
Oop on a brontosaurus, must be brought home and fitted
with uniform and sleeping bag and kit, for he is going to
war. Not the real war—that would cast some melancholy
over the trip. This is only a summer practice for the National Guard, two weeks in the Black Hills like a vacation
(the mother laughs, fitting South Dakota's coyote emblem
the wrong way on his sleeve, and contentedly, as if sewing
baby-garments, does her stitches again); and so you look
forward wholeheartedly to your part in this son-gathering
expedition, your part which consists, as you admit with a
deprecating laugh, mostly of going along for the ride.

Secretly you feel otherwise. Your journey is only two
days, but a day to fruit-flies and to God is as a thousand
years, and space too is experience, like time. From the be-

ginning, swimming awake in the wake of dawn (your wife, resuming country courtesy, treads softly round your altar), splashing costly water on your eyelids (uncertain of bathroom manners where toilets, a recent innovation, flush reluctantly), breakfasting to the hushed flutes of wood doves, you sense in this journey a numinous significance, something to be memorialized beyond mere quantities of mileage. The stacks of homemade buns, the phallic Thermos, the wife's good-bye, the father's blessing ("Good luck," as he puts on his hat for the fields), the sunglasses, the shaving kit, the auto club Great Plains Guidebook unfolding mighty alluviations of glacier and river and road, and the geography of the trip itself, south and north with nature against the course of westering civilization, down the continent's midriff with buffalo and redmen and no others until the harvester crews—this gives an aureole of purpose even to keeping a drowsy driver awake or transporting a boy from work to rituals of war. Suffused with lightness and power, you make with the roughboned farmer beside you (Gerard, pronounced *Jard* like the clashing of gears) an emblem of spirit and flesh like the prairie and cloud horizon, on your right as you roll to the south.

"Farming seems . . . impersonal, nowadays. Nobody builds barns anymore. Only sheds. Quonset huts. I bet the last real barns were built thirty, fifty years ago."

An easy opening but his nod is brief. Perhaps he senses what you now recognize, that in the in-law's extension of sibling rivalry you minimize his job by subsuming it under your own. But acres of morning silence marshal your argument: as the grass breathes quietly, wet with sleep, sunlight speeds infinitesimal packs of energy down conveyor-belts to each green plant. A lark spirals upward, following the phrases of its song, life imitating art. Trees in windbreaks angling stiffly north and west deny the non-Euclidean curves of earth. Thermos-shaped silos, bullets, aim at the sky. The Missouri River, mapped by Lewis and Clark, dammed by Army engineers, is an artificial lake; crossing it, and crossing a line purely intellectual, academic, you enter a new state where people owe allegiances in a different direction and even wildlife is preserved in different seasons, under different rules.

"The modern farmer is citified, really. Half engineer,

half scientist. And market analyst. And politician. Lobbyist. Plants and animals don't have much to do with it."

He smiles as at a falsely clever witticism. "How about Harold?"

Harold, the oldest brother, is known to love the creatures which he raises to slaughter. It is easy to show that Harold's ability to call a hundred Herefords by name, making fine discriminations in spine-length, placement of eyes, and whorls of white hair—or bending over a patch of native sod, to name the individual gramma and buffalo grasses and blue-grass and fescue, annuals and perennials, up to fifteen varieties symbiotically existing in one square foot of "grass"—that this is less instinct or love of earth than sheer intellectual power, categorizing and abstract.

Though eroded grease on his pin-striped bib overalls proclaims him a Quonset and machine, not a barn man, Gerard shrugs and steps on the gas, leaving in his dust a town named for the philosopher Spencer. "Well, Harold always had a memory on him." His bulk on the front seat puts you in his field of gravity, so that you have to lean slightly toward the window. Your point is, the whole ecology of the plains is a web of civilization's weaving—cattle from Scotland and England and Holland, the horse from Spain, the Chinese elm, the Russian olive, the exotic pheasant, the wheat itself, all from Asia, hardly one thing unimported in all the rustic prairie . . . Asia evokes the Guardsman who is the goal of your journey, and with him the images of ships passing on the Pacific, one heavy with bayonets and the other with wheat and pheasants and silver-leafed trees. You swing to an explanation of the excesses done in the name of progress, the making of the dust bowl, the slaughter of buffalo, the ravishment of the Black Hills —these should not be charged to the rational or civilizing principle but to its opposite, a naked instinctive greed. These were mere practical men, their trouble was they didn't *think*.

Gerard keeps his eyes on the road, which glitters now in the sharper angle of the sun. His answer is to ask for lunch, an instinctive rhetoric that forces you to woman's subservience: you serve, he eats and drinks, driving easily with one hand through Greeley, Nebraska. Greeley, a town with shaggy elms and sewers that hump the road, was named for

a journalist who was himself named Horace after the
Roman poet; and as you consider this link between the cul-
tures of Rome and Greeley Gerard says, "Somebody had to
kill them though. Else we couldn't raise any crops."

He means the buffalo. But in the wake of his seriousness
poets, journalists, and all their progeny of wordsmen seem
to expire feet up on the prairie, bull calf and cow, useful
like the bison to exhibit in museums or for the delicacy of
their tongue. Outside the narrow sundrenched streets of St.
Paul Gerard jabs a finger: "There's wheat." It is *his* language, harsh vowels and burred consonants, that has
power. *Thairzweet*. There's wheat, there's wheat; Garden
City has *froze out*, but here by God there's wheat! Green
waves break past the window into individual spears, drilled
in rows. There's wheat. In Red Cloud, home of Willa
Cather, where the sons of pioneers have built a Willa Cather curio shop and museum in an abandoned dry-goods
store where a white-haired lady has lunch alone from wax
paper and Dixie Cup, Gerard stops for gas and lets you
take the wheel.

Downs, Osborne, Luray, Russell, Great Bend, St. John,
Pratt. Map-knowledge is a poor substitute for Gerard's
blood-memory, seasons of pushing the big rigs over weary
hills. Kansas, announced by signs as the home of sunflow-
ers and Miss America, offers empty, rock-edged fields,
farmed by remote control from the irrigated towns. It is a
mistake that no one lives between Downs and Osborne or
walks the twenty-two miles between Osborne and Luray or
touches with his hand the stone fence-posts between Luray
and Russell. Dead houses, gray eyeless skulls where once
Eisenhower and Dorothy of Oz and Olympic distance run-
ners and Miss America lived; thousands in your city hole
like lab-mice while in all non-urban Kansas only a lineman
in tin hat and an orange-vested road crew breathe the
country air, which they taint with fumes of tar. Man should
live in harmony with nature: Gerard agrees, speaks of
shooting deer in Wyoming while his eyes are on the wheat.
Yellow already. Be cutting before Ok'ahoma. It is hot, your
back aches, your eyeballs burn, the white line like a car-
penter's tape zips to your forehead. There is fatigue in
doing nothing but sitting in control of power. In the cool
sky a white hawk swims, sailing with dignity though pur-

sued by small frantic housekeeping birds down a secret
river of air. A truck on its back, wheels and dirty belly sky-
ward amid alarmed red flags, floods you with the sweetness
of existence. Why not live like hawk or bird or Negro boy
on a bicycle (Kansas was a slave state once, but in this boy
in Pratt or the black nurse sashaying through the heat of
Medicine Lodge appears no sullenness like that on the
faces of black strivers in your city, born bitter and consciously oppressed)—why not this simple state of being?
Ah, down here the Mobilgas man speaks softly Southern
and you bless the memory of unpainted wooden signs of
Pentecostals, Baptists, and Brethrens who replace the Mid-
west Gothic Lutherans and Catholics and tight-sphinctered
Reformed, whose metal advertisements back North always
took the shape of shields or arrows. The Methodists have
been with you all the way, like the poor, but down here
they too build churches of wood not brick, speak slow, live
warm and easy like the soft-barked cottonwoods not
ranked in rows but sauntering, graceful, following in lazy
curves the flow of water and the land.

Wheat is being cut. Leathery men and kerchiefed peas-
ant women, the flash of whose bare arms is more seductive
than all Hollywood. Cramped in a crazy speeding furnace
which perverts the sun's love, your right leg growing numb,
you envy the laboring man his nightly sweet-breathed sleep,
still more the exhausting no-nonsense heavy-limbed cou-
pling which you imagine to take place when the sun goes
down in Kansas.

> Oh the people never wed
> Or so I've heard it said
> They just tumble into bed
>   In Kansas.

This tune together with Champlin, Great Name in the
Great Plains, drifts through the brain's dry channels into
Oklahoma. Big-armed combines shoulder you to the ditch,
and their drivers, kings of the road, hold left hands as
blinders to the sun and happily chew one thought, the four-
dollar acres of Kansas tomorrow. You envy them, yes, and
heavy instinctive Gerard, since Nature is the name of all
paradises—but how, without you, would they abstract an

ideal from even the barns wombing their own childhoods, hay cattle and boy one warmth with mice and lantern and cat against the snow? Without you, without vision, they were blinded lemmings who trampled their way to disaster, Quonset huts, war . . .

Gerard takes the wheel. It is a relief to bathe the mind in longing for supper and bed. Fatigue swims out of Chester, Seiling, Taloga. Though your journey began in June it's August, Dakota's yellow dandelions gone to seed, the green wheat burned white, and below the Canadian River's trickle (Drink Canada *Dry*) hardly a stalk uncut. Cicadas sing in the evening heat. Dust blows from fall plowing, burros on the red rock chew brown grass. Hills, horses; tractors, plains. At Hobart conical mountains loom like promises unfulfilled from the horizon you will never reach, and glad of it—Abilene, Laredo, salt and oil, Mexico and the other Americas funneling poverty down to the Horn—the thought of those miles daring to exist to be travelled in other journeys burdens the mind like a concept of stars or religion.

"There they are."

Washed clean for Kansas, trucks bearing Gerard's name stand at roadside tailing docile green elephants. Gerard is renewed; while you stay in the car he braves a farmer's dog to find the trailer parked near a field of pinto beans. There the youngest brother and his crew stow beer-cans and pack guitar, records, dirty bedding, socks, hats, paper-backed history and pornography, moving on. "A bitter run," says the crew, mocking careful epic Gerard; "Ah, 'twas a bitter run." One, who averages less than average at Chadron State, so says the youngest brother, is wearing a Harvard sweat-shirt. Showered, sunburned, using life's first razor, they trust nightfall and a clean truck to bring them the girls of Oklahoma. As for you, after supper with the brothers-in-law (chicken in jackets of batter), after wandering Hobart's dark streets to pay hospitable but accurately profit-taking garagemen and restaurateurs, you lie dirty and relaxed on one of Hobart Hotel's three-dollar beds while Gerard on another sleeps vigorously, his breath threatening the springs. Floating free of him in the rattle of air-conditioning like a soul leaving a body, you have a thought he would never have, that life, like your journey, is half over;

and you ask, sinking asleep, not disappointed but in a
curiously self-congratulatory way, pleased with your discovery, what, oh what have I done, what have I left behind
me but the miles?

Morning brings June again, dark-bellied clouds on a cool
wind. A long-tailed swallow, trailing straw, hovers near the
combine's cutter-bar arm, measuring against hereditary
minuscule blueprints: before she darts away you see the
tiny wing-pits working hard, red against the trim white
chest as if she sweats blood. Everything, the sky, your
body, is washed clean. You travel now with Brian, the
youngest; leaving the others plodding behind you speed to
Chester, where you breakfast on doughnuts (only a nickel
in the wheat flour Bible belt, good measure, pressed down,
running over) and Brian arranges jobs for his crew through
the agency of the cafe waitress.

"He *was* waiting on some fellows from Minnesota. I believe."

Uh-huh. Well, whatever he wants to do. We'll be in
today, is all.

"Well, he ain't but one big field, I know *that's* ready
now . . ."

Uh-huh. Well, far as that goes, we could start within
three, four hours. Maybe less. If he wants to have it done.

"Well, I could *call*, I spose . . ."

We've got two trucks. If he needs any hauling. And two
rigs. If you think he wants it done right away.

"Well, why don't I just call him, then."

Well, I guess it wouldn't hurt. We did four hundred
acres down to Hobart.

Tall, pale, thin-legged, narrow-faced, Brian is different
from his brother. His speech is submissively persistent. At
twenty-three the captain of delicate mortgaged equipment
and a crew of eighteen-year-olds, he rouses your admira-
tion. Unrolling morning miles of Oklahoma you consider
his difference from Gerard: seventeen years younger, born
into war and prosperity, depression dust forgotten, brought
up on TV and flush toilet, his system tuned not to Yankton
but Kansas City and Minneapolis for the Big Leagues
there. He is further from Lewis and Clark by a long generation but dresses more like the West: black grainy high-

heeled boots, tight-legged pants with peaked pockets, three-button-cuffed shirt, suede jacket with outlined shoulder-piece, and a felt Stetson, stylized version of his brother's beat-up straw. Whatever his role, Pecos or Wild Bill or one of the James Boys, he takes it seriously, the back seat is crowded with his costumes; but he talks with you easily in the common tongue of pop tunes and editorials. Trusting you he sleeps, boots off, into Kansas, slumbers through the scene of one of his triumphs, a roadside park where he spent a day replacing, by himself, a piston. A piston is a thing you remember to have occurred in high school physics in a four-stage diagram, and, from bitter experience with repairmen, to involve rings. O Western Ulysses, man of stratagems! Awaking, he offers a cigarette, and suddenly, in his red-and-white package colored like a plug to lure fishermen and largemouthed bass, you see, like the travellers from Emmaus, what resurrection of the West he represents: the Marlboro Man.

Christmas Season
Here's the reason

Buy your tree
Locally!

Canadian trees
Cut before freeze

Without a doubt
They dry out.

St. John Tree Farm
St. John Kan.

Cuts them fresh,
They're the best!

See you in
St. John!

Counting the miles measured by handlettered verses you talk wheat, speculating how long before Gerard reaches each yellow field. At lunch in St. John's Grill and Texaco Station you talk wheat, wheat, praising by implication his work, his independence, his pluck.

"I wouldn't want to do this all my life, though," he says. He pays for two meals, tycooning on a credit card.

"But what else?" He has harvested from Mexico to Canada, from March to December. "What else is there?"

He drives through the oil wells near Great Bend, where donkey engines masked by billboards (GrainBelt Beer, Kill Rootworms Fast!) do the work of a thousand John Henrys.

"Something important," he says. "Like . . . your job."

Your office returns in manila folders, gray fluorescent tubes, sweat smell imbedded in suits because the voice of authority breaks down deodorant.

"Something a hundred other guys can't do."

By a law of life the youngest child seeks new ways to excel: the others are farmers so he's an operator, yes, but excellence is always far off. Boss of two rigs, two trucks, he despairs at the earthquake rumble of outfits from Saskatchewan and Alberta and Colorado moving ten, twelve, sixteen combines and a platoon of men; he can't bear it, he wants, you can tell by his driving, to be first on the road.

"I been thinking about the Army," he says.

There are special deals in the Army where your way is paid through college—he wishes now he'd gone—and some guys make the military a career. Why not? Liberal and peaceful by nature, you hate shouters, and with what weapon should the pacifist attack the military? Moving north in Kansas where five-ranked windbreaks (cedar, olive, cottonwood, olive, cedar) guard the chartreuse wheatfields from the snow, you see how softness needs a shell. All those Pentecostals and Brethren shared their freedom and loved one another nestled within America's tightest system, a place for everyone and everyone in his place, while in the free and open North the grim-lipped Calvinist must place himself. Those neat green dairy farms, islands of rural bliss, are, like the home of every contentment, totalitarian Edens, strapped down and squared away like their tight-capped silos; this Prussian land makes milk for babies, mothers being the first, best militarists. Brian has a mind of his own, this self-made Marlboro Man has the dignity of human freedom too; and so you say nothing.

Once out of Kansas he sleeps, boots off, in the back, trusting you to take him where the mother readies his uniform and kit. No side trips east or west, Chicago decadence or untilled height of the Rockies; the journey is predestined north. In Red Cloud, Nebraska, the Willa Cather museum and curio shop is about to close. An hour to Grand Island, ninety minutes to the head of the sandhill country. You amuse yourself with your allegory, the final proof of which is the allegory itself—for it is at this period of life, when the sun slides slowly north and the journey approaches its end, that we cease testing what has been and planning what must be done, and keep ourselves awake imagining that the whole of it has some meaning, anticipating, perhaps, a smile from those who wait, or homebaked pie in the kitchen bye and bye, when the machine at last stops and the roaring in our ears, the nerves' vibration, the cramp in the legs, dissolves and dwindles away. Life as a recapitulative journey, old age with the freedom of youth, senility as infancy: a pleasing thought as you note how evening echoes morning, how in a lush green field cow leaps upon cow, nature performing civilized perversions, nothing new under the sun, as biologists tell of incest and cannibalism among the lower orders and the noble red elk of Scotland abusing himself on a log. A long aching drive through grass and cattle and horses (patiently doubled, head to withers) with the sun in your eyes: you long for darkness though it means the end of the road. Just north of Spencer, where all are ready for bed, a deer rushes up from the ditch in yellow-blue light—the only deer you have ever seen where the signs warn DEER CROSSING, and you fancy it as a glimpse of beyond. Soon, crossing the Missouri in dusk, the sun glowing blue like a footlight beneath earth's rim, you'll be an hour from the last stop of all, in total dark.

And to what end? To bring a young man one step from peace to war. Yes, and to bring yourself memories: sky, cloud, grass, trees, springtime and harvest, arc of light and orbit of man. And knowledge—ah, twice seven-hundred miles, like seventy years, gives a man a great gust of the world and makes him know what it is to be alive! The Dakota border, a goal you have set. Brian takes the wheel and you sink to a passenger's quiescence, let the dark wind rush

as it will. A star fades in, your eyes close. Is it really knowledge, then, when one does nothing, acts on nothing, feels
nothing? Last night you pissed on the beans in the dark,
playing Henry David Thoreau . . . A whiff of smoke,
Brian's Marlboro. You fall from him as last night Gerard
set you free. Floating on the earth's thin crust, which floats
on fire like a face (Gerard's, Brian's, your own) masking
certain disaster, why should a man put down his hand?
Drowsy, the mind blinks: pheasant in horizontal flight, yel-
low-bibbed lark, fiery wheat, heavy harvesters, red dirt and
white dust, sunlight's stab on glass, gravel, oil, wide Slavic
forehead, Grainbelt, Champlin, Allis-Chalmers, and aloft
with the merest forward effort, a hawk and a boy on a bike,
yes you would do it again, touching nothing, learning nothing, doing nothing at all, but my God what a delight, just to
travel through!

MR. BLUE

ROBERT CREELEY

I don't want to give you only the grotesqueness, not only what it then seemed. It is useless enough to remember but to remember only what is unpleasant seems particularly foolish. I suspect that you have troubles of your own, and, since you have, why bother you with more. Mine against yours. That seems a waste of time. But perhaps mine are also yours. And if that's so, you'll find me a sympathetic listener.

A few nights ago I wrote down some of this, thinking, trying to think, of what had happened. What had really happened like they say. It seemed, then, that some such effort might get me closer to an understanding of the thing than I was. So much that was not directly related had got in and I thought a little noting of what was basic to the problem might be in order. That is, I wanted to analyze it, to try to see where things stood. I'm not at all sure that it got to anything, this attempt, because I'm not very good at it. But you can look for yourselves.

(1) That dwarfs, gnomes, midgets are, by the fact of their SIZE, intense;

(2) that dwarfs, gnomes, midgets cause people LARGER than themselves to appear wispy, insubstantial, cardboard;

(3) that all SIZE tends towards BIG but in the case of dwarfs, gnomes, midgets.

But perhaps best to begin at the beginning. And, to begin, there are two things that you must know. The first of these is that I am, myself, a tall man, somewhat muscular though not unpleasantly so. I have brown hair and brown eyes though that is not altogether to the point here. What you should remember is that I am a big man, as it happens, one of the biggest in the town.

My wife is also large. This is the second. But she is not so much large as large-boned. A big frame. I sound as though I were selling her, but I'm not. I mean, I don't want to sound like that, as though I were trying to impress you that way. It is just that that I don't want to do. That is, make you think that I am defending her or whatever it is that I may sound like to you. In short, she is an attractive woman and I don't think I am the only one who would find her so. She has, like myself, brown hair but it is softer, very soft, and she wears it long, almost to her waist, in heavy braids. But it is like her eyes, I mean, there is that lightness in it, the way it brushes against her back when she is walking. It makes me feel rather blundering, heavy, to look at her. It seems to me my step jars the house when I walk through a room where she is. We have been married five years.

Five years doesn't seem, in itself, a very long time. So much goes so quickly, so many things that I can think of now that then, when they were happening, I could hardly take hold of. And where she comes into it, those things that had to do with her, I find I missed, perhaps, a lot that I should have held to. At least I should have tried. But like it or not, it's done with. Little good to think of it now.

I did try, though, to do what I could. She never seemed unhappy and doesn't even now. Perhaps upset when the baby was sick, but, generally speaking, she's a level woman, calm, good-sense.

But perhaps that's where I'm wrong, that I have that assumption, that I think I know what she is like. Strange that a man shouldn't know his wife but I suppose it could be so, that even having her around him for five years, short as they are, he could still be strange to her and she to him. I think I know, I think I know about what she'd do if this or that happened, if I were to say this to her, or something about something, or what people usually talk about. It's not pleasant doubting your own knowing, since that seems all you have. If you lose that, or take it as somehow wrong, the whole thing goes to pieces. Not much use trying to hold it together after that.

Still I can't take seriously what's happened. I can't but still I do. I wish it were different, that in some way, I were out of it, shaken but at least out. But here I am. The same place.

It was raining, a bad night for anything. Not hard, but enough to soak you if you were out in it for very long. We thought it would probably be closed but when we got there, all the lights were going and I could see some people up in the ferris-wheel, probably wet to the skin. Still they looked as if they were having fun and some of their shouts reached us as we went through the gate and into the main grounds. It was fairly late, about ten or so, another reason why I had thought it would be closed. Another day and the whole works would be gone and that's why she had insisted.

I feel, usually, uncomfortable in such places. I don't like the crowds, at least not the noise of them. They never seem to stop, always jumping, moving, and the noise. Any one of them, alone, or two or three, that's fine. As it happened, we went by a number of our friends, who yelled at us, fine night, or some such thing. I can't remember exactly what the words were. But I didn't like them, of didn't like them then, with that around them, the noise, and their excitement.

No reason, perhaps, to think she knew where she was going. I didn't. I think we followed only the general movement of the people, where they were going. It was packed and very difficult to go anywhere but where you were pushed. So we were landed in front of the tent without much choice and stood, listening to the barker, to see what might be happening.

I can say, and this is part of it, that I didn't want to go in. For several reasons. The main one is that I don't like freaks, I don't like to look at them or to be near them. They seem to have a particular feeling around them, which is against me, altogether. A good many times I've seen others staring, without the slightest embarrassment, at some hunchback, or some man with a deformity that puts him apart from the rest. I don't see how they can do it, how

they can look without any reaction but curiosity. For myself, I want only to get away.

But this time she decided. It seemed that not very much
could be inside the tent. They had advertised a midget, a
knife-thrower, a man with some snakes, and one or two
other things. Nothing like the large circuses and none of
the more horrible things such might offer. So I got the tickets and we followed a few of the others in.

They were just finishing a performance. It was so packed
at the front that we stood at the back, waiting until the
first crowd was ready to leave. I felt tired myself. It must
have been close to eleven at that point. It seemed an effort
there was no reason for. But she enjoyed it, looked all
around, at everyone, smiled at those she knew, waved to
some, kept talking to me, and I would say something or
other to hide my own feeling. Perhaps I should have been
straight with her, told her I was tired, and ducked out. It
would have saved it, or at least got me free. But I kept
standing there, with her, waiting for the show to finish and
another to start.

It did soon, the first crowd moving out, and our own
coming up to take its place. The man on the platform had
got down at the end and now we waited for him to come
back and the new show to begin. There was talking around
us, sounding a little nervous the way most will at those
times when something is being waited for, though what one
can't say with exactness. At this point, I was almost as ex-
pectant as the others. Nothing else to be, perhaps. In any
event, I had got over my other feeling.

The first act was a cowboy with a lariat, rope tricks. Not
much, but he was good with it, could make it spin all kinds
of loops, shrinking them, making them grow right while we
watched him. It was good fun, I thought, not much but
enough. At the end he started stamping with one foot and
at the same time, he slipped his loop off and on it, brought
it up around both feet at the end, jumping and grinning. I
think there may have been some music with it, something
for the beat, but it doesn't matter. The man told us he was
deaf, couldn't hear a thing. There didn't seem to be much
point in telling us that but I guess we're apt to like that adding of what we don't expect.

We enjoyed it, the both of us. It's not often that we can

get out, like that, to see anything. And after the first I forgot about being tired and liked it as much as she did. The next act was the knife-thrower. He could put them all in a circle no bigger than my hand, eight of them, so that they shivered there with a force which surprised me, and each time one hit, she gripped my arm, and I laughed at her nervousness, but it was a funny thing, even so.

Then came the snake act, which wasn't up to the others, or simply that dullness in it, the snakes much the same, doped, I expect, though perhaps I was wrong to think so. Then sort of a juggling act, a man with a number of colored balls and odd-shaped sticks, which he set into a strange kind of movement, tossing them, one after the other, until he must have had ten, somehow, going and all this with an intentness that made us almost clap then, as they did move, through his hands. Altogether a wonder it seemed, his precision, and how it kept him away from us, even though some stood no more than a few feet away. Until at last he stopped them one by one, and then, the last, smiled at us, and we all gave him a good hand.

It's here that I leave, or as I go back to it, this time, or this way, that is, now that I make my way out, through the rest of them, my hand on her arm with just that much pressure to guide her, or that is my intention. Perhaps the lights that make my eyes ache, begin to, or simply, that it's now, this point, that I am happy, that it's ourselves, the two of us, have come to some sort of feel of it, that makes us so. Just that I am, now, running, that it is just that I do.

What she had been doing, or going to that, it was a cigarette she asked me for, and I reached into my pocket for them, had got out the pack, and given her one, and then lit a match for her. She bent a little, got it lit, then looked back to the platform where the juggler had been.

But the trick, that it's him who's there, the midget, as such he is named, but the size, it's that which hits me, at first, that he isn't small, or looking, he must be five feet, or perhaps, a little smaller. Four feet. But not small.

The eyes, catch, get me so into it, that they are so, void, in the head, shaded, the shades like changing shadows, colors coming in to want, to want to be filled. Seem huge. He looks at all of us, moves over us so, to bite, to have something to be there to bite.

But nothing, certainly, to make of it more or more than what I could see, would be, that is, the barker introduced him, and we stood, as we had, in that group in front of him, the boards which made the platform, that roughness, and the poles on which the lights were strung, the wire sagging between them. That is, what is it had come in, as this was, to be not or to make it not as it had been, if it were, as it was, the same place, which I couldn't say or put my finger on, then, but waited like any of the rest.

I could see the muscle of his arm, where the sleeve had been pulled up, rolled, above it, and with his movement, that slightness of tension made him lift it, slightly, from time to time, the muscle tightened and it looked hard, big, below the roll of the sleeve. As my own would. He was smiling, the face somewhat broad, well-shaped, the smile somewhat dreamy, or like sleep, that vagueness, which couldn't be understood.

The barker had laughed, the pitch of it rolled out, on us, and I wondered if he was as drunk as he looked. He was calling the midget, cute, saying, a cute little fellow. He made a joke of it, looking at the women and laughing. Saying, who would like to take him home. There was laughing, they liked the joke, and he carried it further, sensing their tolerance, and played it up. It was the joke he seemed intent on making us remember, the cuteness, the idea of the women.

Taking the cigarettes out of my pocket, the pack crumpled, I held it out to her, but she was intent on what was before us, and I expect that I was myself, and only did what I did, took them out, to somehow break it, to make it break down. It seemed that, that is, that gesture or an act, an action, so meant to serve double, to be a break, but what was it, that is, more than the taking, just that, of the cigarettes, which I didn't want to smoke, had even just put one out. I looked, then, around me at the rest of them and they were looking at him, the midget, and I couldn't see one that noticed I looked, or gave the least sign.

The midget stood still, beside the barker, who staggered a little, under the lights, moved from one side to the other, his face to us, that drunkenness. He was still on the joke, fumbling, and it wore down on us, that weight of it, kept at us, and I wanted to get out. There seemed breaks, lengths of silence, hung there, made the other, the midget, the whole of it, in his own silence, which he kept as a distance around him, that the eyes made actual.

I would have gone, or as I think, I should have in spite of it, simply slipped out, when the others weren't looking, just left and waited for her outside. I can't see that she would have been hurt. That is, I would think, or think I would have that right to, that it would make no difference to her, that is, that she would understand my going, seeing that it had begun to tire me, even became painful to stay. I think of it so, being such, that no difference could be in it, since she was enjoying it, or so it seemed.

I tried to, but the people around pressed too tight, pushed me from the back, all forward, to the one on the platform in front of us. Not the barker, I knew that much, but the other, who pulled them, kept them all, because the barker had somehow fallen altogether to pieces, had just the joke he hung on to, and that was played out. But then he switched it, perhaps feeling it had, and turned to the midget, and said, but you should have some say in this. Which one would you like.

The midget turned, then seemed to pull himself out of it, the distance, out of nothing, the eyes pulled in, to focus, to grow, somehow, smaller, larger. The eyes went over us, the voice, when it came, was breath, a breathing but way back in, wire, tight, taut, the scream and I couldn't hear it, saw only his finger move to point at her, beside me, and wanted to say, he's looking at you, but she was turned away from me, as though laughing, but struck, hit. I looked, a flash, sideways, as it then happened. Looked, he looked at me, cut, the hate jagged, and I had gone, then, into it and that was almost that. But she said, then, she had seen him, earlier, that same day, as he was standing by a store, near the door, I think, as it had opened, and she, there, across the street, saw him motion, the gesture, then, a dance, shuffle, the feet crooked, and the arms, as now, loose, and it was before, as before, but not because of this, that made it, or I thought, so made it, was it, or it was that thing I hung to, when, the show over, they motioned us out, and I pushed a way for her out through the crowd.

A CHASE (ALIGHIERI'S DREAM)

LEROI JONES / Baraka

Place broken: their faces sat and broke each other. As
suns, Sons gone tired in the heart and left the south. The
North, years later she'd wept for him drunk and a man finally they must have thought. In the dark, he was even darker. Wooden fingers running. Wind so sweet it drank him.

Faces broke. Charts of age. Worn thru, to see black
years. Bones in iron faces. Steel bones. Cages of decay.
Cobblestones are wet near the army stores. Beer smells,
Saturday. To now, they have passed so few lovely things.

Newsreel chickens. Browned in the street. I was carrying
groceries back across the manicured past. Back, in a coat.
Sunk, screaming at my fingers. Faces broken, hair waved,
simple false elegance. I must tell someone I love you.
Them. In line near the fence. She sucked my tongue. Red,
actual red, but colored hair. Soft thin voice, and red
freckles. A servant.

You should be ashamed. Your fingers are trembling.
You lied in the garage. You lied yesterday. Get out of the
dance, down the back stairs, the street, and across in the
car. Run past it, around the high building. Court Street,
past the Y, harder, buttoning a cardigan, to Morton Street.
Duck down, behind the car. Let Apple pass; a few others.
Now take off back down Court, the small guys couldn't
run. Cross High, near Graychun's, the Alumni House, donald the fag's, the jews, to Kinney. Up one block, crooked
old jews die softly under the moon. Past them. Past them.
Their tombs and bones. Wet dollars blown against the

fence. Past them, mattie's Dr., waltine, turn at Quitman.
You can slow some, but not too much. Through the Owl
Club, Frankie, Dee's dumb brother, turn, wave at them.
Down the back steps, to dirt, then stone. The poolroom,
eddie smiles, points at his hat, pats his car keys, phone
numbers. Somerset and the projects. To Montgomery and
twist at Barclay. Light people stare. Parties, relationships
forming to be explained later. Casual strangers' faces
known better than any now. Wood jaws sit open, their halls
reek, his fingers tug at yellow cotton pants and slip inside.
One finger her eyes open and close—her mouth opens
moaning deep agitated darkly.

In the middle of the street, straight at the moon. Don't
get close to the buildings. Too many exits, doors, parks.
Straight at the moon, up Barclay. Green tyrolean, grey
bells, bucks. The smoking lights at Spruce. Hip charles cur-
tis. But turn before Herman or Wattley. They pace in wool
jails, wool chains, years below the earth. Dead cocks crawling, eyes turned up in space. Near diane's house and the
trees cradling her hidden flesh. Her fingers, her mouth, her
eyes were all I had. And she screams now through soft
wrinkles for me to take her. A Nun.

Wheeling now, back on
the sidewalk, Saturday drunks spinning by, fish stores
yawned, sprawled niggers dying without matches. Friends,
enemies, strangers, fags, screaming louder than all sound.
Young boys in hallways touching. Bulldaggers hiding their
pussies. Black dead faces slowly ground to dust.

Headlight,
Bubbles, Kennie, Rogie, Junie Boy, T. Bone, Rudy (All
Hillside Place) or Sess, Ray, Lillian, Ungie, Ginger, Shir-
ley, Cedie Abrams. Past them, displaced, blood seeps on
the pavement under marquees. Lynn Hope marches on Bel-
mont Ave. with us all. The Three Musketeers at the National. (Waverly Projects.) Past that. Their arms waving
from the stands. Sun and gravel or the 3 hole opens and it's
more beautiful than Satie. A hip, change speeds, head fake,
stop, cut back, a hip, head fake . . . then only one man
coming from the side . . . it went thru my head a million
times, the years it took, seeing him there, with a good
angle, shooting in, with 3 yards to the sidelines, about 10

home. I watched him all my life close in, and shot to cut, stop or bear down and pray I had speed. Answers shot up, but my head was full of blood and it moved me without talk. I stopped still the ball held almost like a basketball, wheeled and moved in to score untouched.

* * *

A long stretch from Waverly to Spruce (going the other way near Hillside). A long stretch, and steeper, straight up Spruce. And that street moved downtown. They all passed by, going down. And I was burning by, up the hill, toward The Foxes and the milk bar. Change clothes on the street to a black suit. Black wool.

4 corners, the entire world visible from there. Even to the lower regions.

THE ALTERNATIVE

LEROI JONES

This may not seem like much, but it makes a difference. And then there are those who prefer to look
their fate in the eyes.

Between Yes and No
—Camus

The leader sits straddling the bed, and the night, tho innocent, blinds him. (Who is our flesh. Our lover, marched
here from where we sit now sweating and remembering.
Old man. Old man, find me, who am your only blood.)
    Sits straddling the bed under a heavy velvet canopy.
Homemade. The door opened for a breeze, which will not
come through the other heavy velvet hung at the opening.
(Each thread a face, or smell, rubbed against himself with
yellow glasses and fear at their exposure. Death. Death.
They (the younger students) run by screaming. Tho im-
promptu. Tho dead, themselves.
                            The leader, at his bed,
stuck with 130 lbs. black meat sewed to failing bone. A
head with big red eyes turning senselessly. Five toes on each
foot. Each foot needing washing. And hands that dangle to
the floor, tho the boy himself is thin small washed out, he
needs huge bleak hands that drag the floor. And a head full
of walls and flowers. Blinking lights. He is speaking.
                                              "Yeh?"
The walls are empty, heat at the ceiling. Tho one wall is
painted with a lady. (Her name now. In large relief, a
faked rag stuck between the chalk marks of her sex. Finley.
Teddy's Doris. There sprawled where the wind fiddled
with the drying cloth. Leon came in and laughed. Carl
came in and hid his mouth, but he laughed. Teddy said,
"Aw, Man."
            "Come on, Hollywood. You can't beat that.

Not with your years. Man, you're a schoolteacher 10 years
after weeping for this old stinking bitch. And hit with a
aspirin bottle (myth says)."

                                    The leader, is sprawled, dying.
His retinue walks into their comfortable cells. "I have
duraw-ings," says Leon, whimpering now in the buses from
Chicago. Dead in a bottle. Floats out of sight, until the
Africans arrive with love and prestige. "Niggers." They
say. "Niggers." Be happy your ancestors are recognized in
this burg. Martyrs. Dead in an automat, because the boys
had left. Lost in New York, frightened of the burned lady,
they fled into those streets and sang their homage to the
Radio City.

                    The Leader sits watching the window. The
dried orange glass etched with the fading wind. (How
many there then? 13 Rue Madeleine. The Boys Club. They
give, what he has given them. Names. And the black cloth
hung on the door swings back and forth. One pork chop on
the hot plate. And how many there. Here, now. Just the
shadow, waving its arms. The eyes tearing or staring blind-
ly at the dead street. These same who loved me all my
life. These same I find my senses in. Their flesh a wagon
of dust, a mind conceived from all minds. A country, of
thought. Where I am, will go, have never left. A love, of
love. And the silence the question posed each second. "Is
this my mind, my feeling. Is this voice something heavy in
the locked streets of the universe. Dead ends. Where their
talk (these nouns) is bitter vegetable." That is, the suitable
question rings against the walls. Higher learning. That is,
the moon through the window clearly visible. The leader
in seersucker, reading his books. An astronomer of sorts.
"Will you look at that? I mean, really, now, fellows. Cats!"
(Which was Smitty from the City's entree. And him the
smoothest of you American types. Said, "Cats. Cats. What's
goin' on?" The debate.

The leader's job (he keeps it still, above the streets, sum-
mers of low smoke, early evening drunk and wobbling thru
the world. He keeps it, baby. You dig?) was absolute. "I
have the abstract position of watching these halls. Walking
up the stairs giggling. Hurt under the cement steps, weeping . . . is my only task. Tho I play hockey with the broom
& wine bottles. And am the sole martyr of this cause. A.B.,

Young Rick, T.P., Carl, Hambrick, Li'l' Cholley, Phil. O.K. All their knowledge "Flait! More! Way!" The leader's job . . . to make attention for the place. Sit along the sides of the water or lay quietly back under his own shooting vomit, happy to die in a new grey suit. Yes. "And what not."

How many here now? Danny. (brilliant dirty curly Dan, the m.d.) Later, now, where you off to, my man. The tall skinny farmers, lucky to find sales and shiny white shoes. Now made it socially against the temples. This "hotspot" Darien drunk teacher blues . . . "and she tried to come on like she didn't even like to fuck. I mean, you know the kind . . . ." The hand extended, palm upward. I place my own in yours. That cross, of feeling. Willie, in his grinning grave, has it all. The place, of all souls, in their greasy significance. An armour, like the smells drifting slowly up Georgia. The bridge players change clothes, and descend. Carrying home the rolls.

Jimmy Lassiter, first looie. A vector. What is the angle made if a straight line is drawn from the chapel, across to Jimmy, and connected there, to me, and back up the hill again? The angle of progress. "I was talkin' to ol' Mordecai yesterday in a dream, and it's me sayin' 'dig baby, why don't you come off it?' You know."

The line, for Jimmy's sad and useless horn. And they tell me (via phone, letter, accidental meetings in the Village. "Oh he's in med school and married and lost to you, hombre." Ha. They don't dig completely where I'm at. I have him now, complete. Though it is a vicious sadness cripples my fingers. Those blue and empty afternoons I saw him walking at my side. Criminals in that world. Complete heroes of our time. (add Allen to complete an early splinter group. Muslim heroes with flapping pants. Raincoats. Trolley car romances.)

And it's me making a portrait of them all. That was the leader's job. Alone with them. (Without them. Except beautiful faces shoved out the window, sunny days, I ran to meet my darkest girl. Ol' Doll. "Man, that bitch got a goddamn new car." And what not. And it's me sayin' to her, Baby, knock me a kiss.

Tonight the leader is faced with decision. Brown had found him drunk and weeping among the dirty clothes. Some guy with a crippled arm had reported to the farmers (a boppin' gang gone social. Sociologists, artistic arbiters of our times). This one an athlete of mouselike proportions. "You know," he said, his withered arm hung stupidly in the rayon suit, "That cat's nuts. He was sittin' up in that room last night with dark glasses on . . . with a yellow bulb . . . pretendin' to read some abstract shit." (Damn, even the color wrong. Where are you now, hippy, under this abstract shit. Not even defense. That you remain forever in that world. No light. Under my fingers. That you exist alone, as I make you. Your sin, a final ugliness to you. For the leopards, all thumbs jerked toward the sand.) "Man, we do not need cats like that in the frat." (Agreed.)

Tom comes in with two big bottles of wine. For the contest. An outing. "Hugh Herbert and W. C. Fields will now indian wrestle for ownership of this here country!" (Agreed.) The leader loses . . . but is still the leader because he said some words no one had heard of before. (That was after the loss.)

Young Rick has fucked someone else. Let's listen. "Oh, man, you cats don't know what's happenin'." (You're too much, Rick. Much too much. Like Larry Darnell in them ol' italian schools. Much too much.) "Babes" he called them (a poor project across from the convents. Baxter Terrace. Home of the enemy. We stood them off. We Cavaliers. And then, even tho Johnny Boy was his hero. Another midget placed on the purple. Early leader; like myself. The fight of gigantic proportions to settle all those ancient property disputes would have been between us. Both weighing close to 125. But I avoided that like the plague, and managed three times to drive past him with good hooks without incident. Whew, I said to Love, Whew. And Rick, had gone away from them, to school. Like myself. And now, strangely, for the Gods are white our teachers said, he found himself with me. And all the gold and diamonds of the crown I wore he hated. Though, the new wine settled, and his social graces kept him far enough away to ease the hurt of serving a

hated master. Hence "babes," and the constant reference
to his wiggling flesh. Listen.

"Yeh. Me and Chris had these D.C. babes at their cribs."
(Does a dance step with the suggestive flair.) "Oooooo,
that was some good box."

        Tom knew immediately where that
bit was at. And he pulled Rick into virtual madness . . .
lies at least. "Yeh, Rick. Yeh? You mean you got a little
Jones, huh? Was it good?" (Tom pulls on Rick's sleeve
like Laurel and Rick swings.)

"Man, Tom, you don't have to believe it, baby. It's in
here now!" (points to his stomach.)

        The leader stirs. "Hmm,
that's a funny way to fuck." Rick will give a boxing demonstration in a second.

        Dick Smith smiles, "Wow, Rick
you're way," extending his hand, palm upward. "And
what not," Dick adds, for us to laugh. "O.K., you're bad."
(At R's crooked jab.) "Huh, this cat always wants to bust
somebody up, and what not. Hey, baby, you must be
frustrated or something. How come you don't use up all
that energy on your babes . . . and what not?"

        The rest there,
floating empty nouns. Under the sheets. The same death
as the crippled fag. Lost with no defense. Except they sit
now, for this portrait . . . in which they will be portrayed
as losers. Only the leader wins. Tell him that.

Some guys playing cards. Some talking about culture,
i.e., the leader had a new side. (Modesty denies. They sit
around, in real light. The leader in his green glasses, fidget-
ing with his joint. Carl, in a brown fedora, trims his toes
and nails. Spars with Rick. Smells his foot and smiles.
Brady reads, in his silence, a crumpled black dispatch.
Shorter's liver smells the hall and Leon slams the door,
waiting for the single chop, the leader might have to share.
The door opens, two farmers come in, sharp in orange
suits. The hippies laugh, and hide their youthful lies. "Man,
I was always hip. I mean, I knew about Brooks Brothers
when I was 10." (So sad we never know the truth. About
that world, until the bones dry in our heads. Young blond

governors with their "dads" hip at the age of 2. That way.
Which, now, I sit in judgment of. What I wanted those
days with the covers of books turned toward the audience.
The first nighters. Or dragging my two forwards to the
Music Box to see Elliot Nugent. They would say, these
dead men, laughing at us, "The natives are restless," strok-
ing their gouty feet. Gimme culture, culture, culture, and
Romeo and Juliet over the emerson.

How many there now?
Make it 9. Phil's cracking the books. Jimmy Jones and
Pud, two D.C. boys, famous and funny, study "zo" at the
top of their voices. "Hemiptera," says Pud. "Homoptera,"
says Jimmy. "Weak as a bitch," says Phil, "Both your
knowledges are flait."

More than 9. Mazique, Enty, operat-
ing now in silence. Right hands flashing down the cards.
"Uhh!" In love with someone, and money from home.
Both perfect, with curly hair. "Uhh! Shit, Enty, hearts is
trumps."

"What? Ohh, shit!"

"Uhh!", their beautiful hands
flashing under the single bulb.

Hambrick comes with liquor.
(A box of fifths, purchased with the fantastic wealth of
his father's six shrimp shops.) "You cats caint have all
this goddam booze. Brown and I got dates, that's why
and we need some for the babes."

Brown has hot dogs for five. Franks, he says. "Damn,
Cholley, you only get a half of frank . . . and you take
the whole motherfucking thing."

"Aww, man, I'll pay you back." And the room, each
inch, is packed with lives. Make it 12 . . . all heroes; or
dead. Indian chiefs, the ones not waging their wars, like
Clark, in the legal mist of Baltimore. A judge. Old Clark.
You remember when we got drunk together and you fell
down the stairs. Or that time you fell in the punch bowl
puking, and let that sweet yellow ass get away? Boy, I'll
never forget that, as long as I live. (Having died seconds
later, he talks thru his rot.) Yeh, boy, you were always
a card. (White man talk. A card. Who the hell says that,
except that branch office with no culture. Piles of bullion,

and casual violence. To the mind. Nights they kick you
against the buildings. Communist homosexual nigger. "Aw
man, I'm married and got two kids."

What could be hap-
pening? Some uproar. "FUCK YOU, YOU FUNNY
LOOKING SUNAFABITCH."

"Me? Funnylooking? Oh,
wow. Will you listen to this little pointy head bastard
calling *me* funny looking. Hey, Everett. Hey Everett!
Who's the funniest looking . . . me or Keyes?"

"Aww, both you cats need some work. Man, I'm trying
to read."

"Read? What? You gettin' into them books, huh? Barnes
is whippin' your ass, huh? I told you not to take Organic
. . . as light as you are."

"Shit. I'm not even thinking about Barnes. Barnes can
kiss my ass."

"Shit. You better start thinking about him, or you'll
punch right out. They don't need lightweights down in
the valley. Ask Ugly Wilson."

"Look, Tom, I wasn't bothering you."

"Bothering me? Wha's the matter with you ol' Jimmy.
Commere boy, lemme rub your head."

"Man, you better get the hell outta here."

"What? . . . Why? What you gonna do? You can't fight,
you little funny looking buzzard."

"Hey, Tom, why you always bothering ol' Jimmy Wilson.
He's a good man."

"Oh, oh, here's that little light ass Dan sticking up for
Ugly again. Why you like him, huh? Cause he's the only
cat uglier than you? Huh?"

"Tom's the worst looking cat on campus calling me
ugly."

"Well, you are. Wait, lemme bring you this mirror so
you can see yourself. Now, what you think. You can't
think anyway else."

"Aww, man, blow, will you?"

The pork chop is cooked and little charlie is trying
to cut a piece off before the leader can stop him. "Ow,
goddam."

"Well, who told you to try to steal it, jive ass."

"Hey, man, I gotta get somea that chop."

"Gimme some, Ray."

"Why don't you cats go buy something to eat. I didn't ask anybody for any of those hot dogs. So get away from my grease. Hungry ass spooks."

"Wait a minute, fella. I know you don't mean Young Rick."

"Go ask one of those D.C. babes for something to eat. I know they must have something you could sink your teeth into."

Pud and Jimmy Jones are wrestling under Phil's desk. A.B. is playin' the dozen with Leon and Teddy. "Teddy are your momma's legs as crooked as yours?"

"This cat always wants to talk about people's mothers! Country bastard."

Tom is pinching Jimmy Wilson. Dan is laughing at them.

Enty and Mazique are playing bridge with the farmers. "Uhh! Beat that, jew boy!"

"What the fuck is trumps?"

The leader is defending his pork chop from Cholley, Rick, Brady, Brown, Hambrick, Carl, Dick Smith, (S from the City has gone out catting.)

"Who is it?"

A muffled voice, under the uproar, "It's Mister Bush."

"Bush? Hey, Ray . . . Ray."

"Who is it?"

Plainer. "Mister Bush." (Each syllable pronounced and correct as a soft southern american can.) Innocent VIII in his bedroom shoes. Gregory at Canossa, raging softly in his dignity and power. "Mister Bush."

"Ohh, shit. Get that liquor somewhere. O.K., Mr. Bush, just a second. . . . Not there, asshole, in the drawer."

"Mr. McGhee, will you kindly open the door."

"Ohh, shit, the hot plate. I got it." The leader turns a wastepaper basket upside-down on top of the chop. Swings open the door. "Oh, Hello Mister Bush. How are you this evening?" About 15 boots sit smiling toward the door. Come in, Boniface. What news of Luther? In unison, now.

"Hi . . . Hello . . . How are you, Mister Bush?"

"Uh, huh."

He stares around the room, grinding his eyes into their various hearts. An unhealthy atmosphere, this America. "Mr. McGhee, why is it if there's noise in this dormitory it always comes from this room?" Aww, he knows. He wrote me years later in the Air Force that he knew, even then.

"What are you running here, a boys' club?" (That's it.) He could narrow his eyes even in that affluence. Put his hands on his hips. Shove that stomach at you as proof he was an authority of the social grace . . . a western man, no matter the color of his skin. How To? He was saying, this is not the way. Don't act like that word. Don't fail us. We've waited for all you handsome boys too long. Erect a new world, of lies and stocking caps. Silence, and a reluctance of memory. Forget the slow grasses, and flame, flame in the valley. Feet bound, dumb eyes begging for darkness. The bodies moved with the secret movement of the air. Swinging. My beautiful grandmother kneels in the shadow weeping. Flame, flame in the valley. Where is it there is light? Where, this music rakes my talk?

"Why is it, Mr. McGhee, when there's some disturbance in this building, it always comes from here?" (Aww, you said that . . .)

"And what are all you other gentlemen doing in here? Good night, there must be twenty of you here! Really, gentlemen, don't any of you have anything to do?" He made to smile, Ha, I know some of you who'd better be in your rooms right now hitting those books . . . or you might not be with us next semester. Ha.

"O.K., who is that under the sheets?" (It was Enty, a student dormitory director, hiding under the sheets, flat on the leader's bed.) "You, sir, whoever you are, come out of there, hiding won't do you any good. Come out!" (We watched the sheet, and it quivered. Innocent raised his finger.) "Come out, sir!" (The sheet pushed slowly back. Enty's head appeared. And Bush more embarrassed than he.) "Mr. Enty! My assistant dormitory director, good night. A man of responsibility. Go-od night! Are there any more hiding in here, Mr. McGhee?"

"Not that I know of."

"Alright, Mr. Enty, you come with me. And the rest of you had better go to your rooms and try to make some better grades. Mr. McGhee, I'll talk to you tomorrow morning in my office."

The leader smiles, "Yes." (Jive ass.) Bush turns to go, Enty following sadly. "My God, what's that terrible odor . . . something burning." (The leader's chop, and the wastepaper, under the basket, starting to smoke.) "Mr. McGhee, what's that smell?"

"Uhhh," (come-on, baby) "Oh, it's Strothers' kneepads on the radiator! (Yass) They're drying."

"Well, Jesus, I hope they dry soon. Whew! And don't forget, tomorrow morning, Mr. McGhee, and you other gentlemen had better retire, it's 2 in the morning!" The door slams. Charlie sits where Enty was. The bottles come out. The basket is turned right-side up. Chop and most of the papers smoking. The leader pours water onto the mess and sinks to his bed.

"Damn. Now I have to go hungry. Shit."

"That was pretty slick, ugly, the kneepads! Why don't you eat them they look pretty done."

The talk is to that. That elegance of performance. The rite of lust, or self-extinction. Preservation. Some leave, and a softer uproar descends. Jimmy Jones and Pud wrestle quietly on the bed. Phil quotes the *Post's* sports section on Willie Mays. Hambrick and Brown go for franks. Charlie scrapes the "burn" off the chop and eats it alone. Tom, Dan, Ted and the leader drink and manufacture lives for each person they know. We know. Even you. Tom, the lawyer. Dan, the lawyer. Ted, the high-school teacher. All their proper ways. And the leader, without cause or place. Except talk, feeling, guilt. Again, only those areas of the world make sense. Talk. We are doing that now. Feeling: that too. Guilt. That inch of wisdom, forever. Except he sits reading in green glasses. As, "No, no, the utmost share/Of my desire shall be/Only to kiss that air/That lately kissed thee."

"Uhh! What's trumps, dammit!"

As, "Tell me not, Sweet, I am unkind,/That from the nunnery/Of thy chaste breast and quiet mind/To war and arms I fly."

"You talking about a lightweight mammy-tapper, boy, you really king."

Oh, Lucasta, find me here on the bed, with hard pecker and dirty feet. Oh, I suffer, in my green glasses, under the canopy of my loves. Oh, I am drunk and vomity in my room, with only Charley Ventura to understand my grace. As, "Hardly are those words out when a vast image out of *Spiritus Mundi*/Troubles my sight: somewhere in sands of the desert/A shape with lion body and the head of a man/A gaze blank and pitiless as the sun,/Is moving its slow thighs, while all about it/Reel shadows of the indignant desert birds."

Primers for dogs who are learning to read. Tinkle of European teacups. All longing, speed, suffering. All adventure, sadness, stink and wisdom. All feeling, silence, light. As, "Crush, O sea the cities with their catacomb-like corridors/And crush eternally the vile people,/The idiots, and the abstemious, and mow down, mow down/With a single stroke the bent backs of the shrunken harvest!"

"Damn, Charlie, We brought back a frank for everybody . . . now you want two. Wrong sunafabitch!"

"Verde que te quiero verde./Verde viento. Verdes ramas./El barco sobre la mar/y el caballo en la montaña."

"Hey, man, I saw that ol' fagit Bobby Hutchens down in the lobby with a real D.C. queer. I mean a real way-type sissy."

"Huh, man he's just another *actor* . . . hooo."

"That cat still wearing them funny lookin' pants?"

"Yeh, and orange glasses. Plus, the cat always needs a haircut, and what not."

"Hey, man you cats better cool it . . . you talkin' about Ray's main man. You dig?"

"Yeh. I see this cat easin' around corners with the cat all the time. I mean, talkin' some off the wall shit, too, baby."

"Yeh. Yeh. Why don't you cats go fuck yourselves or something hip like that, huh?"

"O.K., ugly Tom, you better quit inferring that shit about Ray. What you trying to say, ol' pointy head is funny or something?"

"Funny . . . how the sound of your voice . . . thri-ills me.
Strange . . ." (the last à la King Cole.)

"Fuck you cats and your funny looking families too."

A
wall. With light at the top, perhaps. No, there is light.
Seen from both sides, a gesture of life. But always more
than is given. An abstract infinitive. To love. To lie. To
want. And that always . . . to want. Always, more than is
given. The dead scramble up each side . . . words or drunkenness. Praise, to the flesh. Rousseau, Hobbes, and their
betters. All move, from flesh to love. From love to flesh.
At that point under the static light. It could be Shostako-
vich in Charleston, South Carolina. Or in the dull windows
of Chicago, an unread volume of Joyce. Some black woman
who will never hear the word *Negress* or remember your
name. Or a thin preacher who thinks your name is Stephen.
A wall. Oh, Lucasta.

"Man, you cats don't know anything
about Hutchens. I don't see why you talk about the cat
and don't know the first thing about him."

"Shit: If he ain't
funny . . . Skippy's a punk."

"How come you don't say that to Skippy?"

"Our Own Boy, Skippy Weatherson. All-coon fullback
for 12 years."

"You tell him that!"

"Man, don't try to change the subject. This cat's trying
to keep us from talking about his boy, Hutchens."

"Yeh, mammy-rammer. What's happenin' McGhee, ol'
man?"

"Hooo. Yeh. They call this cat Dick Brown. Hoooo!"

Rick moves to the offensive. The leader in his book, or
laughs, "Aww, man, that cat ain't my boy. I just don't
think you cats ought to talk about people you don't know
anything about! Plus, that cat probably gets more ass than
any of you silly-ass mother fuckers."

"Hee. That Ray sure can pronounce that word. I mean
he don't say mutha' like most folks . . . he always pro-
nounces the mother *and* the fucker, so proper. And it sure
makes it sound nasty." (A texas millionaire talking.)

"Hutchens teachin' the cat how to talk . . . that's what's
happening. Ha. In exchange for services rendered!"

"Wait, Tom. Is it you saying that Hutchens and my man here are into some funny shit?"

"No, man. It's you saying that. It was me just inferring, you dig?"

"Hey, why don't you cats just get drunk in silence, huh?"

"Hey, Bricks, what was Hutchens doin' downstairs with that cat?"

"Well, they were just coming in the dormitory, I guess. Hutchens was signing in that's all."

"Hey, you dig . . . I bet he's takin' that cat up to his crib."

"Yeh, I wonder what they into by now. Huh! Probably suckin' the shit out of each other."

"Aww, man, cool it, will ya . . . Damn!"

"What's the matter, Ray, you don't dig love?"

"Hey, it's young Rick saying, that we oughta go up and dig what's happenin' up there?"

"Square mother fucker!"

"Votre mere!"

"Votre mere noir!"

"Boy, these cats in French One think they hip!"

"Yeh, let's go up and see what those cats are doing."

"Tecch, aww, shit. Damn, you some square cats, wow! Cats got nothing better to do than fuck with people. Damn!"

Wall. Even to move, impossible. I sit, now, forever where I am. No further. No farther. Father, who am I to hide myself? And brew a world of soft lies.

Again. "Verde que te quiero verde." Green. Read it again Il Duce. Make it build some light here . . . where there is only darkness. Tell them "Verde, que te quiero verde." I want you Green. Leader, the paratroopers will come for you at noon. A helicopter low over the monastery. To get you out.

But my country. My people. These dead souls, I call my people. Flesh of my flesh.

At noon, Il Duce. Make them all etceteras. Extras. The soft strings behind the final horns.

"Hey, Ray, you comin' with us?"

"Fuck you cats. I got other things to do."

"Damn, now the cat's trying to pretend he can read Spanish."

"Yeh . . . well let's go see what's happening cats."

"Cats, Cats, Cats . . . What's happenin'?"

"Hey, Smitty! We going upstairs to peep that ol' sissy Hutchens. He's got some big time D.C. faggot in there with him. You know, we figured it'd be better than 3-D."

"Yeh? That's pretty hip. You not coming, Ray?"

"No, man . . . I'm sure you cats can peep in a keyhole without me."

"Bobby's his main man, that's all."

"Yeh, mine and your daddy's."

Noise. Shouts, and Rick begs them to be softer. For the circus. Up the creaking stairs, except Carl and Leon who go to the freshman dorm to play ping-pong . . . and Ted who is behind in his math.

The 3rd floor of Park Hall, an old 19th-century philanthropy, gone to seed. The missionaries' words dead & hung useless in the air. "Be clean, thrifty, and responsible. Show the anti-Christs you're ready for freedom and God's true word." Peasants among the mulattoes, and the postman's son squats in his glasses shivering at his crimes.

"Hey, which room is his?"

"Three Oh Five."

"Hey, Tom, how you know the cat's room so good? This cat must be sneaking too."

"Huhh, yeh!"

"O.K. Rick, just keep walking."

"Here it is."

"Be cool, bastard. Shut up."

They stood and grinned. And punched each other. Two bulbs in the hall. A window at each end. One facing the reservoir, the other, the fine-arts building where Professor Gorsun sits angry at jazz. "Goddamnit none of that nigger music in my new building. Culture. Goddamnit, ladies and gentlemen, line up and be baptized. This pose will take the hurt away. We are white and featureless under this roof. Praise God, from whom all blessings flow!"

"Bobby. Bobby, baby."

"Huh?"

"Don't go blank on me like that, baby. I was saying something."

"Oh, I'm sorry . . . I guess I'm just tired or something."

"I was saying, how can you live in a place like this. I mean, really, baby, this place is nowhere. Whew. It's like a jail or something eviler."

"Yes, I know."

"Well, why don't you leave it then. You're much too sensitive for a place like this. I don't see why you stay in this damn school. You know, you're really talented."

"Yeh, well, I figured I have to get a degree, you know. Teach or something, I suppose. There's not really much work around for spliv actors."

"Oh, Bobby, you ought to stop being so conscious of being coloured. It really is not fashionable. Ummm. You know you have beautiful eyes."

"You want another drink, Lyle?"

"Ugg. Oh, that cheap bourbon. You know I have some beautiful wines at home. You should try drinking some good stuff for a change. Damn, Bob, why don't you just leave this dump and move into my place? There's certainly enough room. And we certainly get along. Ummm. Such beautiful eyes and hair too."

"Hah. How much rent would I have to pay out there. I don't have penny the first!"

"Rent? No, no . . . you don't have to worry about that. I'll take care of all that. I've got one of those gooood jobs, honey. U.S. guvment."

"Oh? Where do you work?"

"The P.O. with the rest of the fellas. But it's enough for what I want to do. And you wouldn't be an expense. Hmmp. Or would you? You know you have the kind of strong masculine hands I love.

Like you could crush anything you wanted. Lucky I'm on your good side. Hmmp."

          "Well, maybe at the end of this semester I could leave. If the offer still holds then."

          "Still holds? Well why not? We'll still be friends then, I'm certain. Ummm. Say, why don't we shut off that light."

          "Umm. Let me do it. There . . . You know I loved you in Jimmy's play, but the rest of those people are really just kids. You were the only person who really understood what was going on. You have a strong maturity that comes through right away. How old are you, Bobby?"

          "Nineteen."

          "O baby . . . that's why your skin is so soft. Yes. Say, why wait until the end of the semester . . . that's two months away. I might be dead before that, you know. Umm."

The wind moves thru the leader's room, and he sits alone, under the drooping velvet, repeating words he does not understand. The yellow light burns. He turns it off. Smokes. Masturbates. Turns it on. Verde, verde. Te quiero. Smokes. And then to his other source. "Yma's brother," Tom said when he saw it. "Yma Sumac, Albert Camus. Man, nobody wants to go by their right names no more. And a cat told me that chick ain't really from Peru. She was born in Brooklyn man, and her name's Camus too. Amy Camus. This cat's name is probably Trebla Sumac, and he ain't French he's from Brooklyn too. Yeh. Ha!"

In the dark the words are anything. "If it is true that the only paradise is that which one has lost, I know what name to give that something tender and inhuman which dwells within me today."

          "Oh, shit, fuck it. Fuck it." He slams the book against the wall, and empties Hambrick's bottle. "I mean, why?" Empties bottle. "Shiiit."

          When he swings the door open the hall above is screams. Screams. All their

voices, even now right here. The yellow glasses falling on
the stairs, and broken. In his bare feet. "Shiit. Dumb ass
cats!"

"Rick, Rick,
what's the cat doing now?"

"Man, be cool.
Ha, the cat's kissin' Hutchens on the face, man. Um-uh-
mm. Yeh, baby. Damn, he's puttin' his hands all over the
cat. Aww, rotten motherfuckers!"

"What's happen-
ing?"

"Bastards shut
out the lights!"

"Damn."
"Gaw-uhd damn!"
"Hey, let's break
open the door."

"Yeh, HEY, YOU
CATS, WHAT'S HAPPENING IN THERE, HUH?"

"Yeh. Hee, hee.
OPEN UP, FAGGOTS!"

"Whee! HEY
LET US IN, GIRLS!"

Ricky and Jimmy
run against the door, the others screaming and jumping,
doors opening all along the hall. They all come out, screaming as well. "LET US IN. HEY, WHAT'S HAPPENIN',
BABY!" Rick and Jimmy run against the door, and the
door is breaking.

"Who is it? What do you want?" Bobby
turns the light on, and his friend, a balding queer of 40 is
hugged against the sink.

"Who are they, Bobby? What do
they want?"

"Bastards. Damn if I know. GET OUTTA HERE,
AND MIND YOUR OWN DAMN BUSINESS, YOU
CREEPS. Creeps. Damn. Put on your clothes, Lyle!"

"God, they're trying to break the door down, Bobby.
What they want? Why are they screaming like that?"

"GET THE HELL AWAY FROM THIS DOOR,
GODDAMNIT!"

"YEH, YEH. WE SAW WHAT YOU WAS DOIN' HUTCHENS. OPEN THE DOOR AND LET US GET IN ON IT."

"WHEEEEEE! HIT THE FUCKING DOOR, RICK! HIT IT!"

And at the top of the stairs the leader stops, the whole hall full of citizens. Doctors, judges, first negro directors of welfare chain, morticians, chemists, ad men, fighters for civil rights, all admirable, useful men. "BREAK THE FUCKIN' DOOR OPEN, RICK! YEH!"

A wall. Against it, from where you stand, the sea stretches smooth for miles out. Their voices distant thuds of meat against the sand. Murmurs of insects. Hideous singers against your pillow every night of your life. They are there now, screaming at you.

"Ray, Ray, comeon man help us break this faggot's door!"

"Yeh, Ray, comeon!"

"Man, you cats are fools. Evil stupid fools!"

"What? Man, will you listen to this cat."

"Listen, hell, let's get this door. One more smash and it's in. Comeon, Brady, let's break the fuckin' thing."

"Yeh, comeon you cats, don't stand there listenin' to that pointy head clown, he just don't want us to pop his ol' lady!"

"YEH, YEH. LET'S GET IN THERE. HIT IT HIT IT!"

"Goddamnit. Goddamnit, get the fuck out of here. Get outta here. Damnit Rick, you sunafabitch, get the hell out-tahere. Leave the cat alone!"

"Man, don't push me like that, you lil' skinny ass. I'll bust your jaw for you."

"Yeh? Yeh? Yeh? Well you come on, you lyin' ass. This cat's always talking about all his 'babes' and all he's got to do is sneak around peeping in keyholes. You big lying asshole . . . all you know how to do is bullshit and jerk off!"

"Fuck you, Ray."

"Your ugly ass mama."

"Shiit. You wanna go round with me, baby?"

"Comeon. Comeon, big time cocksman, comeon!"

Rick

hits the leader full in the face, and he falls backwards across the hall. The crowd follows screaming at this new feature.

"Aww, man, somebody stop this shit. Rick'll kill Ray!"

"Well, you stop it, man."

"O.K., O.K., cut it out. Cut it out, Rick. You win man. Leave the cat alone. Leave him alone."

"Bad Rick . . . Bad Rick, Bad ass Rick!"

"Well, man, you saw the cat fuckin' with me. He started the shit!"

"Yeh . . . tough cat!"

"Get up Ray."

And then the door does open and Bobby Hutchens stands in the half light in his shower shoes, a broom in his hands. The boys scream and turn their attention back to Love. Bald Lyle is in the closet. More noise. More lies. More prints in the sand, away, or toward some name. I am a poet. I am a rich famous butcher. I am the man who paints the gold balls on the tops of flagpoles. I am, no matter, more beautiful than anyone else. And I have come a long way to say this. Here. In the long hall, shadows across my hands. My face pushed hard against the floor. And the wood, old, and protestant. And their voices, all these other selves screaming for blood. For blood, or whatever it is fills their noble lives.

THE BABYSITTER

ROBERT COOVER

She arrives at 7:40, ten minutes late, but the children, Jimmy and Bitsy, are still eating supper, and their parents are not ready to go yet. From other rooms come the sounds of a baby screaming, water running, a television musical (no words: probably a dance number—patterns of gliding figures come to mind). Mrs. Tucker sweeps into the kitchen, fussing with her hair, and snatches a baby bottle full of milk out of a pan of warm water, rushes out again. "Harry!" she calls. "The babysitter's here already!"

• • •

That's My Desire? I'll Be Around? He smiles toothily, beckons faintly with his head, rubs his fast balding pate. Bewitched, maybe? Or, What's the Reason? He pulls on his shorts, gives his hips a slap. The baby goes silent in mid-scream. Isn't this the one who used their tub last time? Who's Sorry Now, that's it.

• • •

Jack is wandering around town, not knowing what to do. His girlfriend is babysitting at the Tuckers', and later, when she's got the kids in bed, maybe he'll drop over there. Sometimes he watches TV with her when she's babysitting, it's about the only chance he gets to make out a little since he doesn't own wheels, but they have to be careful because most people don't like their sitters to have boyfriends over. Just kissing her makes her nervous. She won't close her eyes because she has to be watching the door all the time. Married people really have it good, he thinks.

"Hi," the babysitter says to the children, and puts her books on top of the refrigerator. "What's for supper?" The little girl, Bitsy, only stares at her obliquely. She joins them at the end of the kitchen table. "I don't have to go to bed until nine," the boy announces flatly, and stuffs his mouth full of potato chips. The babysitter catches a glimpse of Mr. Tucker hurrying out of the bathroom in his underwear.

* * *

Her tummy. Under her arms. And her feet. Those are the best places. She'll spank him, she says sometimes. Let her.

* * *

That sweet odor that girls have. The softness of her blouse. He catches a glimpse of the gentle shadows amid her thighs, as she curls her legs up under her. He stares hard at her. He has a lot of meaning packed into that stare, but she's not even looking. She's popping her gum and watching television. She's sitting right there, inches away, soft, fragrant, and ready: but what's his next move? He notices his buddy Mark in the drugstore, playing the pinball machine, and joins him. "Hey, this mama's cold, Jack baby! She needs your touch!"

* * *

Mrs. Tucker appears at the kitchen doorway, holding a rolled-up diaper. "Now, don't just eat potato chips, Jimmy! See that he eats his hamburger, dear." She hurries away to the bathroom. The boy glares sullenly at the babysitter, silently daring her to carry out the order. "How about a little of that good hamburger now, Jimmy?" she says perfunctorily. He lets half of it drop to the floor. The baby is silent and a man is singing a love song on the TV. The children crunch chips.

* * *

He loves her. She loves him. They whirl airily, stirring a light breeze, through a magical landscape of rose and emerald and deep blue. Her light brown hair coils and wisps softly in the breeze, and the soft folds of her white gown tug at her body and then float away. He smiles in a pulsing crescendo of sincerity and song.

* * *

"You mean she's alone?" Mark asks. "Well, there's two

or three kids," Jack says. He slides the coin in. There's a
rumble of steel balls tumbling, lining up. He pushes a
plunger with his thumb, and one ball pops up in place, hard
and glittering with promise. His stare? to say he loves her.
That he cares for her and would protect her, would shield
her, if need be, with his own body. Grinning, he bends over
the ball to take careful aim: he and Mark have studied this
machine and have it figured out, but still it's not that easy
to beat.

• • •

On the drive to the party, his mind is partly on the girl,
partly on his own high-school days, long past. Sitting at the
end of the kitchen table there with his children, she had
seemed to be self-consciously arching her back, jutting her
pert breasts, twitching her thighs: and for whom if not for
him? So she'd seen him coming out of there, after all. He
smiles. Yet what could he ever do about it? Those good
times are gone, old man. He glances over at his wife, who,
readjusting a garter, asks: "What do you think of our babysitter?"

• • •

He loves her. She loves him. And then the babies come.
And dirty diapers and one goddamn meal after another.
Dishes. Noise. Clutter. And fat. Not just tight, her girdle
actually hurts. Somewhere recently she's read about women
getting heart attacks or cancer or something from too-tight
girdles. Dolly pulls the car door shut with a grunt, strangely irritated, not knowing why. Party mood. Why is her husband humming, "Who's Sorry Now?" Pulling out of the
drive, she glances back at the lighted kitchen window.
"What do you think of our babysitter?" she asks. While her
husband stumbles all over himself trying to answer, she
pulls a stocking tight, biting deeper with the garters.

• • •

"Stop it!" she laughs. Bitsy is pulling on her skirt and he is
tickling her in the ribs. "Jimmy! Don't!" But she is laughing too much to stop him. He leaps on her, wrapping his
legs around her waist, and they all fall to the carpet in
front of the TV, where just now a man in a tuxedo and a
little girl in a flouncy white dress are doing a tapdance together. The babysitter's blouse is pulling out of her skirt,
showing a patch of bare tummy: the target. "I'll spank!"

Jack pushes the plunger, thrusting up a steel ball, and bends studiously over the machine. "You getting any off her?" Mark asks, and clears his throat, flicks ash from his cigarette. "Well, not exactly, not yet," Jack says, grinning awkwardly, but trying to suggest more than he admits to, and fires. He heaves his weight gently against the machine as the ball bounds off a rubber bumper. He can feel her warming up under his hands, the flippers suddenly coming alive, delicate rapid-fire patterns emerging in the flashing of the lights. 1000 WHEN LIT: *now!* "Got my hand on it, that's about all." Mark glances up from the machine, cigarette dangling from his lip. "Maybe you need some help," he suggests with a wry one-sided grin. "Like maybe together, man, we could do it."

• • •

She likes the big tub. She uses the Tuckers' bath salts, and loves to sink into the hot fragrant suds. She can stretch out, submerged, up to her chin. It gives her a good sleepy tingly feeling.

• • •

"What do you think of our babysitter?" Dolly asks, adjusting a garter. "Oh, I hardly noticed," he says. "Cute girl. She seems to get along fine with the kids. Why?" "I don't know." His wife tugs her skirt down, glances at a lighted window they are passing, adding: "I'm not sure I trust her completely, that's all. With the baby, I mean. She seems a little careless. And the other time, I'm almost sure she had a boyfriend over." He grins, claps one hand on his wife's broad gartered thigh. "What's wrong with that?" he asks. Still in anklets, too. Bare thighs, no girdles, nothing up there but a flimsy pair of panties and soft adolescent flesh. He's flooded with vague remembrances of football rallies and movie balconies.

• • •

How tiny and rubbery it is! she thinks, soaping between the boys legs, giving him his bath. Just a funny jiggly little thing that looks like it shouldn't even be there at all. Is that what all the songs are about?

• • •

Jack watches Mark lunge and twist against the machine. Got her running now, racked them up. He's not too excit-

ed about the idea of Mark fooling around with his girlfriend, but Mark's a cooler operator than he is, and maybe,
doing it together this once, he'd get over his own timidity.
And if she didn't like it, there were other girls around. If
Mark went too far, he could cut him off, too. He feels his
shoulders tense: enough's enough, man . . . but sees the
flesh, too. "Maybe I'll call her later," he says.

• • •

"Hey, Harry! Dolly! Glad you could make it!" "I hope
we're not late." "No, no, you're one of the first, come on
in! By golly, Dolly, you're looking younger every day! How
do you do it? Give my wife your secret, will you?" He pats
her on her girdled bottom behind Mr. Tucker's back, leads
them in for drinks.

• • •

8:00. The babysitter runs water in the tub, combs her hair
in front of the bathroom mirror. There's a western on television, so she lets Jimmy watch it while she gives Bitsy her
bath. But Bitsy doesn't want a bath. She's angry and crying
because she has to be first. The babysitter tells her if she'll
take her bath quickly, she'll let her watch television while
Jimmy takes his bath, but it does no good. The little girl
fights to get out of the bathroom, and the babysitter has to
squat with her back against the door and forcibly undress
the child. There are better places to babysit. Both children
mind badly, and then, sooner or later, the baby is sure to
wake up for a diaper change and more bottle. The Tuckers
do have a good color TV, though, and she hopes things will
be settled down enough to catch the 8:30 program. She
thrusts the child into the tub, but she's still screaming and
thrashing around. "Stop it now, Bitsy, or you'll wake the
baby!" "I have to go potty!" the child wails, switching tac-
tics. The babysitter sighs, lifts the girl out of the tub and
onto the toilet, getting her skirt and blouse all wet in the
process. She glances at herself in the mirror. Before she
knows it, the girl is off the seat and out of the bathroom.
"Bitsy! Come back here!"

• • •

"Okay, that's enough!" Her skirt is ripped and she's flushed
and crying. "Who says?" "I do, man!" The bastard goes for
her, but he tackles him. They roll and tumble. Tables tip,

lights topple, the TV crashes to the floor. He slams a hard right to the guy's gut, clips his chin with a rolling left.

● ● ●

"We hope it's a girl." That's hardly surprising, since they already have four boys. Dolly congratulates the woman like everybody else, but she doesn't envy her, not a bit. That's all she needs about now. She stares across the room at Harry, who is slapping backs and getting loud, as usual. He's spreading out through the middle, so why the hell does he have to complain about her all the time? "Dolly, you're looking younger every day!" was the nice greeting she got tonight. "What's your secret?" And Harry: "It's all those calories. She's getting back her baby fat." "Haw haw! Harry, have a heart!"

● ● ●

"Get her feet!" he hollers at Bitsy, his fingers in her ribs, running over her naked tummy, tangling in the underbrush of straps and strange clothing. "Get her shoes off!" He holds her pinned by pressing his head against her soft chest. "No! No, Jimmy! Bitsy, stop!" But though she kicks and twists and rolls around, she doesn't get up, she can't get up, she's laughing too hard, and the shoes come off, and he grabs a stockinged foot and scratches the sole ruthlessly, and she raises up her legs, trying to pitch him off, she's wild, boy, but he hangs on, and she's laughing, and on the screen there's a rattle of hooves, and he and Bitsy are rolling around and around on the floor in a crazy rodeo of long bucking legs.

● ● ●

He slips the coin in. There's a metallic fall and a sharp click as the dial tone begins. "I hope the Tuckers have gone," he says. "Don't worry, they're at our place," Mark says. "They're always the first ones to come and the last ones to go home. My old man's always bitching about them." Jack laughs nervously and dials the number. "Tell her we're coming over to protect her from getting raped," Mark suggests, and lights a cigarette. Jack grins, leaning casually against the door jamb of the phonebooth, chewing gum, one hand in his pocket. He's really pretty uneasy, though. He has the feeling he's somehow messing up a good thing.

• • •

Bitsy runs naked into the livingroom, keeping a hassock between herself and the babysitter. "Bitsy . . . !" the babysitter threatens. Artificial reds and greens and purples flicker over the child's wet body, as hooves clatter, guns crackle, and stagecoach wheels thunder over rutted terrain. "Get outa the way, Bitsy!" the boy complains. "I can't see!" Bitsy streaks past and the babysitter chases, cornering the girl in the back bedroom. Bitsy throws something that hits her softly in the face: a pair of men's undershorts. She grabs the girl scampering by, carries her struggling to the bathroom, and with a smart crack on her glistening bottom, pops her back into the tub. In spite, Bitsy peepees in the bathwater.

• • •

Mr. Tucker stirs a little water into his bourbon and kids with his host and another man, just arrived, about their golf games. They set up a match for the weekend, a threesome looking for a fourth. Holding his drink in his right hand, Mr. Tucker swings his left through the motion of a tee-shot. "You'll have to give me a stroke a hole," he says. "I'll give you a stroke!" says his host: "Bend over!" Laughing, the other man asks: "Where's your boy Mark tonight?" "I don't know," replies the host, gathering up a trayful of drinks. Then he adds in a low growl: "Out chasing tail probably." They chuckle loosely at that, then shrug in commiseration and return to the livingroom to join their women.

• • •

Shades pulled. Door locked. Watching the TV. Under a blanket maybe. Yes, that's right, under a blanket. Her eyes close when he kisses her. Her breasts, under both their hands, are soft and yielding.

• • •

A hard blow to the belly. The face. The dark beardy one staggers. the lean-jawed sheriff moves in, but gets a spurred boot in his face. The dark one hurls himself forward, drives his shoulder into the sheriff's hard midriff, her own tummy tightens, withstands, as the sheriff smashes the dark man's nose, slams him up against a wall, slugs him again! and again! The dark man grunts rhythmically, backs off, then plunges suicidally forward—her own knees draw up protectively—the sheriff staggers! caught low! but instead of following through, the other man steps back—a pistol! the dark one has a pistol! the sheriff draws! shoots from the hip! explosions! she clutches her hands between her thighs—no! the sheriff spins! wounded! the dark man hesitates, aims, her legs stiffen toward the set, the sheriff rolls desperately in the straw, fires: dead! the dark man is dead! groans, crumples, his pistol drooping in his collapsing hand, dropping, he drops. The sheriff, spent, nicked, watches weakly from the floor where he lies. Oh, to be whole! to be good and strong and right! to embrace and be embraced by harmony and wholeness! The sheriff, drawing himself painfully up on one elbow, rubs his bruised mouth with the back of his other hand.

• • •

"Well, we just sorta thought we'd drop over," he says, and winks broadly at Mark. "Who's we?" "Oh, me and Mark here." "Tell her, good thing like her, gotta pass it around," whispers Mark, dragging on his smoke, then flicking the butt over under the pinball machine. "What's that?" she asks. "Oh, Mark and I were just saying, like two's company, three's an orgy," Jack says, and winks again. She giggles. "Oh Jack!" Behind her, he can hear shouts and gunfire. "Well, okay, for just a little while, if you'll both be good." Way to go, man.

• • •

Probably some damn kid over there right now. Wrestling around on the couch in front of his TV. Maybe he should drop back to the house. Just to check. None of that stuff, she was there to do a job! Park the car a couple doors down, slip in the front door before she knows it. He sees the disarray of clothing, the young thighs exposed to the flickering television light, hears his baby crying. "Hey, what's going on here! Get outa here, son, before I call the police!" Of course, they haven't really been doing anything. They probably don't even know how. He stares benignly down upon the girl, her skirt rumpled loosely around her thighs. Flushed, frightened, yet excited, she stares back at him. He smiles. His finger touches a knee, approaches the hem. Another couple arrives. Filling up here with people. He wouldn't be missed. Just slip out, stop back casually to pick up something or other he forgot, never mind what. He remembers that the other time they had this babysitter, she took a bath in their house. She had a date afterwards, and she'd just come from cheerleading practice or something. Aspirin maybe. Just drop quietly and casually into the bathroom to pick up some aspirin. "Oh, excuse me, dear! I only . . . !" She gazes back at him, astonished, yet strangely moved. Her soft wet breasts rise and fall in the water, and her tummy looks pale and ripply. He recalls that her pubic hairs, left in the tub, were brown. Light brown.

• • •

She's no more than stepped into the tub for a quick bath, when Jimmy announces from outside the door that he has to go to the bathroom. She sighs: just an excuse, she knows. "You'll have to wait." The little nuisance. "I can't wait." "Okay, then come ahead, but I'm taking a bath." She supposes that will stop him, but it doesn't. In he comes. She slides down into the suds until she's eye-level with the edge of the tub. He hesitates. "Go ahead, if you have to," she says, a little awkwardly, "but I'm not getting out." "Don't look," he says. She: "I will if I want to."

• • •

She's crying. Mark is rubbing his jaw where he's just slugged him. A lamp lies shattered. "Enough's enough, Mark! Now get outa here!" Her skirt is ripped to the waist, her bare hip bruised. Her panties lie on the floor like a broken balloon. Later, he'll wash her wounds, help her dress, he'll take care of her. Pity washes through him, giving him a sudden hard-on. Mark laughs at it, pointing. Jack crouches, waiting, ready for anything.

• • •

Laughing, they roll and tumble. Their little hands are all over her, digging and pinching. She struggles to her hands and knees, but Bitsy leaps astride her neck, bowing her head to the carpet. "Spank her, Jimmy!" His swats sting: is her skirt up? The phone rings. "The cavalry to the rescue!" she laughs, and throws them off to go answer.

• • •

Kissing Mark, her eyes closed, her hips nudge toward Jack. He stares at the TV screen, unsure of himself, one hand slipping cautiously under her skirt. Her hand touches his arm as though to resist, then brushes on by to rub his leg.

This blanket they're under was a good idea. "Hi! This is Jack!"

· · ·

Bitsy's out and the water's running. "Come on, Jimmy, your turn!" Last time, he told her he took his own baths, but she came in anyway. "I'm not gonna take a bath," he announces, eyes glued on the set. He readies for the struggle. "But I've already run your water. Come on, Jimmy, please!" He shakes his head. She can't make him, he's sure he's as strong as she is. She sighs. "Well, it's up to you. I'll use the water myself then," she says. He waits until he's pretty sure she's not going to change her mind, then sneaks in and peeks through the keyhole in the bathroom door: just in time to see her big bottom as she bends over to stir in the bubblebath. Then she disappears. Trying to see as far down as the keyhole will allow, he bumps his head on the knob. "Jimmy, is that you?" "I—I have to go to the bathroom!" he stammers.

· · ·

Not actually in the tub, just getting in. One foot on the mat, the other in the water. Bent over slightly, buttocks flexed, teats swaying, holding on to the edge of the tub. "Oh, excuse me! I only wanted . . . !" He passes over her astonishment, the awkward excuses, moves quickly to the part where he reaches out to— "What on earth are you doing, Harry?" his wife asks, staring at his hand. His host, passing, laughs. "He's practicing his swing for Sunday, Dolly, but it's not going to do him a damn bit of good!" Mr. Tucker laughs, sweeps his right hand on through the air as though lifting a seven-iron shot onto the green. He makes a *dok!* sound with his tongue. "In there!"

· · ·

"No, Jack, I don't think you'd better." "Well, we just called, we just, uh, thought we'd, you know, stop by for a minute, watch television for thirty minutes, or, or something. " "Who's we?" "Well, Mark's here, I'm with him, and he said he'd like to, you know, like if it's all right, just—" "Well, it's *not* all right. The Tuckers said no." "Yeah, but if we only—" "And they seemed awfully suspicious about last time." "Why? We didn't—I mean, I just thought—" "No, Jack, and that's period." She hangs up.

She returns to the TV, but the commercial is on. Anyway, she's missed most of the show. She decides maybe she'll take a quick bath. Jack might come by anyway, it'd make her mad, that'd be the end as far as he was concerned, but if he should, she doesn't want to be all sweaty. And besides, she likes the big tub the Tuckers have.

* * *

He is self-conscious and stands with his back to her, his little neck flushed. It takes him forever to get started, and when it finally does come, it's just a tiny trickle. "See, it was just an excuse," she scolds, but she's giggling inwardly at the boy's embarrassment. "You're just a nuisance, Jimmy." At the door, his hand on the knob, he hesitates, staring timidly down on his shoes. "Jimmy?" She peeks at him over the edge of the tub, trying to keep a straight face, as he sneaks a nervous glance back over his shoulder. "As long as you bothered me," she says, "you might as well soap my back."

* * *

"The aspirin . . ." They embrace. She huddles in his arms like a child. Lovingly, paternally, knowledgeably, he wraps her nakedness. How compact, how tight and small her body is! Kissing her ear, he stares down past her rump at the still clear water. "I'll join you," he whispers hoarsely.

* * *

She picks up the shorts Bitsy threw at her. Men's underwear. She holds them in front of her, looks at herself in the bedroom mirror. About twenty sizes too big for her, of course. She runs her hand inside the opening in front, pulls out her thumb. How funny it must feel!

* * *

"Well, man, I say we just go rape her," Mark says flatly, and swings his weight against the pinball machine. "Uff! Ahh! Get in there, you mother! Look at that! Hah! Man, I'm gonna turn this baby over!" Jack is embarrassed about the phone conversation. Mark just snorted in disgust when he hung up. He cracks down hard on his gum, angry that he's such a chicken. "Well, I'm game if you are," he says coldly.

* * *

8:30. "Okay, come on, Jimmy, it's time." He ignores her. The western gives way to a spy show. Bitsy, in pajamas, pads into the livingroom. "No, Bitsy, it's time to go to bed." "You said I could watch!" the girl whines, and starts to throw another tantrum. "But you were too slow and it's late. Jimmy, you get in that bathroom, and right now!" Jimmy stares sullenly at the set, unmoving. The babysitter tries to catch the opening scene of the television program so she can follow it later, since Jimmy gives himself his own baths. When the commercial interrupts, she turns off the sound, stands in front of the screen. "Okay, into the tub, Jimmy Tucker, or I'll take you in there and give you your bath myself!" "Just try it," he says, "and see what happens."

• • •

They stand outside, in the dark, crouched in the bushes, peeking in. She's on the floor, playing with the kids. Too early. They seem to be tickling her. She gets to her hands and knees, but the little girl leaps on her head, pressing her face to the floor. There's an obvious target, and the little boy proceeds to beat on it. "Hey, look at that kid go!" whispers Mark, laughing and snapping his fingers softly. Jack feels uneasy out here. Too many neighbors, too many cars going by, too many people in the world. That little boy in there is one up on him, though: he's never thought about tickling her as a starter.

• • •

His little hand, clutching the bar of soap, lathers shyly a narrow space between her shoulderblades. She is doubled forward against her knees, buried in rich suds, peeking at him over the edge of her shoulder. The soap slithers out of his grip and plunks into the water. "I . . . I dropped the soap," he whispers. She: "Find it."

• • •

"I dream of Jeannie with the light brown pubic hair!" "Harry! Stop that! You're drunk!" But they're laughing, they're all laughing, damn! he's feeling pretty goddamn good at that, and now he just knows he needs that aspirin. Watching her there, her thighs spread for him, on the couch, in the tub, hell, on the kitchen table for that matter, he tees off on Number Nine, and—whap!—swats his host's wife on the bottom. "Hole in one!" he shouts. "Harry!" Why can't his goddamn wife Dolly ever get happy-drunk instead of sour-drunk all the time? "Gonna be tough Sun-

day, old buddy!" "You're pretty tough right now, Harry,"
says his host.

• • •

The babysitter lunges forward, grabs the boy by the arms
and hauls him off the couch, pulling two cushions with
him, and drags him toward the bathroom. He lashes out,
knocking over an endtable full of magazines and ashtrays.
"You leave my brother alone!" Bitsy cries and grabs the sitter around the waist. Jimmy jumps on her and down they
all go. On the silent screen, there's a fade-in to a dark pas-
sageway in an old apartment building in some foreign
country. She kicks out and somebody falls between her
legs. Somebody else is sitting on her face. "Jimmy! Stop
that!" the babysitter laughs, her voice muffled.

• • •

She's watching television. All alone. It seems like a good
time to go in. Just remember: really, no matter what she
says, she wants it. They're standing in the bushes, trying to
get up the nerve. "We'll tell her to be good," Mark whispers, "and if she's not good, we'll spank her." Jack giggles
softly, but his knees are weak. She stands. They freeze. She
looks right at them. "She can't see us." Mark whispers tense-
ly. "Is she coming out?" "No," says Mark, "she's going
into—that must be the bathroom!" Jack takes a deep
breath, his heart pounding. "Hey, is there a window back
there?" Mark asks.

• • •

The phone rings. She leaves the tub, wrapped in a towel.
Bitsy gives a tug on the towel. "Hey, Jimmy, get the
towel!" she squeals. "Now stop that, Bitsy!" the babysitter
hisses, but too late: with one hand on the phone, the other
isn't enough to hang on to the towel. Her sudden nakedness
awes them and it takes them a moment to remember about
tickling her. By then, she's in the towel again. "I hope you
got a good look," she says angrily. She feels chilled and
oddly a little frightened. "Hello?" No answer. She glances
at the window—is somebody out there? Something, she saw
something, and a rustling—footsteps?

• • •

"Okay, I don't care, Jimmy, don't take a bath," she says ir-
ritably. Her blouse is pulled out and wrinkled, her hair is
all mussed, and she feels sweaty. There's about a million

things she'd rather be doing than babysitting with these two. Three: at least the baby's sleeping. She knocks on the overturned endtable for luck, rights it, replaces the magazines and ashtrays. The one thing that really makes her sick is a dirty diaper. "Just go on to bed." "I don't have to go to bed until nine," he reminds her. Really, she couldn't care less. She turns up the volume on the TV, settles down on the couch, poking her blouse back into her skirt, pushing her hair out of her eyes. Jimmy and Bitsy watch from the floor. Maybe, once they're in bed, she'll take a quick bath. She wishes Jack would come by. The man, no doubt the spy, is following a woman, but she doesn't know why. The woman passes another man. Something seems to happen, but it's not clear what. She's probably already missed too much. The phone rings.

• • •

Mark is kissing her. Jack is under the blanket, easing her panties down over her squirming hips. Her hand is in his pants, pulling it out, pulling it toward her, pulling it hard. She knew just where it was! Mark is stripping, too. God, it's really happening! he thinks with a kind of pious joy, and notices the open door. "Hey! What's going on here?"

• • •

He soaps her back, smooth and slippery under his hand. She is doubled over, against her knees, between his legs. Her light brown hair, reaching to her gleaming shoulders, is wet at the edges. The soap slips, falls between his legs. He fishes for it, finds it, slips it behind him. "Help me find it," he whispers in her ear. "Sure Harry," says his host, going around behind him. "What'd you lose?"

• • •

Soon be nine, time to pack the kids off to bed. She clears the table, dumps paper plates and leftover hamburgers into the garbage, puts glasses and silverware into the sink, and the mayonnaise, mustard, and ketchup in the refrigerator. Neither child has eaten much supper finally, mostly potato chips and ice cream, but it's really not her problem. She glances at the books on the refrigerator. Not much chance she'll get to them, she's already pretty worn out. Maybe she'd feel better if she had a quick bath. She runs water into the tub, tosses in bubblebath salts, undresses. Before pushing down her panties, she stares for a moment at the

smooth silken panel across her tummy, fingers the place
where the opening would be if there were one. Then she
steps quickly out of them, feeling somehow ashamed, un-
hooks her brassiere. She weighs her breasts in the palms of
her hands, watching herself in the bathroom mirror, where,
in the open window behind her, she sees a face. She
screams.

* * *

She screams: "Jimmy! Give me that!" "What's the matter?"
asks Jack on the other end. "Jimmy! Give me my towel!
Right now!" "Hello? Hey, are you still there?" "I'm sorry,
Jack," she says, panting. "You caught me in the tub. I'm
just wrapped in a towel and these silly kids grabbed it
away!" "Gee, I wish I'd been there!" "Jack—!" "To protect
you, I mean." "Oh, sure," she says, giggling. "Well, what
do you think, can I come over and watch TV with you?"
"Well, not right this minute," she says. He laughs lightly.
He feels very cool. "Jack?" "Yeah?" "Jack, I . . . I think
there's somebody outside the window!"

* * *

She carries him, fighting all the way, to the tub, Bitsy pum-
meling her in the back and kicking her ankles. She can't
hang on to him and undress him at the same time. "I'll
throw you in, clothes and all, Jimmy Tucker!" she gasps.
"You better not!" he cries. She sits on the toilet seat, locks
her legs around him, whips his shirt up over his head before he knows what's happening. The pants are easier. Like
all little boys his age, he has almost no hips at all. He hangs
on desperately to his underpants, but when she succeeds in
snapping these down out of his grip, too, he gives up, starts
to bawl, and beats her wildly in the face with his fists. She
ducks her head, laughing hysterically, oddly entranced by
the spectacle of that pale little thing down there, bobbing
and bouncing rubberlike about the boy's helpless fury and
anguish.

* * *

"Aspirin? Whaddaya want aspirin for, Harry? I'm sure they
got aspirin here, if you—" "Did I say aspirin? I meant uh,
my glasses. And, you know, I thought, well, I'd sorta check
to see if everything was okay at home." Why the hell is it
his mouth feels like it's got about six sets of teeth packed in
there, and a tongue the size of that liverwurst his host's

wife is passing around? "Whaddaya want your glasses for, Harry? I don't understand you at all!" "Aw, well, honey, I was feeling kind of dizzy or something, and I thought—" "Dizzy is right. If you want to check on the kids, why don't you just call on the phone?"

• • •

They can tell she's naked and about to get into the tub, but the bathroom window is frosted glass, and they can't see anything clearly. "I got an idea," Mark whispers. "One of us goes and calls her on the phone, and the other watches when she comes out." "Okay, but who calls?" "Both of us, we'll do it twice. Or more."

• • •

Down forbidden alleys. Into secret passageways. Unlocking the world's terrible secrets. Sudden shocks: a trapdoor! a fall! or the stunning report of a rifle shot, the *whaaii-ii-ing!* of the bullet biting concrete by your ear! Careful! Then edge forward once more, avoiding the light, inch at a time, now a quick dash for an open doorway—*look out!* there's a knife! a struggle! no! the long blade glistens! jerks! thrusts! *stabbed!* No, no, it missed! The assailant's down, yes! the spy's on top, pinning him, a terrific thrashing about, the spy rips off the assailant's mask: *a woman!*

• • •

Fumbling behind her, she finds it, wraps her hand around it, tugs. "Oh!" she gasps, pulling her hand back quickly, her ears turning crimson. "I . . . I thought it was the soap!" He squeezes her close between his thighs, pulls her back toward him, one hand sliding down her tummy between her legs. I Dream of Jeannie— "I have to go to the bathroom!" says someone outside the door.

• • •

She's combing her hair in the bathroom when the phone rings. She hurries to answer it before it wakes the baby. "Hello, Tuckers." There's no answer. "Hello?" A soft click. Strange. She feels suddenly alone in the big house, and goes in to watch TV with the children.

• • •

"Stop it!" she screams. "Please, stop!" She's on her hands and knees, trying to get up, but they're too strong for her. Mark holds her head down. "Now, baby, we're gonna teach you how to be a nice girl," he says coldly, and nods at

Jack. When she's doubled over like that, her skirt rides up her thighs to the leg bands of her panties. "C'mon, man, go! This baby's cold! She needs your touch!"

● ● ●

Parks the car a couple blocks away. Slips up to the house, glances in his window. Just like he's expected. Her blouse is off and the kid's shirt is unbuttoned. He watches, while slowly, clumsily, childishly, they fumble with each other's clothes. My God, it takes them forever. "Some party!" "You said it!" When they're more or less naked, he walks in. "Hey! What's going on here?" They go white as bleu cheese. Haw haw! "What's the little thing you got sticking out there, boy?" "Harry, behave yourself!" No, he doesn't let the kid get dressed, he sends him home bareassed. "Bareassed!!" He drinks to that. "Promises, promises," says his host's wife. "I'll mail you your clothes, son!" He gazes down on the naked little girl on his couch. "Looks like you and me, we got a little secret to keep, honey," he says cooly. "Less you wanna go home the same way your boyfriend did!" He chuckles at his easy wit, leans down over her, and unbuckles his belt. "Might as well make it two secrets, right?" "What in God's name are you talking about, Harry?" He staggers out of there, drink in hand, and goes to look for his car.

● ● ●

"Hey! What's going on here?" They huddle half-naked under the blanket, caught utterly unawares. On television: the clickety-click of frightened running feet on foreign pavements. Jack is fumbling for his shorts, tangled somehow around his ankles. The blanket is snatched away. "On your feet there!" Mr. Tucker, Mrs. Tucker, and Mark's mom and dad, the police, the neighbors, everybody comes crowding in. Hopelessly, he has a terrific erection. So hard it hurts. Everybody stares down at it.

● ● ●

Bitsy's sleeping on the floor. The babysitter is taking a bath. For more than an hour now, he'd had to use the bathroom. He doesn't know how much longer he can wait. Finally, he goes to knock on the bathroom door. "I have to use the bathroom." "Well, come ahead, if you have to." "Not while you're in there." She sighs loudly. "Okay, okay, just a minute," she says, "but you're a real nuisance, Jimmy!" He's holding on, pinching it as tight as he can. *"Hurry!"* He holds his breath, squeezing shut his eyes. No. Too late. At last, she opens the door. "Jimmy!" "I *told* you to hurry!" he sobs. She drags him into the bathroom and pulls his pants down.

• • •

He arrives just in time to see her emerge from the bathroom, wrapped in a towel, to answer the phone. His two kids sneak up behind her and pull the towel away. She's trying to hang onto the phone and get the towel back at the same time. It's quite a picture. She's got a sweet ass. Standing there in the bushes, pawing himself with one hand, he lifts his glass with the other and toasts her sweet ass, which his son now swats. Haw haw, maybe that boy's gonna shape up, after all.

• • •

They're in the bushes, arguing about their next move, when she comes out of the bathroom, wrapped in a towel. They can hear the baby crying. Then it stops. They see her running, naked, back to the bathroom like she's scared or something. "I'm going in after her, man, whether you're with me or not!" Mark whispers, and he starts out of the bushes. But just then, a light comes sweeping up through the yard, as a car swings in the drive. They hit the dirt, hearts pounding. "Is it the cops?" "I don't know!" "Do you think they saw us?" "Sshh!" A man comes staggering up the walk from the drive, a drink in his hand, stumbles on in the kitchen door and then straight into the bathroom. "It's Mr. Tucker!" Mark whispers. A scream. "Let's get outa here, man!"

• • •

9:00. Having missed most of the spy show anyway and having little else to do, the babysitter has washed the dishes and cleaned the kitchen up a little. The books on the refrigerator remind her of her better intentions, but she decides that first she'll see what's next on TV. In the livingroom, she finds little Bitsy sound asleep on the floor. She lifts her gently, carries her into her bed, and tucks her in. "Okay, Jimmy, it's nine o'clock, I've let you stay up, now be a good boy." Sullenly, his sleepy eyes glued still to the set, the boy backs out of the room toward his bedroom. A drama comes on. She switches channels. A ballgame and a murder mystery. She switches back to the drama. It's a love story of some kind. A man married to an aging invalid wife, but in love with a younger girl. "Use the bathroom and brush your teeth before going to bed, Jimmy!" she calls, but as quickly regrets it, for she hears the baby stir in its crib.

• • •

Two of them are talking about mothers they've salted away in rest homes. Oh boy, that's just wonderful, this is one helluva party. She leaves them to use the john, takes advantage of the retreat to ease her girdle down awhile, get a few good deep breaths. She has this picture of her three kids carting her off to a rest home. In a wheelbarrow. That sure is something to look forward to, all right. When she pulls her girdle back up, she can't seem to squeeze into it. The host looks in. "Hey, Dolly, are you all right?" "Yeah, I just can't get into my damn girdle, that's all." "Here, let me help."

• • •

She pulls them on, over her own, standing in front of the bedroom mirror, holding her skirt bundled up around the waist. About twenty sizes too big for her, of course. She pulls them tight from behind, runs her hand inside the opening in front, pulls out her thumb. "And what a good boy am I!" She giggles: how funny it must feel! Then, in the mirror, she sees him: in the doorway behind her, sullenly watching. "Jimmy! You're supposed to be in bed!" "Those are my daddy's!" the boy says. "I'm gonna tell!"

• • •

"Jimmy!" She drags him into the bathroom and pulls his pants down. "Even your shoes are wet! Get them off!" She soaps up a warm washcloth she's had with her in the bathtub, scrubs him from the waist down with it. Bitsy stands in the doorway, staring. "Get out! Get out!" the boy screams at his sister. "Go back to bed, Bitsy. It's just an accident." "Get out!" The baby wakes and starts to howl.

• • •

The young lover feels sorry for her rival, the invalid wife; she believes the man has a duty toward the poor woman and insists she is willing to wait. But the man argues that he also has a duty toward himself: his life, too, is short, and he could not love his wife now even were she well. He embraces the young girl feverishly; she twists away in anguish. The door opens. They stand there grinning, looking devilish, but pretty silly at the same time. "Jack! I thought I told you not to come!" She's angry, but she's also glad in a way: she was beginning to feel a little too alone in the big house, with the children all sleeping. She should have taken that bath, after all. "We just came by to see if you were being a good girl," Jack says and blushes. The boys glance at each other nervously.

• • •

She's just sunk down into the tubful of warm fragrant suds, ready for a nice long soaking, when the phone rings. Wrapping a towel around her, she goes to answer: no one there. But now the baby's awake and bawling. She wonders if that's Jack bothering her all the time. If it is, brother, that's the end. Maybe it's the end anyway. She tries to calm the baby with the half-empty bottle, not wanting to change it until she's finished her bath. The bathroom's where the diapers go dirty, and they make it stink to high heaven. "Shush, shush!" she whispers, rocking the crib. The towel slips away, leaving an airy empty tingle up and down her backside. Even before she stoops for the towel, even before she turns around, she knows there's somebody behind her.

• • •

"We just came by to see if you were being a good girl," Jack says, grinning down at her. She's flushed and silent, her mouth half open. "Lean over," says Mark amiably. "We'll soap your back, as long as we're here." But she just huddles there, down in the suds, staring up at them with big eyes.

• • •

"Hey! What's going on here?" It's Mr. Tucker, stumbling through the door with a drink in his hand. She looks up from the TV. "What's the matter, Mr. Tucker?" "Oh, uh, I'm sorry, I got lost—no, I mean, I had to get some aspirin. Excuse me!" And he rushes past her into the bathroom, caroming off the livingroom door jamb on the way. The baby awakes.

• • •

"Okay, get off her, Mr. Tucker!" "Jack!" she cries, "what are *you* doing here?" He stares hard at them a moment: so that's where it goes. Then, as Mr. Tucker swings heavily off, he leans into the bastard with a hard right to the belly. Next thing he knows, though, he's got a face full of an old man's fist. He's not sure, as the lights go out, if that's his girlfriend screaming or the baby . . .

• • •

Her host pushes down on her fat fanny and tugs with all his might on her girdle, while she bawls on his shoulder: "I don't *wanna* go to a rest home!" "Now, now, take it easy, Dolly, nobody's gonna make you—" "Ouch! Hey, you're hurting!" "You should buy a bigger girdle, Dolly." "You're telling me?" Some other guy pokes his head in. "Whatsamatter? Dolly fall in?" "No, she fell out. Give me a hand."

• • •

By the time she's chased Jack and Mark out of there, she's lost track of the program she's been watching on television. There's another woman in the story now for some reason. That guy lives a very complicated life. Impatiently, she switches channels. She hates ballgames, so she settles for the murder mystery. She switches just in time, too: there's a dead man sprawled out on the floor of what looks like an office or a study or something. A heavyset detective gazes up from his crouch over the body: "He's been strangled." Maybe she'll take that bath, after all.

• • •

She drags him into the bathroom and pulls his pants down. She soaps up a warm washcloth she's had in the tub with her, but just as she reaches between his legs, it starts to spurt, spraying her arms and hands. "Oh, Jimmy! I thought you were done!" she cries, pulling him toward the toilet and aiming it into the bowl. How moist and rubbery it is! And you can turn it every which way. How funny it must feel!

• • •

"Stop it!" she screams. "Please stop!" She's on her hands and knees and Jack is holding her head down. "Now we're gonna teach you how to be a nice girl," Mark says and lifts her skirt. "Well, I'll be damned!" "What's the matter?" asks Jack, his heart pounding. "Look at this big pair of men's underpants she's got on!" "Those are my daddy's!" says Jimmy, watching them from the doorway. "I'm gonna tell!"

• • •

People are shooting at each other in the murder mystery,

but she's so mixed up, she doesn't know which ones are the good guys. She switches back to the love story. Something seems to have happened, because now the man is kissing his invalid wife tenderly. Maybe she's finally dying. The baby wakes, begins to scream. Let it. She turns up the volume on the TV.

• • •

Leaning down over her, unbuckling his belt. It's all happening just like he's known it would. Beautiful! The kid is gone, though his pants, poor lad, remain. "Looks like you and me, we got a secret to keep, child!" But he's cramped on the couch and everything is too slippery and small. "Lift your legs up, honey. Put them around my back." But instead, she screams. He rolls off, crashing to the floor. There they all come, through the front door. On television, somebody is saying: "Am I a burden to you, darling?" "Dolly! My God! Dolly, I can explain . . . !"

• • •

The game of the night is Get Dolly Tucker Back in Her Girdle Again. They've got her down on her belly in the livingroom and the whole damn crowd is working on her. Several of them are stretching the girdle, while others try to jam the fat inside. "I think we made a couple inches on this side! Roll her over!" Harry?

• • •

She's just stepped into the tub, when the phone rings, waking the baby. She sinks down in the suds, trying not to hear. But that baby doesn't cry, it screams. Angrily, she wraps a towel around herself, stamps peevishly into the baby's room, just letting the phone jangle. She tosses the baby down on its back, unpins its diapers hastily, and gets yellowish baby stool all over her hands. Her towel drops away. She turns to find Jimmy staring at her like a little idiot. She slaps him in the face with her dirty hand, while the baby screams, the phone rings, and nagging voices argue on the TV. There are better things she might be doing.

• • •

What's happening? Now there's a young guy in it. Is he after the young girl or the old invalid? To tell the truth, it looks like he's after the same man the women are. In disgust, she switches channels. "The strangler again," growls the fat detective, hands on hips, staring down at the body of a half-naked girl. She's considering either switching back to the love story or taking a quick bath, when a hand suddenly clutches her mouth.

* * *

"You're both chicken," she says, staring up at them. "But what if Mr. Tucker comes home?" Mark asks nervously.

* * *

How did he get here? He's standing pissing in his own goddamn bathroom, his wife is still back at the party, the three of them are, like good kids, sitting in there in the livingroom watching TV. One of them is his host's boy Mark. "It's a good murder mystery, Mr. Tucker," Mark said, when he came staggering in on them a minute ago. "Sit still!" he shouted, "I am just home for a moment!" Then whump thump on into the bathroom. Long hike for a wee-wee, Mister. But something keeps bothering him. Then it hits him: the girl's panties hanging like a broken balloon from the rabbit-ear antennae on the TV! He barges back in there, giving his shoulder a helluva crack on the livingroom door jamb on the way—but they're not hanging there any more. Maybe he's only imagined it. "Hey, Mr. Tucker," Mark says flatly. "Your fly's open."

* * *

The baby's dirty. Stinks to high heaven. She hurries back to the livingroom, hearing sirens and gunshots. The detective is crouched outside a house, peering in. Already, she's completely lost. The baby screams at the top of its lungs. She turns up the volume. But it's all confused. She hurries back in there, claps an angry hand to the baby's mouth. "Shut up!" she cries. She throws the baby down on its back, starts to unpin the diaper, as the baby tunes up again. The phone rings. She answers it, one eye on the TV. "What?" The baby cries so hard it starts to choke. Let it. "I said, hi, this is Jack!" Then it hits her: oh no! the diaper pin!

* * *

"The aspirin . . . " But she's already in the tub. Way down in the tub. Staring at him through the water. Her tummy looks pale and ripply. He hears sirens, people on the porch.

* * *

Jimmy gets up to go to the bathroom and gets his face

slapped and smeared with baby poop. Then she hauls him
off to the bathroom, yanks off his pajamas, and throws him
into the tub. That's okay, but next she gets naked and acts
like she's gonna get in the tub, too. The baby's screaming
and the phone's ringing like crazy and in walks his dad.
Saved! he thinks, but, no, his dad grabs him right back out
of the tub and whales the dickens out of him, no questions
asked, while she watches, then sends him—*whack!*—back
to bed. So he's lying there, wet and dirty and naked and
sore, and he still has to go to the bathroom, and outside his
window he hears two older guys talking. "Listen, you know
where to do it if we get her pinned?" "No! Don't you?"

* * *

"Yo ho heave ho! *Ugh!*" Dolly's on her back and they're
working on the belly side. Somebody got the great idea of
buttering her down first. Not to lose the ground they've
gained, they've shot it inside with a basting syringe. But
now suddenly there's this big tug-of-war under way between those who want to stuff her in and those who want to
let her out. Something rips, but she feels better. The odor
of hot butter makes her think of movie theaters and popcorn. "Hey, has anybody seen Harry?" she asks. "Where's
Harry?"

* * *

Somebody's getting chased. She switches back to the love
story, and now the man's back kissing the young lover
again. What's going on? She gives it up, decides to take a
quick bath. She's just stepping into the tub, one foot in, one
foot out, when Mr. Tucker walks in. "Oh, excuse me! I
only wanted some aspirin . . . " She grabs for a towel, but
he yanks it away. "Now, that's not how it's supposed to
happen, child," he scolds. "Please! Mr. Tucker . . . !" He
embraces her savagely, his calloused old hands clutching
roughly at her backside. "Mr. Tucker!" she cries, squirming. "Your wife called—!" He's pushing something between
her legs, hurting her. She slips, they both slip—something
cold and hard slams her in the back, cracks her skull, she
seems to be sinking into a sea . . .

* * *

They've got her over the hassock, skirt up and pants down.
"Give her a little lesson there, Jack baby!" The television

lights flicker and flash over her glossy flesh. 1000 WHEN
LIT. Whack! Slap! Bumper to bumper! He leans into her,
feeling her come alive.

• • •

The phone rings, waking the baby. "Jack, is that you?
Now, you listen to me—" "No, dear, this is Mrs. Tucker.
Isn't the TV awfully loud?" "Oh, I'm sorry, Mrs. Tucker!
I've been getting—" "I tried to call you before, but I
couldn't hang on. To the phone, I mean. I'm sorry, dear."
"Just a minute, Mrs. Tucker, the baby's—" "Honey, listen!
Is Harry there? Is Mr. Tucker there, dear?"

• • •

"Stop it!" she screams and claps a hand over the baby's
mouth. "Stop it! Stop it! *Stop it!*" Her other hand is full of
baby stool and she's afraid she's going to be sick. The
phone rings. "No!" she cries. She's hanging on to the baby,
leaning woozily away, listening to the phone ring. "Okay,
okay," she sighs, getting ahold of herself. But when she lets
go of the baby, it isn't screaming any more. She shakes it.
Oh no . . .

• • •

"Hello?" No answer. Strange. She hangs up and, wrapped
only in a towel, stares out the window at the cold face staring in—she screams!

• • •

She screams, scaring the hell out of him. He leaps out of
the tub, glances up at the window she's gaping at just in
time to see two faces duck away, then slips on the
bathroom tiles, and crashes to his ass, whacking his head
on the sink on the way down. She stares down at him,
trembling, a towel over her narrow shoulders. "Mr. Tucker! Mr. Tucker, are you all right . . . ?" Who's Sorry Now?
Yessir, who's back is breaking with each . . . He stares up
at the little tufted locus of all his woes, and passes out,
dreaming of Jeannie . . .

• • •

The phone rings. "Dolly! It's for you!" "Hello?" "Hello,
Mrs. Tucker?" "Yes, speaking." "Mrs. Tucker, this is the
police calling . . ."

• • •

It's cramped and awkward and slippery, but he's pretty
sure he got it in her, once anyway. When he gets the suds

out of his eyes, he sees her staring up at them. Through the water. "Hey, Mark! Let her up!"

•   •   •

Down in the suds. Feeling sleepy. The phone rings, startling her. Wrapped in a towel, she goes to answer. "No, he's not here, Mrs. Tucker." Strange. Married people act pretty funny sometimes. The baby is awake and screaming. Dirty, a real mess. Oh boy, there's a lot of things she'd rather be doing than babysitting in this madhouse. She decides to wash the baby off in her own bathwater. She removes her towel, unplugs the tub, lowers the water level so the baby can sit. Glancing back over her shoulder, she sees Jimmy staring at her. "Go back to bed, Jimmy." "I have to go to the bathroom." "Good grief, Jimmy! It looks like you already have!" The phone rings. She doesn't bother with the towel—what can Jimmy see he hasn't already seen?— and goes to answer. "No, Jack, and that's final." Sirens, on the TV, as the police move in. But wasn't that the channel with the love story? Ambulance maybe. Get this over with so she can at least catch the news. "Get those wet pajamas off, Jimmy, and I'll find clean ones. Maybe you better get in the tub, too." "I think something's wrong with the baby," he says. "It's down in the water and it's not swimming or anything."

•   •   •

She's staring up at them from the rug. They slap her. Nothing happens. "You just tilted her, man!" Mark says softly. "We gotta get outa here!" Two little kids are standing wide-eyed in the doorway. Mark looks hard at Jack. "No, Mark, they're just little kids . . . !" "We gotta, man, or we're dead."

•   •   •

"Dolly! My God! Dolly, I can explain!" She glowers down at them, her ripped girdle around her ankles. "What the four of you are doing in the bathtub with *my* babysitter?" she says sourly. "I can hardly wait!"

•   •   •

Police sirens wail, lights flash. "I heard the scream!" somebody shouts. "There were two boys!" "I saw a man!" "She was running with the baby!" "My God!" somebody screams "they're *all* dead!" Crowds come running. Spotlights probe the bushes.

• • •

"Harry, where the hell you been?" his wife whines, glaring blearily up at him from the carpet. "I can explain," he says. "Hey, whatsamatter, Harry?" his host asks, smeared with butter for some goddamn reason. "You look like you just seen a ghost!" Where did he leave his drink? Everybody's laughing, everybody except Dolly, whose cheeks are streaked with tears. "Hey, Harry, you won't let them take me to a rest home, will you, Harry?"

• • •

10:00. The dishes done, children to bed, her books read, she watches the news on television. Sleepy. The man's voice is gentle, soothing. She dozes—awakes with a start: a babysitter? Did the announcer say something about a babysitter?

• • •

"Just want to catch the weather," the host says, switching on the TV. Most of the guests are leaving, but the Tuckers stay to watch the news. As it comes on, the announcer is saying something about a babysitter. The host switches channels. "They got a better weatherman on four," he explains. "Wait!" says Mrs. Tucker. "There was something about a babysitter . . . !" The host switches back. "Details have not yet been released by the police," the announcer says. "Harry, maybe we'd better go . . ."

• • •

They stroll casually out of the drugstore, run into a buddy of theirs. "Hey! Did you hear about the babysitter?" the guy asks. Mark grunts, glances at Jack. "Got a smoke?" he asks the guy.

• • •

"I think I hear the baby screaming!" Mrs. Tucker cries, running across the lawn from the drive.

• • •

She wakes, startled, to find Mr. Tucker hovering over her. "I must have dozed off!" she exclaims. "Did you hear the news about the babysitter?" Mr. Tucker asks. "Part of it," she says, rising. "Too bad, wasn't it?" Mr. Tucker is watching the report of the ball scores and golf tournaments. "I'll drive you home in just a minute, dear," he says. "Why, how nice!" Mrs. Tucker exclaims from the kitchen. "The dishes are all done!"

• • •

"What can I say, Dolly?" the host says with a sigh, twisting the buttered strands of her ripped girdle between his fingers. "Your children are murdered, your husband gone, a corpse in your bathtub, and your house is wrecked. I'm sorry. But what can I say?" On the TV, the news is over, and they're selling aspirin. "Hell, *I* don't know," she says. "Let's see what's on the late late movie."

TERGVINDER'S STONE

W. S. MERWIN

One time my friend Tergvinder brought a large round boulder into his living room. He rolled it up the steps with the help of some two-by-fours, and when he got it out into the middle of the room, where some people have coffee tables (though he had never had one there himself) he left it. He said that was where it belonged.

It is really a plain-looking stone. Not as large as Plymouth Rock by a great deal, but then it does not have all the claims of a big shaky promotion campaign to support. That was one of the things Tergvinder said about it. He made no claims at all for it, he said. It was other people who called it Tergvinder's Stone. All he said was that according to him it belonged there.

His dog took to peeing on it, which created a problem (Tergvinder had not moved the carpet before he got the stone to where he said it belonged). Their tomcat took to squirting it, too. His wife fell over it quite often at first and it did not help their already strained marriage. Tergvinder said there was nothing to be done about it. It was in the order of things. That was a phrase he seldom employed, and never when he conceived that there was any room left for doubt.

He confided in me that he often woke in the middle of the night, troubled by the ancient, nameless ills of the planet, and got up quietly not to wake his wife, and walked through the house naked, without turning on any lights. He said that at such times he found himself listening, listening, aware of how some shapes in the darkness emitted low sounds like breathing, as they never did by day. He said he had become aware of a hole in the darkness in the middle of the living room, and out of that hole a breathing, a mournful dissatisfied sound of an absence waiting for what belonged to it, for something it had never seen and could not conceive of, but without which it could not rest. It was a sound, Tergvinder said, that touched him with fellow-feeling, and he had undertaken—oh, without saying anything to anybody—to assuage, if he could, that wordless longing that seemed always on the verge of despair. How to do it was another matter, and for months he had circled the problem, night and day, without apparently coming any closer to a solution. Then one day he had seen the stone. It had been there all the time at the bottom of his drive, he said, and he had never really seen it. Never recognized it for what it was. The nearer to the house he had got it, the more certain he had become. The stone had rolled into its present place like a lost loved one falling into arms that had long ached for it.

Tergvinder says that now on nights when he walks through the dark house he comes and stands in the living room doorway and listens to the peace in the middle of the floor. He knows its size, its weight, the touch of it, something of what is thought of it. He knows that it is peace. As he listens, some hint of that peace touches him too. Often, after a while, he steps down into the living room and goes and kneels beside the stone and they converse for hours in silence—a silence broken only by the sound of his own breathing.

PORCUPINES
AT THE UNIVERSITY

DONALD BARTHELME

" 'And now the purple dusk of twilight time/steals across the meadows of my heart,' " the Dean said.

His pretty wife, Paula, extended her long graceful hands full of Negro-nis.

A scout burst into the room, through the door. "Porcupines!" he shouted.

"Porcupines what?" the Dean asked.

"Thousands and thousands of them. Three miles down the road and comin' fast!"

"Maybe they won't enroll," the Dean said. "Maybe they're just passing through."

"You can't be sure," his wife said.

"How do they look?" he asked the scout, who was pulling porcupine quills out of his ankles.

"Well, you know. Like porcupines."

"Are you going to bust them?" Paula asked.

"I'm tired of busting people," the Dean said.

"They're not people," Paula pointed out.

"*De bustibus non est disputandum,*" the scout said.

"I suppose I'll have to do something," the Dean said.

Meanwhile the porcupine wrangler was wrangling the porcupines across the dusty and overbuilt West.

Dust clouds. Yips. The lowing of porcupines.

"Git along theah li'l porcupines."

And when I reach the great porcupine canneries of the

East, I will be rich, the wrangler reflected. I will sit on the front porch of the Muchlebach Hotel in New York City and smoke me a big seegar. Then, the fancy women.

"All right you porcupines step up to that yellow line."

There was no yellow line. This was just an expression the wrangler used to keep the porcupines moving. He had heard it in the Army. The damn-fool porcupines didn't know the difference.

The wrangler ambled along reading the ads in a copy of *Song Hits* magazine. "Play Harmonica in 5 Mins.!" and so forth.

The porcupines scuffled along making their little hops. There were four–five thousand in the herd. Nobody had counted exactly.

An assistant wrangler rode in from the outskirts of the herd. He too had a copy of *Song Hits* magazine, in his hip pocket. He looked at the head wrangler's arm, which had a lot of little holes in it.

"Hey Griswold."

"Yeah?"

"How'd you get all them little holes in your arm?"

"You ever try to slap a brand on a porky-pine?"

Probably the fancy women will be covered with low-cut dresses and cheap perfume, the wrangler thought. Probably there will be hundreds of them, hundreds and hundreds. All after my medicine bundle containing my gold and my lucky drill bit. But if they try to rush me I will pull my guitar. And sing them a song of prairie virility.

"Porcupines at the university," the Dean's wife said. "Well, why not?"

"We don't have *facilities* for four or five thousand porcupines," the Dean said. "I can't get a dial tone."

"They could take Alternate Life Styles," Paula said.

"We've already got too many people in Alternate Life Styles," the Dean said, putting down the telephone. "The hell with it. I'll bust them myself. Singlehanded. Lye."

"You'll get hurt."

"Nonsense, they're only porcupines. I'd better wear my old clothes."

"Bag of dirty shirts in the closet," Paula said.

The Dean went into the closet.

Bags and bags of dirty shirts.

"Why doesn't she ever take these shirts to the laundry?"

Griswold, the wrangler, wrote a new song in the saddle:

> Fancy woman fancy woman
> How come you don't do right
> I oughta rap you in the mouth
>   for the way you acted
> In the porte-cochere of the Trinity
>   River Consolidated
>   General High last Friday
> Nite.

I will sit back and watch it climbing the charts, he said to himself. As recorded by Merle Travis. First, it will be a Bell Ringer. Then, the Top Forty. Finally a Golden Oldie.

"All right you porcupines. Git along."

The herd was moving down a twelve-lane trail of silky-smooth concrete. Signs along the trail said things like "NEXT EXIT 5 MI." "RADAR IN USE."

"Griswold, some of them motorists behind us is gettin' awful edgy."

"I'm runnin' this here porky-pine drive," Griswold said, "and I say we better gettum off the road."

The herd was turned onto a broad field of green grass. Green grass with white lime lines on it at ten-yard intervals.

The Ed Sullivan show, the wrangler thought. Well, Ed, how I come to write this song, I was on a porky-pine drive. The last of the great porky-pine drives you might say. We had four-five thousand head we'd fatted up along the Tuscalora and we was headin' for New York City.

The Dean loaded a gleaming Gatling gun capable of delivering three hundred and sixty rounds a minute. The Gatling gun sat in a mule-drawn wagon and was covered with an old piece of canvas. Formerly it had sat on a concrete slab in front of the R.O.T.C. Building.

First, the Dean said to himself, all they see is this funky

old wagon pulled by this busted-up old mule. Then, I whip
off the canvas. There stands the gleaming Gatling gun capable of delivering three hundred and sixty rounds a minute. My hand resting lightly, confidently on the crank.
They shall not pass, I say. *Ils ne passeront pas*. Then, the
porcupine hide begins to fly.

I wonder if these rounds are still good?

The gigantic Gatling gun loomed over the herd like an immense piece of bad news.

"Hey Griswold."

"What?"

"He's got a gun."

"I *see* it," Griswold said. "You think I'm blind?"

"What we gonna do?"

"How about vamoosing?"

"But the herd—"

"Them li'l porcupines can take care of their own selves,"
Griswold said. "God damn it. I guess we better parley." He
got up off the grass, where he had been stretched full
length, and walked toward the wagon.

"What say potner?"

"Look," the Dean said. "You can't enroll those porcupines. It's out of the question."

"That so?"

"It's out of the question," the Dean repeated. "We've
had a lot of trouble around here. The cops won't even
speak to me. We can't *take* any more trouble." The Dean
glanced at the herd. "That's a mighty handsome herd you
have there."

"Kind of you," Griswold said. "That's a mighty handsome mule *you* got."

They both gazed at the Dean's terrible-looking mule.

Griswold wiped his neck with a red bandanna. "You
don't want no porky-pines over to your place, is that it?"

"That's it."

"Well we don't *go* where we ain't wanted," the wrangler
said. "No call to throw down on us with that . . . *machine*
there."

The Dean looked embarrassed.

"You don't know Mr. Ed Sullivan, do you?" Griswold
asked. "He lives around here somewheres, don't he?"

"I haven't had the pleasure," the Dean said. He thought for a moment. "I know a booker in Vegas, though. He was one of our people. He was a grad student in comparative religion."

"Maybe we can do a deal," the wrangler said. "Whichaway is New York City?"

"Well?" the Dean's wife asked. "What were their demands?"

"I'll tell you in a minute," the Dean said. "My mule is double-parked."

The herd turned onto the Cross-Bronx Expressway. People looking out of their cars saw thousands and thousands of porcupines. The porcupines looked like badly engineered vacuum-cleaner attachments.

Vegas, the wrangler was thinking. Ten weeks at Caesar's Palace at a sock 15 Gs a week. "The Ballad of the Last Drive." Leroy Griswold singing his smash single, "The Ballad of the Last Drive."

"Git along theah li'l porcupines."

The citizens in their cars looked at the porcupines, thinking: What is wonderful? Are these porcupines wonderful? Are they significant? Are they what I need?

ROBERT KENNEDY
SAVED FROM DROWNING

DONALD BARTHELME

K. at His Desk

He is neither abrupt with nor excessively kind to associates.
Or he is both abrupt and kind.

The telephone is, for him, a whip, a lash, but also a con-
duit for soothing words, a sink into which he can hurl gallons of syrup if it comes to that.

He reads quickly, scratching brief comments ("Yes,"
"No") in corners of the paper. He slouches in the leather
chair, looking about him with a slightly irritated air for
new visitors, new difficulties. He spends his time sending
and receiving messengers.

"I spend my time sending and receiving messengers," he
says. "Some of these messages are important. Others are
not."

Described by Secretaries

A: "Quite frankly I think he forgets a lot of things. But
the things he forgets are those which are inessential. I even
think he might forget deliberately, to leave his mind free.
He has the ability to get rid of unimportant details. And he
does."

B: "Once when I was sick, I hadn't heard from him, and
I thought he had forgotten me. You know usually your
boss will send flowers or something like that. I was in the
hospital, and I was mighty blue. I was in a room with another girl, and *her* boss hadn't sent her anything either.
Then suddenly the door opened and there he was with the

biggest bunch of yellow tulips I'd ever seen in my life. And the other girl's boss was with him, and he had tulips too. They were standing there with all those tulips, smiling."

Behind the Bar

At a crowded party, he wanders behind the bar to make himself a Scotch and water. His hand is on the bottle of Scotch, his glass is waiting. The bartender, a small man in a beige uniform with gilt buttons, politely asks K. to return to the other side, the guests' side, of the bar. "You let one behind here, they all be behind here," the bartender says.

K. Reading the Newspaper

His reactions are impossible to catalogue. Often he will find a note that amuses him endlessly, some anecdote involving, say, a fireman who has propelled his apparatus at record-breaking speed to the wrong address. These small stories are clipped, carried about in a pocket, to be produced at appropriate moments for the pleasure of friends. Other manifestations please him less. An account of an earthquake in Chile, with its thousands of dead and homeless, may depress him for weeks. He memorizes the terrible statistics, quoting them everywhere and saying, with a grave look: "We must do something." Important actions often follow, sometimes within a matter of hours. (On the other hand, these two kinds of responses may be, on a given day, inexplicably reversed.)

The more trivial aspects of the daily itemization are skipped. While reading, he maintains a rapid drumming of his fingertips on the desktop. He receives twelve newspapers, but of these, only four are regarded as serious.

Attitude Toward His Work

"Sometimes I can't seem to do anything. The work is there, piled up, it seems to me an insurmountable obstacle, really out of reach. I sit and look at it, wondering where to begin, how to take hold of it. Perhaps I pick up a piece of paper, try to read it but my mind is elsewhere, I am thinking of something else, I can't seem to get the gist of it, it seems meaningless, devoid of interest, not having to do with human affairs, drained of life. Then, in an hour, or even a moment, everything changes suddenly: I realize I only have to *do* it, hurl myself into the midst of it, proceed mechanically, the first thing and then the second thing, that it is simply a matter of moving from one step to the next, plowing through it. I become interested, I become excited, I work very fast, things fall into place, I am exhilarated, amazed that these things could ever have seemed dead to me."

Sleeping on the Stones of Unknown Towns (Rimbaud)

K. is walking with that familiar slight dip of the shoulders, through the streets of a small city in France or Germany. The shop signs are in a language which alters when inspected closely, MOBEL becoming MEUBLES for example, and the citizens mutter to themselves with dark virtuosity a mixture of languages. K. is very interested, looks closely at everything, at the shops, the goods displayed, the clothing of the people, the tempo of street life, the citizens themselves, wondering about them. What are their water needs?

"In the West, wisdom is mostly gained at lunch. At lunch, people tell you things."

The nervous eyes of the waiters.

The tall bald cook, white apron, white T-shirt, grinning through an opening in the wall.

"Why is that cook looking at me?"

Urban Transportation

"The transportation problems of our cities and their rapidly expanding suburbs are the most urgent and neglected transportation problems confronting the country. In these heavily populated and industrialized areas, people are dependent on a system of transportation that is at once complex and inadequate. Obsolete facilities and growing demands have created seemingly insoluble difficulties and present methods of dealing with these difficulties offer little prospect of relief."

K. Penetrated with Sadness

He hears something playing on someone else's radio, in another part of the building.

The music is wretchedly sad; now he can (barely) hear it, now it fades into the wall.

He turns on his own radio. There it is, on his own radio, the same music. The sound fills the room.

Karsh of Ottawa

"We sent a man to Karsh of Ottawa and told him that we admired his work very much. Especially, I don't know, the Churchill thing and, you know, the Hemingway thing, and all that. And we told him we wanted to set up a sitting for K. sometime in June, if that would be convenient for him, and he said yes, that was okay, June was okay, and where did we want to have it shot, there or in New York or where. Well, that was a problem because we didn't know exactly what K.'s schedule would be for June, it was up in the air, so we tentatively said New York around the fifteenth. And he said, that was okay, he could do that. And he wanted to know how much time he could have, and we said, well, how much time do you need? And he said he didn't know, it varied from sitter to sitter. He said some people were very restless and that made it difficult to get just the right shot. He said there was one shot in each sitting that was, you know, the key shot, the right one. He said he'd have to see, when the time came."

Dress

He is neatly dressed in a manner that does not call attention to itself. The suits are soberly cut and in dark colors. He must at all times present an aspect of freshness difficult to sustain because of frequent movements from place to place under conditions which are not always the most favorable. Thus he changes clothes frequently, especially shirts. In the course of a day he changes his shirt many times. There are always extra shirts about, in boxes.

"Which of you has the shirts?"

A Friend Comments: K.'s Aloneness

"The thing you have to realize about K. is that essentially he's absolutely alone in the world. There's this terrible loneliness which prevents people from getting too close to him. Maybe it comes from something in his childhood, I don't know. But he's very hard to get to know, and a lot of people who think they know him rather well don't really know him at all. He says something or does something that surprises you, and you realize that all along you really didn't know him at all.

"He has surprising facets. I remember once we were out in a small boat. K. of course was the captain. Some rough weather came up and we began to head back in. I began worrying about picking up a landing and I said to him that I didn't think the anchor would hold, with the wind and all. He just looked at me. Then he said: 'Of course it will hold. That's what it's for.' "

K. on Crowds

"There are exhausted crowds and vivacious crowds.

"Sometimes, standing there, I can sense whether a particular crowd is one thing or the other. Sometimes the mood of the crowd is disguised, sometimes you only find out after a quarter of an hour what sort of crowd a particular crowd is.

"And you can't speak to them in the same way. The variations have to be taken into account. You have to say something to them that is meaningful to them *in that mood.*"

Gallery-going

K. enters a large gallery on Fifty-seventh Street, in the Fuller Building. His entourage includes several ladies and gentlemen. Works by a geometricist are on show. K. looks at the immense, rather theoretical paintings.

"Well, at least we know he has a ruler."

The group dissolves in laughter. People repeat the remark to one another, laughing.

The artist, who has been standing behind a dealer, regards K. with hatred.

K. Puzzled by His Children

The children are crying. There are several children, one about four, a boy, then another boy, slightly older, and a little girl, very beautiful, wearing blue jeans, crying. There are various objects on the grass, an electric train, a picture book, a red ball, a plastic bucket, a plastic shovel.

K. frowns at the children whose distress issues from no source immediately available to the eye, which seems indeed uncaused, vacant, a general anguish. K. turns to the mother of these children who is standing nearby wearing hip-huggers which appear to be made of linked marshmallows studded with diamonds but then I am a notoriously poor observer.

"Play with them," he says.

This mother of ten quietly suggests that K. himself "play with them."

K. picks up the picture book and begins to read to the children. But the book has a German text. It has been left behind, perhaps, by some foreign visitor. Nevertheless K. perseveres.

"A ist der Affe, er isst mit der Pfote." ("A is the Ape, he eats with his Paw.")

The crying of the children continues.

A Dream

Orange trees.

Overhead, a steady stream of strange aircraft which resemble kitchen implements, bread boards, cookie sheets, colanders.

The shiny aluminum instruments are on their way to complete the bombing of Sidi-Madani.

A farm in the hills.

Matters (from an Administrative Assistant)

"A lot of matters that had been pending came to a head right about that time, moved to the front burner, things we absolutely had to take care of. And we couldn't find K. Nobody knew where he was. We had looked everywhere. He had just withdrawn, made himself unavailable. There was this one matter that was probably more pressing than all the rest put together. Really crucial. We were all standing around wondering what to do. We were getting pretty nervous because this thing was really. . . . Then K. walked in and disposed of it with a quick phone call. A quick phone call!"

Childhood of K. as Recalled by a Former Teacher

"He was a very alert boy, very bright, good at his studies, very thorough, very conscientious. But that's not unusual; that describes a good number of the boys who pass through here. It's not unusual, that is, to find these qualities which are after all the qualities that we look for and encourage in them. What *was* unusual about K. was his compassion, something very rare for a boy of that age—even if they have it, they're usually very careful not to display it for fear of seeming soft, girlish. I remember though, that in K. this particular attribute was very marked. I would almost say that it was his strongest characteristic."

Speaking to No One but Waiters, He—

"The dandelion salad with bacon, I think."
"The *rysstafel.*"
"The poached duck."
"The black bean puree."
"The cod fritters."

K. Explains a Technique

"It's an expedient in terms of how not to destroy a situation which has been a long time gestating, or, again, how *to* break it up if it appears that the situation has changed, during the gestation period, into one whose implications are not quite what they were at the beginning. What I mean is that in this business things are constantly altering (usually for the worse) and usually you want to give the impression that you're not watching this particular situation particularly closely, that you're paying no special attention to it, until you're ready to make your move. That is, it's best to be sudden, if you can manage it. Of course you can't do that all the time. Sometimes you're just completely wiped out, cleaned out, totaled, and then the only thing to do is shrug and forget about it."

K. on His Own Role

"Sometimes it seems to me that it doesn't matter what I do, that it is enough to exist, to sit somewhere, in a garden for example, watching whatever is to be seen there, the small events. At other times, I'm aware that other people, possibly a great number of other people, could be affected by what I do or fail to do, that I have a responsibility, as we all have, to make the best possible use of whatever talents I've been given, for the common good. It is not enough to sit in that garden, however restful or pleasurable it might be. The world is full of unsolved problems, situations that demand careful, reasoned and intelligent action. In Latin America, for example."

As Entrepreneur

The original cost estimates for burying the North Sea pipeline have been exceeded by a considerable margin. Everyone wonders what he will say about this contretemps which does not fail to have its dangers for those responsible for the costly miscalculations, which are viewed in many minds as inexcusable.

He says only: "Exceptionally difficult rock conditions."

With Young People

K., walking the streets of unknown towns, finds himself among young people. Young people line these streets, narrow and curving, which are theirs, dedicated to them. They are everywhere, resting on the embankments, their guitars, small radios, long hair. They sit on the sidewalks, back to back, heads turned to stare. They stand implacably on street corners, in doorways, or lean on their elbows in windows, or squat in small groups at that place where the sidewalk meets the walls of buildings. The streets are filled with these young people who say nothing, reveal only a limited interest, refuse to declare themselves. Street after street contains them, a great number, more displayed as one turns a corner, rank upon rank stretching into the distance, drawn from the arcades, the plazas, staring.

He Discusses the French Writer, Poulet

"For Poulet, it is not enough to speak of *seizing the moment*. It is rather a question of, and I quote, 'recognizing in the instant which lives and dies, which surges out of nothingness and which ends in dream, an intensity and depth of significance which ordinarily attaches only to the whole of existence.'

"What Poulet is describing is neither an ethic nor a prescription but rather what he has discovered in the work of Marivaux. Poulet has taken up the Marivaudian canon and squeezed it with both hands to discover the essence of what may be called the Marivaudian being, what Poulet in fact calls the Marivaudian being.

"The Marivaudian being is, according to Poulet, a pastless futureless man, born anew at every instant. The instants are points which organize themselves into a line, but what is important is the instant, not the line. The Marivaudian being has in a sense no history. Nothing follows from what has gone before. He is constantly surprised. He cannot predict his own reaction to events. He is constantly being *overtaken* by events. A condition of breathlessness and dazzlement surrounds him. In consequence he exists in a certain freshness which seems, if I may say so, very desirable. This freshness Poulet, quoting Marivaux, describes very well."

K. Saved from Drowning

K. in the water. His flat black hat, his black cape, his sword are on the shore. He retains his mask. His hands beat the surface of the water which tears and rips about him. The white foam, the green depths. I throw a line, the coils leaping out over the surface of the water. He has missed it. No, it appears that he has it. His right hand (sword arm) grasps the line that I have thrown him. I am on the bank, the rope wound round my waist, braced against a rock. K. now has both hands on the line. I pull him out of the water. He stands now on the bank, gasping.

"Thank you."

VIEWS OF MY FATHER WEEPING

DONALD BARTHELME

An aristocrat was riding down the street in his carriage. He ran over my father.

•

After the ceremony I walked back to the city. I was trying to think of the reason my father had died. Then I remembered: he was run over by a carriage.

•

I telephoned my mother and told her of my father's death. She said she supposed it was the best thing. I too supposed it was the best thing. His enjoyment was diminishing. I wondered if I should attempt to trace the aristocrat whose carriage had run him down. There were said to have been one or two witnesses.

•

Yes it is possible that it is not my father who sits there in the center of the bed weeping. It may be someone else, the mailman, the man who delivers the groceries, an insurance salesman or tax collector, who knows. However, I must say, it resembles my father. The resemblance is very strong. He is not smiling through his tears but frowning through them. I remember once we were out on the ranch shooting peccadillos (result of a meeting, on the plains of the West, of the collared peccary and the nine-banded armadillo). My father shot and missed. He wept. This weeping resembles that weeping.

•

"Did you see it?" "Yes but only part of it. Part of the

time I had my back turned." The witness was a little girl, eleven or twelve. She lived in a very poor quarter and I could not imagine that, were she to testify, anyone would credit her. "Can you recall what the man in the carriage looked like?" "Like an aristocrat," she said.

•

The first witness declares that the man in the carriage looked "like an aristocrat." But that might be simply the carriage itself. Any man sitting in a handsome carriage with a driver on the box and perhaps one or two footmen up behind tends to look like an aristocrat. I wrote down her name and asked her to call me if she remembered anything else. I gave her some candy.

•

I stood in the square where my father was killed and asked people passing by if they had seen, or knew of anyone who had seen, the incident. At the same time I felt the effort was wasted. Even if I found the man whose carriage had done the job, what would I say to him? "You killed my father." "Yes," the aristocrat would say, "but he ran right in under the legs of the horses. My man tried to stop but it happened too quickly. There was nothing anyone could do." Then perhaps he would offer me a purse full of money.

•

The man sitting in the center of the bed looks very much like my father. He is weeping, tears coursing down his cheeks. One can see that he is upset about something. Looking at him I see that something is wrong. He is spewing like a fire hydrant with its lock knocked off. His yammer darts in and out of all the rooms. In a melting mood I lay my paw on my breast and say, "Father." This does not distract him from his plaint, which rises to a shriek, sinks to a pule. His range is great, his ambition commensurate. I say again, "Father," but he ignores me. I don't know whether it is time to flee or will not be time to flee until later. He may suddenly stop, assume a sternness. I have kept the door open and nothing between me and the door, and moreover the screen unlatched, and on top of that the motor running, in the Mustang. But perhaps it is not my father weeping there, but another father: Tom's father, Phil's father, Pat's father, Pete's father, Paul's father. Apply some sort of test, voiceprint reading or

My father throws his ball of knitting up in the air. The orange wool hangs there.

My father regards the tray of pink cupcakes. Then he jams his thumb into each cupcake, into the top. Cupcake by cupcake. A thick smile spreads over the face of each cupcake.

Then a man volunteered that he had heard two other men talking about the accident in a shop. "What shop?" The man pointed it out to me, a draper's shop on the south side of the square. I entered the shop and made inquiries. "It was your father, eh? He was bloody clumsy if you ask me." This was the clerk behind the counter. But another man standing nearby, well-dressed, even elegant, a gold watchchain stretched across his vest, disagreed. "It was the fault of the driver," the second man said. "He could have stopped them if he had cared to." "Nonsense," the clerk said, "not a chance in the world. If your father hadn't been drunk—" "He wasn't drunk," I said. "I arrived on the scene soon after it happened and I smelled no liquor."

This was true. I had been notified by the police, who came to my room and fetched me to the scene of the accident. I bent over my father, whose chest was crushed, and laid my cheek against his. His cheek was cold. I smelled no liquor but blood from his mouth stained the collar of my coat. I asked the people standing there how it had happened. "Run down by a carriage," they said. "Did the driver stop?" "No, he whipped up the horses and went off down the street and then around the corner at the end of the street, toward King's New Square." "You have no idea as to whose carriage . . ." "None." Then I made the arrangements for the burial. It was not until several days later that the idea of seeking the aristocrat in the carriage came to me.

I had had in my life nothing to do with aristocrats, did

not even know in what part of the city they lived, in their
great houses. So that even if I located someone who had
seen the incident and could identify the particular aristocrat involved, I would be faced with the further task of
finding his house and gaining admittance (and even then,
might he not be abroad?). "No, the driver was at fault,"
the man with the gold watchchain said. "Even if your father was drunk—and I can't say about that, one way or another, I have no opinion—even if your father was drunk,
the driver could have done more to avoid the accident. He
was dragged, you know. The carriage dragged him about
forty feet." I had noticed that my father's clothes were torn
in a peculiar way. "There was one thing," the clerk said,
"don't tell anyone I told you, but I can give you one hint.
The driver's livery was blue and green."

•

It is someone's father. That much is clear. He is fatherly.
The gray in the head. The puff in the face. The droop in
the shoulders. The flab on the gut. Tears falling. Tears falling. Tears falling. Tears falling. More tears. It seems that
he intends to go further along this salty path. The facts suggest that this is his program, weeping. He has something in
mind, more weeping. O lud lud! But why remain? Why
watch it? Why tarry? Why not fly? Why subject myself? I
could be somewhere else, reading a book, watching the
telly, stuffing a big ship into a little bottle, dancing the Pig.
I could be out in the streets feeling up eleven-year-old girls
in their soldier drag, there are thousands, as alike as pen-
nies, and I could be— Why doesn't he stand up, arrange
his clothes, dry his face? He's trying to embarrass us. He
wants attention. He's trying to make himself interesting. He
wants his brow wrapped in cold cloths perhaps, his hands
held perhaps, his back rubbed, his neck kneaded, his wrists
patted, his elbows anointed with rare oils, his toenails
painted with tiny scenes representing God blessing America. I won't do it.

•

My father has a red bandana tied around his face cover-
ing the nose and mouth. He extends his right hand in which
there is a water pistol. "Stick 'em up!" he says.

•

But blue and green livery is not unusual. A blue coat

with green trousers, or the reverse, if I saw a coachman wearing such livery I would take no particular notice. It is true that most livery tends to be blue and buff, or blue and white, or blue and a sort of darker blue (for the trousers). But in these days one often finds a servant aping the more exquisite color combinations affected by his masters. I have even seen them in red trousers although red trousers used to be reserved, by unspoken agreement, for the aristocracy. So that the colors of the driver's livery were not of much consequence. Still it was something. I could now go about in the city, especially in stables and gin shops and such places, keeping a weather eye for the livery of the lackeys who gathered there. It was possible that more than one of the gentry dressed his servants in this blue and green livery, but on the other hand, unlikely that there were as many as half a dozen. So that in fact the draper's clerk had offered a very good clue indeed, had one the energy to pursue it vigorously.

•

There is my father, standing alongside an extremely large dog, a dog ten hands high at the very least. My father leaps on the dog's back, straddles him. My father kicks the large dog in the ribs with his heels. "Giddyap!"

•

My father has written on the white wall with his crayons.

•

I was stretched out on my bed when someone knocked at the door. It was the small girl to whom I had given candy when I had first begun searching for the aristocrat. She looked frightened, yet resolute; I could see that she had some information for me. "I know who it was," she said. "I know his name." "What is it?" "First you must give me five crowns." Luckily I had five crowns in my pocket; had she come later in the day, after I had eaten, I would have had nothing to give her. I handed over the money and she said, "Lars Bang." I looked at her in some surprise. "What sort of name is that for an aristocrat?" "His coachman," she said. "The coachman's name is Lars Bang." Then she fled.

•

When I heard this name, which in its sound and appearance is rude, vulgar, not unlike my own name, I was seized with repugnance, thought of dropping the whole business, although the piece of information she had brought had just cost me five crowns. When I was seeking him and he was yet nameless, the aristocrat and, by extension, his servants, seemed vulnerable: they had, after all, been responsible for a crime, or a sort of crime. My father was dead and they were responsible, or at least involved; and even though they were of the aristocracy or servants of the aristocracy, still common justice might be sought for; they might be required to make reparation, in some measure, for what they had done. Now, having the name of the coachman, and being thus much closer to his master than when I merely had the clue of the blue and green livery, I became afraid. For, after all, the unknown aristocrat must be a very powerful man, not at all accustomed to being called to account by people like me; indeed, his contempt for people like me was so great that, when one of us was so foolish as to stray into the path of his carriage, the aristocrat dashed him down, or permitted his coachman to do so, dragged him along the cobblestones for as much as forty feet, and then went gaily on his way, toward King's New Square. Such a man, I reasoned, was not very likely to take kindly to what I had to say to him. Very possibly there would be no purse of money at all, not a crown, not an öre; but rather he would, with an abrupt, impatient nod of his head, set his servants upon me. I would be beaten, perhaps killed. Like my father.

●

But if it is not my father sitting there in the bed weeping, why am I standing before the bed, in an attitude of supplication? Why do I desire with all my heart that this man, my father, cease what he is doing, which is so painful to me? Is it only that my position is a familiar one? That I remember, before, desiring with all my heart that this man, my father, cease what he is doing?

●

Why . . . there's my father! . . . sitting in the bed there! . . . and he's *weeping!* . . . as though his heart would burst! . . . Father . . . how is this! . . . who has wounded you? . . . name the man! . . . why I'll . . . I'll . . . here, Father, take this handkerchief! . . . and this handkerchief! . . . and this handkerchief! . . . I'll run for a towel . . . for a doctor . . . for a priest . . . for a good fairy . . . is there . . . can you . . . can

I . . . a cup of hot tea? . . . bowl of steaming soup? . . . shot of Calvados? . . . a joint? . . . a red jacket? . . . a blue jacket? . . . Father, please! . . . look at me, Father . . . who has insulted you? . . . are you, then, compromised? . . . ruined? . . . a slander is going around? . . . an obloquy? . . . a traducement? . . . 'sdeath!' . . . I won't permit it! . . . I won't abide it! . . . I'll . . . move every mountain . . . climb . . . every river . . . etc.

●

My father is playing with the salt and pepper shakers, and with the sugar bowl. He lifts the cover off the sugar bowl, and shakes pepper into it.

●

Or: My father thrusts his hand through a window of the doll's house. His hand knocks over the doll's chair, knocks over the doll's chest of drawers, knocks over the doll's bed.

●

The next day, just before noon, Lars Bang himself came to my room. "I understand that you are looking for me." He was very much of a surprise. I had expected a rather burly, heavy man, of a piece with all of the other coachmen one saw sitting up on the box; Lars Bang was, instead, slight, almost feminine-looking, more the type of the secretary or valet than the coachman. He was not threatening at all, contrary to my fears; he was almost helpful, albeit with the slightest hint of malice in his helpfulness. I stammeringly explained that my father, a good man although subject to certain weaknesses, including a love of the bottle, had been run down by an aristocrat's coach, in the vicinity of King's New Square, not very many days previously; that I had information that the coach had dragged him some forty feet; and that I was eager to establish certain facts about the case. "Well then," Lars Bang said, with a helpful nod, "I'm your man, for it was my coach that was involved. A sorry business! Unfortunately I haven't the time right now to give you the full particulars, but if you will call round at the address written on this card, at six o'clock in the evening, I believe I will be able to satisfy you." So saying, he took himself off, leaving me with the card in my hand.

●

I spoke to Miranda, quickly sketching what had happened. She asked to see the white card; I gave it to her, for the address meant nothing to me. "Oh my," she said. "17 rue du Bac, that's over by the Vixen Gate—a very special quarter. Only aristocrats of the highest rank live there, and common people are not even allowed into the great park that lies between the houses and the river. If you are found wandering about there at night, you are apt to earn yourself a very severe beating." "But I have an appointment," I said. "An appointment with a coachman!" Miranda cried, "how foolish you are! Do you think the men of the watch will believe that, or even if they believe it (you have an honest enough face) will allow you to prowl that rich quarter, where so many thieves would dearly love to be set free for an hour or so, after dark? Go to!" Then she advised me that I must carry something with me, a pannier of beef or some dozen bottles of wine, so that if apprehended by the watch, I could say that I was delivering to such and such a house, and thus be judged an honest man on an honest errand, and escape a beating. I saw that she was right; and going out, I purchased at the wine merchant's a dozen bottles of a rather good claret (for it would never do to be delivering wine no aristocrat would drink); this cost me thirty crowns, which I had borrowed from Miranda. The bottles we wrapped round with straw, to prevent them banging into one another, and the whole we arranged in a sack, which I could carry on my back. I remember thinking, how they rhymed, fitted together, *sack* and *back*. In this fashion I set off across the city.

•

There is my father's bed. In it, my father. Attitude of dejection. Graceful as a mule deer once, the same large ears. For a nanosecond, there is a nanosmile. Is he having me on? I remember once we went out on the ups and downs of the West (out past Vulture's Roost) to shoot. First we shot up a lot of old beer cans, then we shot up a lot of old whiskey bottles, better because they shattered. Then we shot up some mesquite bushes and some parts of a Ford pickup sombody'd left lying around. But no animals came to our party (it was noisy, I admit it). A long list of animals failed to arrive, no deer, quail, rabbit, seals, sea lions, condylarths. It was pretty boring shooting up mesquite bushes, so we hunkered down behind some rocks, Father and I, he

hunkered down behind his rocks and I hunkered down behind my rocks, and we commenced to shooting at each
other. That was interesting.

•

My father is looking at himself in a mirror. He is wearing a large hat (straw) on which there are a number of
blue and yellow plastic jonquils. He says: "How do I
look?"

•

Lars Bang took the sack from me and without asking
permission reached inside, withdrawing one of the straw-
wrapped bottles of claret. "Here's something!" he exclaimed, reading the label. "A gift for the master, I don't
doubt!" Then, regarding me steadily all the while, he took
up an awl and lifted the cork. There were two other men
seated at the pantry table, dressed in the blue-and-green livery, and with them a dark-haired, beautiful girl, quite
young, who said nothing and looked at no one. Lars Bang
obtained glasses, kicked a chair in my direction, and
poured drinks all round. "To your health!" he said (with
what I thought an ironical overtone) and we drank. "This
young man," Lars Bang said, nodding at me, "is here seeking our advice on a very complicated business. A murder, I
believe you said?" "I said nothing of the kind. I seek information about an accident." The claret was soon exhausted.
Without looking at me, Lars Bang opened a second bottle
and set it in the center of the table. The beautiful dark-
haired girl ignored me along with all the others. For my
part, I felt I had conducted myself rather well thus far. I
had not protested when the wine was made free of (after
all, they would be accustomed to levying a sort of tax on
anything entering through the back door). But also I had
not permitted his word "murder" to be used, but instead
specified the use of the word "accident." Therefore I was,
in general, comfortable sitting at the table drinking the
wine, for which I have no better head than had my father.
"Well," said Lars Bang, at length, "I will relate the circumstances of the accident, and you may judge for yourself as
to whether myself and my master, the Lensgreve Aklefeldt,
were at fault." I absorbed this news with a slight shock. A
count! I had selected a man of very high rank indeed to put
my question to. In a moment my accumulated self-confi-

dence drained away. A count! Mother of God, have mercy
on me.

•

There is my father, peering through an open door into
an empty house. He is accompanied by a dog (small dog;
not the same dog as before). He looks into the empty
room. He says: "Anybody home?"

•

There is my father, sitting in his bed, weeping.

•

"It was a Friday," Lars Bang began, as if he were telling
a tavern story. "The hour was close upon noon and my
master directed me to drive him to King's New Square,
where he had some business. We were proceeding there at
a modest easy pace, for he was in no great hurry. Judge of
my astonishment when, passing through the drapers'
quarter, we found ourselves set upon by an elderly man,
thoroughly drunk, who flung himself at my lead pair and
began cutting at their legs with a switch, in the most vicious
manner imaginable. The poor dumb brutes reared, of
course, in fright and fear, for," Lars Bang said piously,
"they are accustomed to the best of care, and never a blow
do they receive from me, or from the other coachman, Rik,
for the count is especially severe upon this point, that his
animals be well-treated. The horses, then, were rearing and
plunging; it was all I could do to hold them; I shouted at
the man, who fell back for an instant. The count stuck his
head out of the window, to inquire as to the nature of the
trouble; and I told him that a drunken man had attacked
our horses. Your father, in his blindness, being not content
with the mischief he had already worked, ran back in
again, close to the animals, and began madly cutting at
their legs with his stick. At this renewed attack the horses,
frightened out of their wits, jerked the reins from my
hands, and ran headlong over your father who fell beneath
their hooves. The heavy wheels of the carriage passed over
him (I felt two quite distinct thumps), his body caught
upon a projection under the boot, and he was dragged
some forty feet, over the cobblestones. I was attempting,
with all my might, merely to hang on to the box, for, having taken the bit between their teeth, the horses were in no

mood to tarry; nor could any human agency have stopped them. We flew down the street . . ."

My father is attending a class in good behavior.

"Do the men rise when friends greet us while we are sitting in a booth?"

"The men do not rise when they are seated in a booth," he answers, "although they may half-rise and make apologies for not fully rising."

". . . the horses turning into the way that leads to King's New Square; and it was not until we reached that place that they stopped and allowed me to quiet them. I wanted to go back and see what had become of the madman, your father, who had attacked us; but my master, vastly angry and shaken up, forbade it. I have never seen him in so fearful a temper as that day; if your father had survived, and my master got his hands on him, it would have gone ill with your father, that's a certainty. And so, you are now in possession of all the facts. I trust you are satisfied, and will drink another bottle of this quite fair claret you have brought us, and be on your way." Before I had time to frame a reply, the dark-haired girl spoke. "Bang is an absolute bloody liar," she said.

Etc.

MYTHOLOGY: WONDER WOMAN

STEVE KATZ

Wonder Woman was a dike, but she was nice. If she hadn't been a dike she might have been nice, but she wouldn't have been Wonder Woman, and vice-versa. Of all the interesting stories about Wonder Woman, the most delightful is the tale of how she ended the war in Vietnam. When she started to end it it wasn't over but when she was through it was finished. Except nobody believed a dike could end the war. They went on killing like the bunch of rowdies they believed in. Finally everybody was crowded into the bloodshed till there was no one left on earth except Wonder Woman and one slow-moving little squirt with asthma. She met him on the road, where you meet everyone these days in case of emergency. He was trying to push his car uphill at a total stalemate when Wonder Woman surprised him.

"What's the big idea, buster," she intoned.

The car slid backwards into a warehouse of surplus feathers. "I'm not very anxious," he said.

"You're the last man here on earth so you should be bawling your ass off."

"You too should be weeping, for you are the last woman on earth as far as is imaginable." He leaned on the shoulder of the freeway.

"If you want to have the straight goop, I'm Wonder Woman, the dike." She blew on her wristlets. "But why do you insist on pushing around that old jalopy, when here for the asking are all these Cadillacs and Chaparrals?"

"My analyst is dead," he roared.

"Just hop in and drive one of them away, and don't bother me."

"There's no place I want to go. It's death, death, everywhere death. All the people are dead as doornails. I never thought I'd live to see the day."

"At least the traffic is light. Haw Haw." Wonder Woman fixed her comb and prepared to leave.

"I guess I could drive East through Canada. I always wanted to drive East through Canada, and why not? It's a beautiful country and a friendly place. Thank you for the wonderful idea, Wonder Woman." He reached a long arm out and dragged himself over to a solid blue Mercedes 300 and tipped out the ex-driver. The motor gurgled when he hit the switch.

Wonder Woman split for elsewhere. She visited the hangouts of her old consorts: Cynthia the Sphincter was dead, as were Julie and Fatty and Leslie the Mars Bar. She went to Pittsburgh. She headed for Santa Cruz. She got to Albany. She hit Moose Jaw. She stopped in Philly. She took in New York City. She crossed to Budapest. Copenhagen was empty. Damascus was empty. Kuala Lumpur was through. The little wheezer had been right. She journeyed to New Delhi. She hit Kyoto in the spring. She left for Singapore. She hustled to Djakarta. They all were dead. Everyone was dead. She decided to take in a movie. Best of all was a revival of the old blue whisker comedies, which she took in with a cup of buttered popcorn that tasted disturbingly fresh. Without her cohorts she fell into a fit of depression. Then she saw an airplane overhead and shot it down in her excitement. Luckily there was nobody aboard except for one newspaper. The flyer read TALK BUYS MUD FLACK and the headlines, REVERSE PUMP MURTY. The mention of Pump Murty kept Wonder Woman's chin up. "So," she thought. "Even at the end the old guy could wrap a rice patch."* Then she fell into a fit of depression. All around her heavy machinery was hanging out as if it had a contract to work. "For naught. For naught. For naught," she sighed and then hopped onto a Caterpillar D8 and started pushing everything aside until she uncovered the remains of a familiar solid blue Mercedes. She rolled it over

---

*special dike talk or professional dyke jargon.

and over down a side street. Poor little guy. "Fuck ambition," she screamed, standing up and waving her arms
around. Suddenly the bulldozer veered out of control into a
huge man-made wall which toppled on top of her knocking
her for a loop, and squooshing her down in a pit of depression. When she came to she wasn't herself but was being
cared for by a slowpoke with asthma. "There now," he
said. "You had quite a seizure."

"Where am I?" Wonder Woman queried. "And what
kind of special clothing is this?"

"You are Wonder Woman, the last dike on earth," said
the slow one. "Admired and esteemed by the whole world,
which is me."

"Chubby chance of that, you handsome stud, you fistful
of nuts," and she threw her weakened arms around his
neck. He mopped her lecherous brow with droplets from a
nearby rivulet. She began to sigh and swivel. He worked on
her clothes with a hacksaw till they fell apart like a shutter.
He was staring at the last cunt on earth. He untied from his
leg the last cock on earth and when she saw it she sizzled.
"Do something filthy dirty right away."

"But you're Wonder Woman, the dike," he slobbered,
holding his cock at arm's length. Just then she passed a
sonorous and intoxicating flatus that drugged them into an
ecstatic embrace, pumping and sucking like it was the end
of the world. He wondered if she was still Wonder Woman
if she wasn't a dike, but was so nice. She cooked his dinner
and mended his sock and then they started to have babies,
and the babies they had were made of gold.

EXCEPT FOR THE SICKNESS I'M QUITE HEALTHY NOW. YOU CAN BELIEVE THAT

THOMAS GLYNN

This morning a man came to my door and asked if I had taken a bath. I told him I was an artist and he left. I called Sinkowiz and asked him what that meant but he didn't know. I like to know what things mean, their deeper significance. So then I asked my slum landlord, Solomon Golub, but he only lied and said it was the man from the water department. Someday I'll tell you about Golub, king of the slum landlords, but not now. Not with the pain I've got. Funny how a room can turn around. I mean you can stand in one place, with your feet on solid floor, and the room can spin around like a top. Ever watch colors then? Red, green, violet, they all turn into blue. The pain helps and then sometimes when I'm not on my feet the paints will change colors and tubes and those goddam rats are partial to navy blue, they eat right through the tubes, metal, plastic and all and then gorge on the paint.
Stark came over last night and I showed him my new picture. He said it was all right except for the red. He says that just to gall me, Stark does. I say what red and he says there and points to a place which is blue and I say that's blue and he says red. Stark! What does he know. He can't even walk on the ground. If you watch him closely you see that he walks on air. Two inches of air. How can anybody who walks on air know anything about painting? Still, I ask him, sucker that I am. Lately I am asking more people like that. Even Golub, who likes art if it can cover up a bad hole in the wall. Next time you see Stark, look at his pants.

They come down over his heels, brushing the ground. How can anyone tell he's walking on air if his pants are too long and touch the ground? He tries to hide it. He's embarrassed about walking on air.

Stark sews. He has a showing at the Stampfli of old sheets. They're all stained, his sheets. Also, a showing of laundry tickets at the Almalfi.

Did you ever see Stark and Golub argue? Stark is five feet four and Golub is five feet six. But with Stark two inches off the ground he comes up level to Golub. They stand and shout, mouth to mouth, and Golub puts his hands on Stark's shoulders and pushes him the remaining two inches down to the ground, but unless he keeps his hands there Stark just pops up again, crew cut to crew cut with Golub. Being artists, they both argue economics. Stark lives below me, a tenant of madman Golub. Golub is trying to put hot water in our lofts so he can raise the rent. Each day the plumbers come, and each night Stark and I are busy with pipe wrenches undoing their work. Once the hot water is in and running the rent goes up. So far we are even with the plumbers, but Golub is thinking of adding more to keep ahead. That's Golub. Always thinking.

Another thing about blue. My model has varicose veins which fascinate me. Did you ever see a really good showing? I don't mean the beginnings, those immature spiderwebs with their picky little microscopic traces. I'm talking about your great over-hanging ropes, your great knotted, clotted masses of bulging misshappen inoperative veins that are congealed like wet cotton. What shades of blue! From dark to light, sea to sky, fire to ice. The picture I'm working on now, with my model bent over so that from the rear I can see her patch, is all varicose vein. Title: Varicose Veins at Sunrise. I keep her standing all day in a tub of cold water. It brings texture, adds depth to the blue tubes. She's fifty-three, afraid I'll fire her and get a younger girl. I talk about breasts that stay up and flesh that holds together and she breaks down, blubbering. But I wouldn't have a younger model. Give me the flesh that shifts, the breasts that sag!

Snow is blue, and when you walk on snow that's blue on blue, but of course Stark doesn't make any tracks when he walks so he can't know what I'm talking about. But snow is pale blue really, the color of chipped china or faded blotters. I thought of that yesterday during the heat wave. If I feel up to it, and the pain isn't so bad, I put snow in my pictures, lots of fat flakes with a footprint or two. If Jenny can shiver when I paint so much the better. She has rheumatism and shivering comes easy to her. I make it simple by keeping her in a bucket of water, her large blistered feet rubbing the sides of the rusty iron tub. Sometimes if I leave a window open in the dead of winter, which I'm liable to do, it looks like a colony of mice is running underneath her skin. Then when I see her shake I get inspired and often do six or seven competed nudes in one day. Titles: Jenny Shivering in a Bucket of Water. Jenny Under Delusions of Cold, Jenny's Veins, Jenny Without Food for Three Days (and its corollary, Jenny Fainting from Lack of Food and Falling Head First into the Iron Bucket), Blue Jenny, Jenny in Between, and my big one, Jenny Jumps. The last one is the size of my wall. I wanted to do a big picture and nailed canvas to one of the walls, propping chairs and tables and ladders against it so I could hop around on my one good leg and fill the canvas with lines. I had Jenny jumping from one of the ceiling beams in the loft. I wanted to get that look people have on their face when they go through the air. Have you seen that look? It's like modeling a face in damp seersucker shorts. The mouth has this absent-minded look about it, the eyes seem to be hurricane centers. Jenny jumped, her blubber trailing behind, adding buoyancy, floating like potato angels. Jenny is all fluff and old chocolate, and when she jumps, she expands. This is art, that expansion. I'm doing a sequel to Jenny Jumps. Jenny Lands. Setting: Old broken cement, blistered sidewalk all cracks and acne, dry bones for plants and rust-red blood scattered like pandemonium seeds. In the middle, in parts, lies Jenny, full of hope, her mouth bleeding belief and the shock of the real blended miraculously into her limbs. Great stores of curious onlookers and large cities burning in the background, crucifixions and pilgrims walking, bombs exploding and lovers opening letters. The surroundings of Jenny. It will be the greatest thing. I or anybody, has done yet. It's what I've been trying to say for years.

Golub says he'll buy it to cover a hole in the wall.

I'll take praise wherever I can find it.

Stark, who should know, says Jenny Lands can hang side by side with Giambo.

I'll tell you more about Golub as soon as the pain goes away. Golub sleeps during the day on a small canvas cot upstairs. If Stark or I feel like waking him we pound on the pipes with a monkey wrench until he stirs. With that noise he'll run out into the street thinking his building is falling down, and just to convince him we sometimes throw things out the window. Packing crates and type fonts and baby carriages with little nephews. Then he'll run to the phone booth and call the Health Department, complaining that the "Roooskeeies are coming," and he's getting the first bomb.

I don't think I told you about the pain. There are two kinds. Professional and amateur. In between is Golub. I'll talk about that later.

Half the numbers under ten are prime, so there must be a connection there somewhere. But try to tell that to Stark! I asked him about emotion in painting. I told him I thought it was a net full of feelings, some of which poked fingers and toes into the picture. All he said was that I had too much blue. Here here here and here he said, too much blue. Change this to vermilion, this to ochre, that to beige, and this to sienna. I leave him alone he kicks my paintings. I have to put ropes around him he comes into the studio. He doesn't understand blue. Paint by the stars he says. He pulls out his astrology handbook, a Carrol Richter special, mumbles some Latin names and comes up with exact dates and times when I should paint. Stark, floating two inches off the ground, says I should paint on the twenty-third of March at two-thirty in the afternoon, again on the twenty-fifth at seven, and then wait until the sixteenth of April when I can paint the whole day.

One day I showed him a new picture which he said was out of my horoscope and kicked a hole in it before I could hit him with my iron easel. I painted around the hole. But what can you do with a critic?

When Stark gets excited he rises, and if he's really enthusiastic about something he floats up to the ceiling. Jumping after him doesn't do any good, he'll just bob along the ceiling like a moth after cotton candy.

Remember that faggot farmboy in Nebraska who killed eleven people? I'm doing a series on him. Three-quarter profile set in plaster of Paris surrounded by a movie marquee, rerun of an old George Brent picture. Halloween death mask and magic lantern eyes under dime store plastic rims and larger than life proboscis. Munger leveling his gun and out pops a flag, *love*. I like things surrounding other things in my pictures, and I like people hiding, using masks and stepping out of dark alleys wearing capes and frightening drunks. But try to get *that* into a painting. And that's just the beginning. When you add up the trading stamps and the formica counters and the bedwetters and the high school Spanish teachers, where does that leave you? In Toledo with El Greco. The canvas isn't big enough. I'll have to block off the intersections and lay my linen in the streets, paint with dripping buckets from tenement roofs.

Stark is taking lessons to fly, so he can't understand. When you look down, what can you see? Only birdshit and slugs, if you happen to be a bird. I tell Stark, what do you want to fly for? He thinks it will help his art. When I try to explain about art he's bumping his head against the ceiling. So who can you talk to about art?

Much more on Golub later.

Sinkowiz is calling now. I think I'll tell him about the pain. Did you know the monarch butterfly will go thousands of miles just to get a good piece of ass?

Talking to Golub after I've taken down his pipes. I take him up to my studio and show him my paintings. I flip through canvas after canvas, put slivers in my fingers, and smile. Golub is not one of your wishy-washy art owners. He buckles his shoes every morning. Buttons on his pants. Who can beat lead pipe enlightenment like that?

When Stark floats, he fills himself up like a blowfish. Huff and puff, taking in great balloons of air, inflating his cheeks. His skin distends, his face changes from purple to red to pink. He floats above our heads, a network of veins. Golub looking up.

Golub would be a hunchback if he had the choice, but lacking the will to deform he stares popeyed. I have a thing in yellow. Title: Golub Staring. I have a hole in my floor where I build most of my fires and I put him in this. There were three stages. Golub in the hole, me painting over him on the floor, and Jenny above both of us on a swing. I fixed it so Golub could look up her dress and when he did, then I had the look I wanted. I could have titled it Golub Staring Under Jenny's Dress or Golub in Discomfort, but I liked the neutral tones of Golub Staring better. His forehead is freckled, and what occupies the center of the picture is this forehead, this sandy, speckled forehead. The more I looked at his forehead the more it reminded me of a beach, so I painted it as a beach. Sand, with grey wood and broken shells and faded glass. I didn't use a brush but scraped large clumps of crusty oil on the canvas. I used paint that had dried, sticking it on in sections, like a statue. I mixed some sand in with the paint, and far off, in a wrinkle of the left brow, I had a beach city burning, concrete bunkers exploding and dog legs falling through storm clouds and old newspapers with faded ocean print spelling forgotten tragedies buried under the sand. All that was on Golub's forehead, staring up. And much more. Golub has acne, pits of flesh that insult the eyes, his adolescent blitzkrieg. These became pop bottles with lost notes inserted by myopic teenage girls who worked from dawn to dusk in glass factories dreaming of orgasms. Old bones (naturally), insect bodies blowing like dry bamboo in the Philippine wind, spittle damp and bubbly drawing together hundreds of grains into a small spitball. Women's liquids, deposited in secret places, harsh droppings, folded under thin straw-colored leaves and spent in quick spurts. All that was on Golub's forehead. I worked fast, in a rage, throwing paint, building this forehead up like a plaster wall. And underneath, dim but not lost, two faint firefly eyes shining through the wind, looking hopefully up at Jenny.

Sinkowiz gave me a good price for it, almost enough to pay off my lawsuit.

If Stark takes to flying too much I can't have him in my studio. I made that resolution yesterday.

The pain starts in the left leg and runs up through the right testicle like a silver wire, where it shorts over to the left ball, down the right leg where it gathers in little hair balls, which is what happens if you're not careful and swallow hair. Then the surface of the leg goes bad, and no matter how you slap it, from thigh to knee, nothing is felt, you might as well have plastic for skin. I told the doctors about it and they told me it was sciatica compounded by a pinched vein. I thanked them and paid my bill, slapping my leg, which still felt like plastic. When the pain comes I can't talk much and that's not because it hurts. Pain is squeezed out of me and coats my walls. I have an aching knee over by the window that must take up a good four square feet. It's almost an inch thick, and on bad nights it vibrates, crumbling the plaster in its tendon fingers. I sit smoking, watching it. How can I paint then, watching that wall shake, my knee ache, with such pain? Pain jumps too, and one flew out my window and landed on a bum below, crippling his other leg. Sometimes when the pain comes I try to paint my big picture, but often the walls shake so that nothing is steady.

Jenny talks with Golub and that's when I'm sure they're plotting something even though all Golub can talk about is lead pipes. And his driving tests. Golub is a great conversationalist. He fascinates. He is beyond the bore. With him it is a matter of reality, like dropping a plumb line to the center of the earth. What you find there you talk about. Golub dropped and found. Lead pipes and driving tests. Take your number three lead pipe, he'd say, and indeed I had already taken it the night before and dropped it out the window, letting it fall in the cellar doorway where he and I have our agreement. Did I tell you about the agreement? Take your number three lead pipe, he says, talking as if he had a cigar in his mouth. Conforms to your ASA specifications as cited in code number thirty-seven of the plumbing and heating contractors. Golub tells me all about lead pipes, about shear strengths and thread pitch, about decay factors and incessant vibration strain. I like that last one, the one about incessant vibration strain. I thought it applied somehow. To something. I let it roll around on my tongue, coating the consonants with saliva and tickling the s's on the roof of my mouth. Golub has a winner there, in that incessant vibration strain.

Goddamn that Stark!

He's getting to act more like a bird every day. Soon as he comes in the first thing he wants to do is fly up to a rafter and drop bird shit on the forks. No manners at all and he's constantly shedding. What good is he up there, on the rafters? I brought him down one evening with my Crossman, lead pellet in the wing, because he was making tracks over my canvas.

Golub tells me about his driving lessons. What he does with the clutch and how he turns the wheel with one hand and signals with the other. Golub's feet on the pedals: small, tiny little hooves gloved in leather and reaching a delicate point at the front. Golub has weak legs and can't press the pedals hard enough, too cheap for power brakes and automatic transmission. Last Tuesday during one of his road tests he smashed into a bread truck. I got a call on the phone and rushed down, paints in hand. Used a lot of yellow and red. Noticed that when metal bends it turns yellow. Used the flat of the spatula, quick strokes like cutting turkey. Golub leaning his head through the cracked window, thoughtfully bleeding and I had a tube of vermilion that did the job nicely. I like the warm shine of vermilion, and the rich sheen before it dries. I have since tried to rework it in blue, but a certain power is missing.

Golub fails driver's tests with alarming regularity. Stark came down from the ceiling long enough to make a suggestion. He told me to look for connections. Before I could ask him what with what, he flew back up again, and since he's out of range of the Crossman I'll have to be content with that enigmatic phrase. Typical of Stark.

I didn't tell you about my big picture yet. Invited Steinmentz up to talk about it. He's the only one left. He's a cigar store clerk downstairs and I suspect also a friend of Golub's, but what can you do when you're trapped? Steinmetz listens to me, sucking his teeth. He's good at lit matches, and just this week almost burnt down my studio. That would have gotten Stark out, but I'll have to watch Steinmetz because I think he talks to Golub. Did I ever tell you why Golub is always taking driving tests? Clutch chatter and low octane knock are second nature to him. He wishes he could get his hands greasy.

Stark just dropped another egg. Two since this morning.

Steinmetz brought his mother over, and that's something even Sinkowiz won't do. His mother is Danish and smokes cigars and that's how he got his start in the business, but of course he's German. She wears long black gabardine dresses that come down to her ankles and has a small charcoal mustache at the corner of her mouth. I wanted to do a picture of her and Steinmetz, title: Steinmetz's Mother, but with him in the picture since I thought he was a part of her. All blacks and shoe-polish browns, like the one I did of Golub's feet, title: Golub's Feet on the Pedals, size eight pumps in soft calfskin, hand stitched and shivering, dancing in the air. I painted Golub's feet from underneath, to get the character, and I wanted to do the same with Steinmetz's Mother, showing old smoke and forgotten tobacco and falling folds of gabardine, locked rooms and stained books with bitter scenes, *Who is to remember this?* hanging over the drawing room like a long Danish winter night. But try to get that in. All black and brown and colors they don't have yet. Try to mix them!

Anyway I couldn't do it, working in blue now and I don't see those lips in anything but long brown rolled cadavers of tobacco wrappers.

Golub tells me that Stark refuses to pay rent since he's a bird. I can see he thinks Stark is setting a dangerous precedent.

My big picture, the one with *everything* in, is going to be in blue. I told Sinkowiz about it and he says he's got a buyer lined up but the only one I can talk to about it now is Steinmetz's mother. I've given up on Steinmetz. He spends all his time sucking his teeth. Yesterday he swallowed two fillings, gold, and his bowel movements are watched with great eagerness.

The big picture. Everything has to be in it. I've decided to do a falling picture. Things falling. I think blue will put that across best. How big should the canvas be? Don't know. Might have to knock out a wall. What falls? Jenny, Golub's Feet, Steinmetz's Mother. But that's just a start.

I used to get invitations from Sinkowiz to go to openings, but now he feels I work best through a front. I still haven't met his mother. She wears chrome-rimmed glasses, and her face, like my leg, is plastic. I'd love to see that face, but Sinkowiz is adamant. No mother, no plastic face.

People will fall two ways in my painting. Head first or feet first. Eisenhower will fall head first, but Jenny and the Virgin Mary will fall feet first. Steinmetz's mother wanted to know if she could fall in my picture and I said yes. Not that I consider this a compromise since I'd planned to have

her falling anyway. I gave her a choice of head or feet first,
and she took head first. She's afraid that if she falls feet first
her dress will billow up over her head. Everybody is in
blue, the Duke of Windsor is in navy-blue plus fours while
his wife is in sky blue tennis shorts and an off-blue polo
shirt. Naturally they fall holding hands. Steinmetz came up
and he wants to fall too, though he'll settle for whatever
way I put him, feet or head first. He'd like to fall with his
cigars. Golub wants to fall too, but he wants to fall with his
driving lessons, and I told him that just people will be falling in this picture. He wants to know if he could fall with a
gearshift lever in his hand, maybe a brake pedal or two. I'll
have to think about that. I think I'll put Golub falling in
between Mao Tse-tung and DeGaulle. He asked if he
could fall in his blue serge, and I told him yes. Sinkowiz
came up and wanted to know how the big one was coming
and I told him, but he wanted to see. Funny about Sinkowiz, he never listens to words. He has ears, but I think
they're sealed over on the inside. He must read lips. I think
I'll have Sinkowiz falling in my picture, upside down next
to Eisenhower, reading his lips. Sinkowiz would fall good.
He has that look about his face, the look of someone used
to falling, eyeballs detached, cheeks inflated like a para-
chute, hair grabbing for air. Some people are good at falling, and some not. I'll show this in my picture. My picture
takes place in an elevator shaft. Everybody crowding in at
the top, falling in the middle. There is no landing. Nobody
ever lands. There will be arms and legs and dog heads
twirling past elevator cables, some people will slide, holding
onto the greased cables with bloody hands and a look of
automated horror. Others will ignore the cables and fall
like Buddhists burning in Saigon, arrow sure. The grabbers
will reach out, twirl, shiver, and fall like animated cart-
wheels in a firecracker carnival. Everyone will fall in my
picture. Heads of state, models, safecrackers, highway pa-
trolmen. I'm considering other things falling. Alarm clocks
and forks and crutches.
Stark came down and wants to know if he can fall, but I
told him no. Then he told me I could fly if I wanted to. He
told me to fill my cheeks with air and breathe fast. I tried
but only my heels came off the ground. We talked about
blue and Stark said that black was blue, that everything

was black and that was why he was flying. He laid an egg and flew back up to the ceiling.

The painting is turning out to be larger than I thought. It already covers two walls, and everyone who sees it wants to fall in it. Jenny wants to fall in her furs and I asked if she meant that old muskrat coat she wears. Like all old people when they get upset, Jenny's nostrils flutter and go pale, the tissue drained of blood. Blue again. I told her she could fall in her furs. She's happy.

If you look towards the center of your nose and press the corner of your eye, you can see a small cornea of the visible spectrum. Newton in the Optics.

Steinmetz's mother wanted to know why people fell and I asked her if she knew Sinkowiz's mother but she said she never associated with anyone who had a plastic face. I can see why. Hers is leather. Cracked and peeling, like a blue Michelangelo ceiling, with faint flakes that fall like flesh showers on her teacup. She takes no notice. Still, we can talk.

She speaks in blue syllables, like old river icicles. She takes one bony peeling hand and reaches inside her dress, the black gabardine crinkling like a forest fire. Fingers fumble, feeling old linen and immigrant undergarments. When she finds the word she wants, she has no hesitancy in bringing it out, holding it between her dead fish fingers like a cracked amethyst. We spent one evening talking of Japan. She attributed her old age to cigar smoking.

Did I tell you the Pope, His Holiness, is falling in my picture? To be sure. Along with the entire College of Cardinals and selected artifacts of Vatican City. They fall feet first, their robes billowing up like mushrooms. His Holiness holds a miter in one hand and a fork in the other. It is Friday and he is eating cod.

Sinkowiz came and said the picture was too big. It now covers three walls, and I have half the upper chamber of the New York State Legislature falling along with two dozen rock-and-roll stars, five respected surgeons, and ten policemen, arm in arm, who are ceremoniously trampling on a select group of Ban the Bomb demonstrators. Sinkowiz saw the last vignette and wanted to know if I was going political and I told him I would if I could. Did you ever notice the look on someone's face when they get testy? All wound up, like a rusty screw that's been worked on backwards? That's Sinkowiz. I'm having reservations about him. He talks with Golub too much, and lately is getting very commercial. Stark thinks commerce is good for art but after my last arrest I don't agree.

Jenny's teeth hurt. I told her they would. At her age what can you expect. She took them out and showed them to me. They were hurting. She has arguments with her teeth several times a day. She says they make her say things she doesn't want to say.

I told her I'd put her teeth in the picture, falling.

Golub tried to hit me with a lead pipe.

With Sinkowiz, it's the mouth. I tried to explain that to him the other day. I told him, look Sinkowiz, your mouth is shaped like a saucer and that's why you say what you do. It may be the last we'll see of Sinkowiz. O.K. with me. Have been trusting him less since he started brushing his teeth.

Yesterday we celebrated the King of Denmark's birthday and everybody came. Steinmetz and Steinmetz's mother, Jenny, and even Golub, who brought his own control panel with him. Golub is very intent on passing his driving test. Wherever he goes he takes his steering wheel, pedals, windshield, gear shift lever, and bench seat. We had ice cream and cake and Jenny passed out party hats, shiny little elastic domes with a rubber that fit around the neck. Golub sat shifting gears and making Plymouth noises. He takes his test on a Plymouth, six cylinder, though at the present he's having clutch trouble. Stark flew down and read a poem though he's no poet. Jenny gave him a hat and he complained about the elastic. Someday I'll have to have a good talk with Stark.

Why do old men walk in the streets in winter?

Last night Sinkowiz came and knocked on my door, late at night. I had trouble with some of the chains, and at least one padlock had rusted shut, but I finally got the door open. Sinkowiz asked me if I believed in art for art's sake, and I told him I might. Who knows? He said if I did I should cut up my big picture and sell the pieces. I let him into the main studio because I liked a vein that was throbbing on the side of his temple. It wasn't a big vein, actually about the size of a fingernail, but it jumped up and down

like a snail strangling. Someday I'll tell you more about
Sinkowiz. That he's a prick, in the aforementioned sense,
you know, but did you know that he wears white hair sil-
vered and has a camel's hair coat which he's thrown up on
three times already? His face is the color of shiny pigskin,
and that always fascinates me. I'm a sucker for Sinkowiz's
face, I must admit. It's like new money rubbed into old
leather. There's a sheen about it, soft, as if he spent his entire life crying in expensive sand. So I let him in and sat
him on a kitchen chair over which hung an electric light
bulb, swaying on the end of a frayed line. Sinkowiz's head
danced on the floor like a sea horse in a storm as the bulb
swung first one way and then the other. When the bulb was
at one end of its arc I could see that vein, throbbing like
salmon sperm, dark blue, the color of the Baltic. At the
other end of the arc the vein was hidden in the shadow of
his head, beating, but beating unseen. I wanted to reach
over and touch his vein. All I could think of was electricity
and telephone lines. Sinkowiz blubbered on about how he
had to have that picture to sell, that he was committed to
sell it, that he needed the money, that it was too big to sell
in its present size. It now covers all four walls and the end
is not in sight. It's heading for the roof, my canvas, my res-
urrected linen, unfolding its scroll like equator up to the
heavens. But with his vein and my unfinished canvas and
Sinkowiz's blubbering, I had to set up a new canvas. I
worked fast, sketching him in charcoal. Titanium blue, zinc
red, and some old yellow that has been drying up in a forgotten tube. I started with a brush but couldn't get the paint
on fast enough to match the frenzy of that throbbing so I
moved on to a spatula and then fingers, trying to keep up
with the mad army of blood that raced through that temple. Let me tell you what I put in. First of all electricity
running through frayed lines, sputtering, and then shadows
crossing soft faces, old olives, the sun in Sicily, expensive
conversations, and of course Sinkowiz's face in triplicate,
pleading, smiling, crying, being soothed by costly salves
and rubbed with blushing liquids from near-nude virgins.
Hair like hoarfrost, looked at in mirrors, often combed. If
you look closely at Sinkowiz's face you'll find it's hideously
smoothed by small scars, brushed shining like light leather
over upholstery. And the vein, beating its own metronome,

reckoning the cost of cocktails and canvas, calligraphy and Corot.

I finished at five a.m., and Sinkowiz was asleep, so I wrapped his lank, slack body in the dirty camel's hair coat and carried him over to my couch. I pulled the coat around his shoulders with the feeling I was wrapping a piece of fish.

No more room in the studio.

I'm painting on the roof. Set up curtain stretchers weighted down with bricks. Stark flies up now and then to see how I'm coming. I show him the new fallers. The mayor and the city council, five rabbis making liberal pronouncements, a dozen candy store owners, innumerable mothers with babes in arms, two thousand Gideon Bibles placed here for your convenience and enlightenment, and seven irreproachable Miss America contestants.

Word has gotten out about my picture, and everybody wants to fall in it. Stark sells tickets and Jenny seats them in a chair, or tells them to stand. There is no longer room on the roof, so I let the painting drape down the side of the building. Last night it rained, altering the composition of one section. Stark is against touching it up. He feels that whatever happens *is*, and should be left. I can see now that this painting will have no end. I hate to disappoint Sinkowiz and the mortgage on his Long Island home.

An accident.

Better explain about it from the ending. We had a fire. Golub keeps insisting that I had a fire, but he says that for the benefit of the insurance agent who stands perpetually at his elbow. The insurance agent says he can't understand how the fire got started, but it's perfectly simple. Stark did it. Of course he really didn't do it, but since we're going backwards to explain (which is really the only way to explain), he did it. How did he start it the agent asks. With the ash from his cigar I say. The agent tells me that birds don't smoke but I try to explain to him that Stark is no bird. Temporarily, a phase. Behind all those feathers stands Stark, the real commercial menace. Now why is Stark smoking a cigar? Easy. He is upset. And where did he get the cigar? Another easy one. Steinmetz and his mother, Steinmetz's mother, went in halvsies on a box of slim Panatellas, Stark's favorites. Stark goes for your riverboat-gambler cigar, and likes to fiddle with a gold watchchain when he smokes. For the benefit of the insurance agent, I explained why Stark was upset. This was because of the argument I was having with Golub. Now why was I having an argument with Golub? Simple. Because I was having an argument with Sinkowiz. Golub and I were arguing over what Sinkowiz had said. I told Golub he couldn't hear because he keeps his driving gloves in his ears. He doesn't have pockets on his pants. So the only place he can keep his gloves are in his ears. They hang down to his shoulders, easily the world's longest, with deep folds in which he keeps all the things he normally would keep in his pockets. But as a result of this he has trouble hearing. Maybe that's why he fails his driving tests. Try to take something out of his ears and he says his ears get cold. His earmuffs look like knee-length socks. What were Sinkowiz and I arguing about? About Golub's ears. Sinkowiz claims they're normal ears, like everyone else's. He says they don't hang down, but I claim they do. When ears hang, they hang. No one can tell you different. I tell Golub he should face his long ears. Then he could accept disappointment.

Golub wants to set up a driving school in my studio. He has a plan to buy old junks and haul them up here for beginners. Golub loves driving. He figures with his own driving school he'll be able to pass his driving tests. How can you argue with a man who carries gearshift knobs in his ears?

Steinmetz's mother wants to know if this is all real, and she has a point there. Jenny argues yes, but then she always was an incurable romantic. Steinmetz doesn't say much. Did I tell you his eyebrows and hair were completely burned off? Steinmetz's mother thinks the whole idea of people falling is unreal. She suggested I do old ladies with lap dogs, or something classic like Man Brushing His Wig, or Portia Surprised. She's a great one for people being surprised. She says that real people are always being surprised. But this she says, waving a bony peeling hand in front of my people falling picture, this is not real. I tried to tell her that people are always falling.

They even fall surprised.

New fallings: five generals in full battle dress, seven postmen delivering dead letters, twenty precocious epileptics.

Golub is upset.

I tried to hit him over the head with a lead pipe. He also claims I tried to tie his ears in knots. He is currently pushing a Studebaker into my studio. It's wedged rather tightly in the elevator door.

At eight a.m. Golub is out in the rear of the elevator, feet wedged against the elevator wall, polished little landlord hands on the rear bumper of the Studebaker trying to push it into the studio. And me? I stand on the floor trying to push it back into the elevator. Golub gives a grunt, pushes, and a small drop of businessman's sweat drops from his oily brow. At ten we break for coffee, at twelve for lunch, and by special agreement we knock off at four. He's persistent, this Golub, and shows amazing strength for a landlord. The Studebaker is three inches in his favor. I calculated this amount to a bumper so I cut it off with my acetylene torch and threw it in the back yard. Golub claims he'll sue. He comes back with a lawyer, who helps him push.

Sinkowiz came over and helped me push, but he's like a lawyer, no back or shoulder muscles to speak of. Again he's crying for the big picture.

Fat men keep coming into the ground floor, but never leaving. I can see them now, wedged bulging hip to portly shoulder, Golub's Dachau. If the pain wasn't so bad I'd go downstairs and let them out. Golub's probably hoarding them, for the time when there'll be a shortage of fat men.

When fat men fall, they flutter. I've shown that. Sizzling little pork butterflies.

Steinmetz finally gave me the idea!

He sucks his teeth, but he sucks a new set each day. He has seven sets of false teeth. A Monday set, a Tuesday set, and so on. That means he returns to his sucked teeth. I call them Steinmetz's Revolving Sucked False Teeth.

The same thing with my picture. Mount it on a gigantic revolving drum, spectators at the apex. My Revolving Falling People.

And I'll soon start on the drum too, when the fire in the elevator shaft dies down and the claws on my hand turn back into fingers.

MOMENTUM

RONALD SUKENICK

His room in the slum.

This is perhaps naive;
distortion occurs in
    the moment
as in memory;
the mind is quick
the feelings quicker;
but I want the moment
    live
in its dishonesty,
minimal affectation:
correction in re-
    flection.

More: constriction of
life paralysis of
    vitality—

okay here we go   i don't
want to whisper this   i want
to hear my natural speaking
voice the way it really
sounds   also i can see myself
here in a full-length mirror as i
speak   there's another mirror
too   so that i can't really lose
sight of myself as i sit down on
my bed or lie down or walk
around   i want to say this as it
comes without premeditation
because i want to say it before
i lose it   or not so much say it
as tell it   tell it to myself so
i'll have it down   so that i can
come back to it again and re
capture it   so the speed of the
tape is my form   keep talk
ing as the tape records non
stop   tuesday   it wasn't
merely that i had to go up
there to find a place for us to
live in the summer   i had
been in a condition of somno
lence   stupor perhaps   more
like it   going to bed late at

the garotte of the slum,
the garret of the mind.

Tunnel—skyline: N.Y.'s
tight rectumtangles.

He leaveth the City,
his bane & his home.
Coleridge, Lowry,
can we join hands?

Delaware Water Gap,
   wide
river, fruit trees
flowering: summer
   via spring.
Kittatinny Mts.—
sadist counselors, me
a skinny kid, proto-
   wordsworthian:
morning clouds stretch
   & rise sleepy from
   mt. tops.

The terminal with its
corrupt loafers the
City again.

night three or four getting
ten hours sleep waking up to
ward noon or past one o'clock
sometimes   and i wanted to
break that   i got to the
bus station no time to buy
anything to bring along to
eat just beckett i got on the
bus only one other passenger
an old lady uneventful
through the tunnel the view of
the skyline down the turn
pike through new jersey some
other city newark maybe pa
terson one of those picked
up several more passengers
very ugly here the city the cit
ies the industry i wanted not
to look at it the roadside stands
the mechanics the garages the
custard palaces ice cream ham
burgers bee urgers fish and
chimps so i got out beckett
and tried to read it was lousy
reading on the bus it hurt my
eyes we were getting into the
country anyway i put away
beckett long overdue at the
library what ten cents a day i
stared at the country it was
nice being in the country
again by the time we got to
scranton at five i was head
achey from hunger the nasty
lunchcounter man in the scran
ton terminal from whom i
bought some cigarillos then
on to ithaca via another
bus sitting in second seat in
front of me a student from
the west indies next to him
sits down this middle-aged la

dy she hadn't been on the last bus nor was he i think the moment she sits down she starts talking and she didn't stop till we arrived the guy hardly said twenty words the whole trip three hours or something like that she was talking about her life she was english she had been brought up in oxford she explained how oxford had been very pretty but then they moved in an auto factory and then a steel factory to supply the auto factory she married an amer ican or i guess a canadian and they came to this country she was one of those english ec centrics her hangup was oxy gen she described the whole story of her life in terms of getting enough oxygen once living in new jersey for ex ample they had rented a house she made her husband give it up because of the facto ry smoke they had to move to new york new york wasn't so bad because she said the sea air it was full of oxygen at night after she was married she went to visit her in-laws somewhere in the backwoods of canada they were menno nites they didn't want their son to marry outside their reli gion they were very strict a sect but they were very nice to her she said only they put her into a room into which coal gas from the furnace

Eccentricity: a trope
of freedom traumatized
by conformity.

It is true that in New
   York one feels
freer at night:
official reality dozes
   if watchfully;
foghorns, the sense of
   ships to/from
distant ports, one
   breathes more easily.

I had seen large num-
bers of horses
in the mountains,
untended in the fields,
unsaddled,
moving in herds.

escaped every night she
would get sick and apparent
ly in fact according to her coal
gas can be lethal   so there she
was getting sicker and sicker
and finally one day her hus
band's youngest sister came in
and let slip something about
the coal gas that it was escap
ing into the room and when
she asked why she hadn't been
told about this the girl said her
parents told her that if it was
god's will to take her then he
would take her and the matter
was really out of their
hands   she thought that was
pretty cruel   her search for ox
ygen was taking her up to
ithaca   her husband who had
taught english and was now in
the college administration busi
ness was i think administrating
in new york but she had taken
it upon herself to come to itha
ca and see if they couldn't both
get jobs working for the uni
versity   and she kept asking
the student about ithaca
whether it was big whether
it had much industry in
short   whether or not there
was enough oxygen   at first i
thought this lady was a real
nut   naturally she believed in
reincarnation   her husband she
said was a very nice man
but he was very cranky and
nasty and he couldn't get along
with people and she thought
perhaps he would learn that
in his next life   she was also

There are times I
feel I'm suffocating
my breath comes shal-
low panting I think
of a man I heard of
dying with a heart
attack gasping I
can't breathe I
can't breathe.
There's nothing wrong
with my heart.

Like Odysseus 10 years

a socialist   a proselytizing so
cialist   after a while it struck
me though that her ideas after
all weren't so insane   that they
were pretty humane   what was
wrong with a proselytizing soci
alist   reincarnation well that's
harmless   and after all she had
a point about oxygen   in a way
i feel and i would come to feel
more after being in ithaca that
my life too all our lives was
a struggle for sufficient oxy
gen   ithaca   i hope i'm say
ing all i want to say   katz
wasn't home   i called   his wife
answered   seemed glad to hear
from me i walked over just long
enough to drop my bags   nice
girl   pretty too   up to the cam
pus   i took a cab   no other
way of getting up the hill this
time of night   about nine   no
buses   incredible   i was walk
ing in a dream   in memory ra
ther   nothing was real because
everything was exactly the same
   it wasn't real because it was
all in my mind   johnny's big
red grill the royal palm across
the street still there   i felt as
if i could put my hand right
through them   they weren't
there—they were in my head
and the food in johnny's as bad
as ever   things began to settle
into place   present and past
made connections located one
another so to speak   adamov
was there in johnny's   walked
in a little after me   i had seen
him the week before with mutu

Real means locating
the present in terms
of the past
locating the self
in terms of the
present.
Wordsworth, Proust.

al friends sitting next to the
stage in a kitchen while he lec
tured about the modern french
theater and two hundred algeri
ans drowned in the seine by the
french police things were be
coming real again i walked
over the gorge onto cam
pus again the feeling of walk
ing through memory the feel
ing that everything was in my
head but then the big new
modern library again things
began to fall into place the
past vis à vis the present i
looked at the night view the
lights in the valley a few glim
mering lights in the hill oppo
site distant the students
going from dormitory to li
brary across the big cam
pus the girls i was interested
in mostly some nice looking
ones a different genre from
the city a different genre
from other colleges too they
looked like they lived in the
country they looked like they
lived in a country club heal
thy sunburned lithe the libra
ry tower more impressive than
i remembered more beautiful
even perhaps the discovery
that the old library was not go
thic but romanesque i hadn't
known the difference before i
got katz out of his carrel in the
new library very luxe very
air conditioned sculpture by
lipschitz katz glad to see
me so it seemed that cheered
me up hard to contact katz

with words   do better with a
slap on the shoulder   telling
a story maybe a joke not
evasive but oblique wednes
day   for the first time in
months it seems i get up as early
as eight thirty   not only up but
wide awake   the outside is
flooded with sunlight the air
totally different   from new
york fresh race into the
bathroom shave not quite in
time to catch katz   linger a bit
over coffee then take a bus
up   the campus in the daytime
quite different   more real   cla
rity   again the girls   not quite
so dazzling as last night   begin
ning to get used to them   still
quite a few pretty ones   coffee
in the straight and one of those
great glazed doughnuts they do
n't make them like that any
where else why   as usual as al
ways coffee in the straight in the
morning a laxative effect   up
to the john   back out to the
terrace   just sitting   the view
of the valley i think of
wordsworth   hard to get in
touch with people looking for
an apartment   i call from the
straight go back to the terrace
sit there incredible sunlight
blue sky back to the phones
first few apartments very dis
couraging   rickety old wooden
places with creepy landladies
looking at everybody as they
go up and down the stairs
cramped quarters firetraps
too much money   discouraging

car ads look hopeful though
maybe i'll be able to get a car
here too   the students are dif
ferent   the good students i
mean about five percent of
them maybe as usual apart
from the fraternities they clus
ter in the straight in johnny's
in apartments   now the girls
are allowed to stay out ov
ernight stay in the apart
ments   seniors even some of
them can live out poetry fic
tion published in the student
magazine that ten years ago
would have gotten you thrown
out just like that thing about
a girl masturbating in front of
a creative writing class on the
teacher's desk with the tea
cher's grade book published in
the magazine katz told me
about it and me ten years ago a
national issue a huge fuss be
tween administration and the
arts just because i wrote bird
shit in a story not only that
though the spirit of berkeley
demonstrations vietnam santo
domingo pacifists anti rotc ro
tc it really does me good to
see students demonstrating
against rotc poor marty
marching up and down in
barton hall hour after hour al
ways some new violation
did he ever catch up on the
penalty hours he had to march
in barton hall disgusting im
agine going to college to march
with a rifle in barton hall
alone back and forth they

even have trouble finding things
to demonstrate against it seems
tant mieux the big thing a
demonstration the other day in
barton hall at the presidential
review of rotc at which about
80 demonstrators sat down on
the floor so they couldn't
march against them the damn
fraternities mobilized twenty
five-hundred students apparent
ly in a murderous mood
carrying signs kill kill kill drop
the bomb etc somewhat anti
semitic too good old fraterni
ties violence prevented only by
the campus patrol protecting the
demonstrators dick gregory
was coming up to give a speech
there were demonstrators there
too people demonstrating for
dick gregory against dick greg
ory and then a whole sorority
full of nice girls demonstrating
against the anti-gregory demon
strators an unusual sorority
withdrew from the national
that was complaining they took
in too many negroes and no
doubt jews too now one won
ders why don't they dissolve
the sorority and just become
people place shown to me by
a law school student a creepy
guy vaguely in favor of the
demonstrations but he told me
they were just creating more
enemies he wanted everybody
to be nice and well-behaved
nobody should cause trouble
seemed to be the idea obvious
ly worried that somehow he

might get involved there might
be repercussions of course he
had liberal ideas but he didn't
want his career to get messed
up by things changing too
much no chaos couldn't af
ford that a crummy place any
way later on standing in front
of the straight waiting for a guy
to pick me up in a car to look
at another car that he had
somewhere on the outskirts i
was watching somebody mak
ing a speech some undergrad
uate guitar group singing civil
rights songs trying to get people
to the dick gregory thing
which in turn was a benefit for
some harlem project or for
some southern project i don't re
member which drive out with
a new yorky type shows me
his car total wreck wants
150 for it every time you get
near the thing you tear your
clothes the body was in such
bad shape couldn't try it out
because he didn't have plates i
didn't have time gave me ad
vice on apartments bargain he
said bargain them down
they have to get rid of them
cheap for the summer i
asked him then if he'd take
125 for the car he guessed he
would i never saw him
again he told me he goes
swimming in the reservoir
where i swam with ***** at
dusk and saw a loon that
night at katz's his kids clam
bering all over him like one of

his stories   i couldn't imagine
katz with three kids i'd never
seen him with his kids   what
would he be like   well there
it was   it was like katz with
three kids   nice to see ob
viously had an empathy with
children   his own   anyway
the younger one coos when
he talks   they're three boys
that afternoon late after a long
exhausting search up and down
the famous hill i found some
thing   i thought   i might
like   collegetown's ugly one
apartment house   not really
an apartment house although
there are enough apartments in
it   but not really an apartment
house by new york standards
four floors made of white con
crete   apartment on the first
floor pretty cheap cheaper than
i   expected   memories   con
nected with that house   espe
cially this one in the crescent
drive   in the   front   meeting
***** i was in front of the
house she was at onc end of
the drive a white sweater as i
remember running towards me
must have been glad to see me
i guess she liked me i remember
as she ran how her breasts
bounced her big silky breasts
silky nipples the french influ
ence no doubt as i now realized
the bouncing a french brassiere
  all through collegetown mem
ories   all the places still there
******'s   apartment   down
stairs how much smaller i was

then how little how little i
knew how much bigger she
was than me and of course i
knew it which was why i was
afraid of her as indeed there
was good reason to be and
****'s old place the site so to
speak of my first mistress my
first real sex if not exactly
my first fuck **** sneaking
out at night to snip her neigh
bor's giant tulips and bring
them to me katz's wife makes
spice bread all her own bread
only white bread in packages
in ithaca and sour bread
too and chala for the week
end late that night i close
the deal on the apartment the
thing that really won me
over and despite not because
of the memories the fact that
the gorge so close i saw a
beautiful bird there red beak
red head i walked down
along a path overlooking falls
rapids pools trees above the
gorges here and there still quite
primeval and at the top above
the falls tennis courts in the
middle of the woods i imagine
myself walking through the
gorge up to the courts playing
a while back into the gorge to

Looking back with
some urgency to find
a place to write
Is this the gorge
where Bogotay
died the year
after I left I
find no room &

then discover that
p. 12 I missed in
pagination was
that your ghost
Joe then let this
space be a memorial
death is white a
blank a young man's
death a page unwritten
therefore a propos
besides you were no
architect never even
finished that but a
tinkerer over jobs
undone like your car
your brother I think
finished it it turned
up like a ghost in
Cambridge it was the
tinkering you liked
you never meant to
finish life why else
were you shooting
rapids in a flood
damn fool tinkering
as you would say you
built a boat in your
bedroom I helped you
hoist it out &
left it on the lawn
en route to L.A.
where we sped around
on the crazy carcass
of your unfinished car.

There seems to be an
error of chronology
here: I think this
happened the night
before. That too

cool off in a pool and back to
the house   so i take the apart
ment i pick up steve in his car
rel   at the same moment i'm
meeting him i raise my hand in
greeting he raises his hand but
in greeting someone behind me
next to me a nice-looking young

has its value—to
capture the present
with the collusion
of the past. Let
it stand.

Or was my lust still
weak, a mere tickling
of the surface, a
thing of the eye?
A queer painter once
told me that sight is
the most sensual
of the senses: I
aksed him, What
about touch?

From Wordsworth one

girl   a senior but she looks a
lot younger than that   i say
why don't you come along
with us we all go for a
beer   i was coming on strong
girl obviously impressed   after
a while in johnny's nothing to
say   all the tension suddenly
getting expressed being here
breaking through the memory
barrier the effort of finding a
place the fact of finding it the
displacement from new york
not much left to be charming
    to a girl for whom in any
case my desire would be merely
carnal   if that   not much for
me there   by this time i'm ab
solutely sick of cornell   the
scenery is beautiful   the gorg
es wonderful   that's it   every
thing else depresses me espe
cially all the deja views   i
feel trapped here   the students
make me feel   claustropho
bic   i wish i were back in new
york   still at every table in
johnny's   the talk about the
demonstration in barton hall
the booing of Johnson's foreign
policy spokesman   that's en
couraging that makes me feel
good   making him show his
true colors who has flown the
flag of liberalism for how long
twenty or thirty years   just an
other pricky billionaire   talk
ing too low too slow   next day
thursday   up every morning at
nine this is fantastic i don't
even get tired oh i get tired but i
recuperate   more and more en

passes inevitably
to Lawrence: from
health of habitat to
health of the animal
itself.

ergy of course i know this that
activity generates energy for
por just dissipates it i know
it and yet in new york of
course i forget it or if not for
get it just know incapable of
doing anything about it the
sunlight the view of the val
ley still another stage looking
at the students that is first i
was dazzled by the girls then
quite sick of them now i
begin to single different ones
out my lusts are scattered all
across the campus a beautiful
indian girl i keep seeing a
graduate student katz tells
me daughter of some impor
tant indian government per
son incredibly expensive cloth
ing she wears saris one of
the few indian girls i've ever
found attractive after a few
days she gets to know me by
sight she's interested a hard
look in the eyes she gives me
mysterious dark brown eyes
another girl an older one
must be somebody's wife
eating along in johnny's not
far from my table looking at
me out of the corner of her
eye this one really good-look
ing an actress face elegant
figure i could go over and
ask her if she wants to have a
drink or if i could join
her no doubt she wants me
to would she say no so
what if i handled it right
she'd say yes and yet i'm
not really on the make

here it interests me but it
doesn't interest me really she
leaves i cheer up on the ter
race i look at more cars i
begin to cancel out ads in the
papers i get it down to a
choice between a few i'm be
ginning to feel better and bet
ter i think it's the oxygen
really i'm finally getting
enough oxygen here away
from new york that after
noon i see a ford that looks
good but there are a few oth
er cars i want to check at
some point or other i meet the
leader of the student demon
strations briefly obviously a
new york jew he's supposed
to be all sensibility the guy
with the charisma i can see
that in his face i wonder how
conscious is he how much
does it matter that he's the
center of things how much is
he interested in power at
heart how much is he inter
ested in the inevitable fringe
vulgarities of such a posi
tion how much is he like or
unlike myself when ten years
ago i was briefly a campus
hero of sorts and girls would
come up to me as i would walk
across campus and my imme
diate reflex was to be as nasty
as possible for which i al
ways kicked myself after
wards because some of them
were pretty and one i re
member throwing herself
away on some shmuck who i

had seen around a lot and
lusted after i was uncertain
about him the charismatic
guy extremely difficult to get
through that ten years and see
what things are really
like though here i have a
double view my paranoia for
ex mple ten years ago with re
gard to fraternity types the
real americans the square-jaw
ed arrogant types the blond
girls with money and pedigree
some where behind them my
paranoia of these types which
after leaving i had thought stu
pid now i see was not only
absolutely justified but in
fact i have it again of these
students from whom i have
nothing at the moment at all to
fear but who id do fear and i
know now as i knew then in
stinctively with good rea
son hard to get through that
ten years what would i have
thought of that girl i met the
other day not merely that
there was no contact nothing
there for me but possibly that
she was an idiot even despite
her sharpness her intelli
gence the fact that she took
all the right positions maybe
   in fact no doubt and this is a
comfort if i got to know her i
think i would think the same of
her now as one way or another
i would have thought of her
then one sees the same
types one has the impulse to
tap them on the shoulder and

The chaos of my mind.

call them by the same
names   one is convinced they
would answer to them   and
yet there is this differ
ence   the spirit the demonstra
tions   the rebellion much
healthier   that night at dinner
i decide which car to buy   i
feel that i'm somewhat out of
contact with my host and host
ess my mind is always on other
things business the cars
the apartments   is this what
it's like to be a businessman
i call lynn i had called her be
fore   last night to tell her i got
an apartment   she'll wire me
money for the car   at the end
of dinner i decide which car to
get   despite the suspicious ra
diator the ford   when was it
that i began to feel good   es
sentially i think it was when i
woke up the first morning at
eight thirty   the sunlight out
side the oxygen   still the ten
sion of the car but that's al
most over   next morning i
close the deal   by then i'm ex
hausted   this is friday i go
to all the necessary offices do
all the necessary things   i'm
really knocked out   i pick up
the car put the plate on say
goodbye   go to a gas station
get some gas open the
hood   the radiator that had
supposedly just been fixed was
spurting a steady stream of
water   a regular geyser   when
was it i started feeling so
good   was it during the

walk in the gorge i think so
or was it the continual buzz
among the students in college
town in the straight the enclave
of intellectuals or bohemians
or whatever they were was it
that sitting on the terrace the
other day waiting to get in
touch with someone with a
car a group of students
couldn't quite figure out the
boys their haircuts may be
the beatle influence obvious
ly campus intellectuals dunga
rees and so on only their style
of dress their style in gen
eral had a kind of chic to
it the boys looked sort of pret
ty i tried to place them among
people i had known ten years
ago these types were different
  they would have been dirt
ier they would have been less
self-conscious or self-conscious
in a different way what would
i have thought of these peo
ple then i couldn't quite make
them out the girls though one
of them a blond not bad
looking i could place her all
right the blond one cuddling
up to her pretty boyfriend es
caped from a sorority brains
enough to know that the more
interesting people didn't have
anything to do with fraterni
ty sorority life essentially not
very different from her ex-so
rority sisters in five years you
would hardly know the differ
ence i knew girls like that
the other was different nice

looking girl baby face sexy
body very young   but whereas
the others seemed to be playact
ing she seemed to be uninterest
ed in acting any particular role
    they were talking about the
demonstrations in barton hall
    she had been one of the sit
tees   her case had come up be
fore some disciplinary board
    apparently as she explained it
they were reprimanded   they
considered this a light sentence
    two students looking up the
sky very blue   wispy clouds
jet bomber refueling in midair
    way up   tiny white outlines
against blue vapor trail   you
could see them one plane flying
slightly behind the other   now
i'm lying on the bed   in full
view of the full-length mir
ror   closed off here   lynn on
the phone in the other room
    planes overhead   below   un
der the bomber   the issue
stop the war in viet nam   san
to domingo rotc   one's sense of
the enormous privilege of the
students here   a country club
grownups would pay large
sums of money to come here
sit on the terrace drinking
beer   a sense of awe   at the
lightness with which i held this
privilege   when i was here
ready to throw it away so
easily   i was quite aghast at
this   suppose i had done
so   in fact i had done so   and
was saved only by a quirk of
faculty administration politics

the ten years' difference   ob
viously i would do the same
thing again   they had been
reprimanded   she was explain
ing carefully   she sympathized
with the dean in charge   he
wasn't bad he had to do his
job he was conservative but he
was sympathetic she could un
derstand his position   the stu
dents in front of the straight
talking the other day   there
was a petition they were getting
a lot of signatures against
the demonstrations   two white
guys were telling a black girl
there are quite a few more
blacks here now   a negro in
the john the other day   i typed
him as one of the athletes   still
the kind of negro there because
he could play football or was
good at track   singing of all
things old man river in the
john   very palsy walsy with a
negro porter cleaning things up
there as if they really had
something in common   and i
guess they did   but this girl one
of the new types apparently
there for no reason but that
she was smart   explaining that
it would do no good to get up
a counterpetition because in
any case they were the minori
ty   taking advantage a little of
being able to be authoritative
because she was black   knew i
was listening too showing off
for me   i could see that   the
bomber refueling overhead   a
kid taking the line that perhaps

it would be better not to irri
tate people any further at the
moment   baby face explaining
carefully and patiently why
this was no good it was a
doubt raised not out of interest
in the issue but out of a desire
to be part of this group which
apparently had some pres
tige i would not have been so
patient i would have ignored
the question totally i didn't
like the boys they were too
pretty there was a kind of
chic involved there was a
false note it wasn't merely the
issue a kid came over he
could have been in tep the
jewish fraternity he probably
wasn't but he was coming on
like a fraternity boy singing
whatever he had to say really
coming on the other boys the
pretty ones joined in took up
this tone after a while the girl
got up without saying anything
and walked away looking
bored the   pseudofraternity
type yelled after her you just
don't like us because we're
jewish still that issue   later on
i found out that she too was
jewish she had said that they
were giggling in the dean's of
fice because all the demon
strators turned out to have
jewish names and they were all
from brooklyn or the bronx
the mechanic said he could
solder the radiator two dollars
or so i believe it turned out to
be four which is usually what

two dollars or so means in the
mouth of a mechanic he was
an old type very rustic robert
frost would have liked him i
had to have the emergency
brake cable tightened i came
back an hour later he had fin
ished soldering the radiator just
finishing the emergency brake
i said how are the rest of the
brakes apparently in fixing
up the emergency they had dis
covered that the brakes were
no good at all dangerous in
fact sixty bucks the car was
150 i had felt bad when i
tried to bargain the guy down
to 125 he was such a nice
guy all the people with used
cars up there for sale were
very nice except the first car i
looked at the new york
guy who ended up giving me
advice on bargaining and who
was obviously trying to get rid
of a wreck but the natives
were very nice a middle-aged
lady out of small town usa
very respectable very helpful
very honest no doubt a
couple of kids from maybe
pennsylvania with a morris
minor they bought from an
english professor at swarth
more the guy i bought my
car from nicest of all every
body with a good reason for
selling the car just got a new
one couldn't pass it up and so
on he'd put a lot of money
into that car he said he was
only selling it that cheap be

cause well in effect that was all
he could get for it   could it be
that these nice people were
cheats in their nice way   isn't
just that the great american
hypocrisy   maybe   maybe not
   anyway there i was with
a sixty-dollar brake job on my
hands   and god knows what
else   this rustic type standing
there looking at the car and
saying   yep the gutless fif
ty-eight don't know why ford
ever made that car   i should
have felt worse   but i knew
the routine so well   i kept say
ing to myself something like
it's all part of the fun of own
ing a car   an essentially amer
ican experience buying a used
car mechanics with their am
biguous smiles of concern the
clap on the shoulder from the
buyer as you drive off the feel
ing of never knowing and
never being able to know
whether he didn't know eith
er   or whether it was just that
he didn't want to know   i
should have felt worse   but it
wasn't only that i knew the
routine   it was   the   oxy
gen   the oxygen was buoying
me up   i drove around   i
found a cheaper place   a for
ty-dollar estimate made an ap
pointment to bring the car
back that night   went back to
katz's exhausted   i still felt
good   i was feeling better and
better   it was the oxygen the

trees the sunlight the students with their demonstrations katz's kids clambering over him like one of his stories his wife mak ing bread her shyness   after din ner we went up to a campus place a student place overlook ing the lake the falls one of the falls   in this place a girl with huge boobs shorts and a cap pistol looking disheveled   walk ing around with her enormous breasts shooting off her cap pis tol   a mathematician with an other cap pistol must be some kind of fad   said he was drunk

we went outside we were go ing to a party   the mathemati cian not only had a cap pistol but in his car he also had a whip   a bullwhip   he showed us how he snapped the bull whip and fired the pistol at the same time   the impression was supposed to be that was the way he dealt with women i believe

we went to the party an architects' party always a lively bunch   katz knew a lot of people there   i found i really couldn't face it i had something to drink the people were doing the twist or whatever version it is now   lively   lots of nice looking girls   there was the girl on the terrace baby face   was it her eyes   in a sensational dress   showing the exaggerated s of her figure   i asked her where the drinks were she told me i wanted to say more   i felt too stupid   i would have

Out of place, even ten years ago I felt too stupid— the F. Scott Fitz- gerald scene: magic parties, dashing girls.

liked to have gotten to know
her i was curious i had said
one night at dinner that i heard
this student talking in this im
pressively clearheaded way and
i wondered if there were stu
dents who at that age she
looked like a freshman   when
i was here who could have been
that clearheaded at that age i
went over to katz that's the girl
i was talking about i
said more punch appeared i
drank two or three glasses
some girl attached her

This, of course, is
inexcusably gross—
it is a way in which
I am inexcusably gross.

self to me not very pret
ty a familiar type brooklyn
intellectual must have known
hundreds like her - who i also
didn't like i got mildly
rude she went - away for a
while   and then   came
back katz seemed to know all
the pretty girls at the party i
spotted him at the other side of
the room talking to my cling
ing intellectual acquaintance
and the clearheaded girl i
went over the liquor luckily
was getting to me i barged
into the middle of the conver
sation explaining that i could
never be one of the cool facul
ty types like katz because i
couldn't get myself to act stu
pid enough unless i got drunk
that wasn't a nice thing to say
nobody minded the clear
headed girl was very drunk
she knew she was very drunk
she was having fun being
very drunk this time i got in

to a conversation with her a
three-way conversation me her
and the plain girl she's wear
ing my ear rings i'm wearing
hers which do you like better
  it was turning into a competi
tive thing katz had disappeared
  i was enjoying myself i like
yours better i said to the pretty
girl and pointed out how that
was a two-way compliment
and felt myself very sauve i
was enjoying myself the girls
were friends each was trying
to get me away from the oth
er i overplayed it the pretty
girl got bored again as she had
on the terrace and there i was
again left with that brooklyn
intellectual those hundreds of
brooklyn intellectual girls i
got away somehow i bumped
into the pretty girl again she
told me she was very drunk i
asked her for a cigarette she
said it was her last cigarette and
said with me that's really a sign
of affection she was coming
on she wasn't making any se
crets about it either i said
when do you have to get back
twelve thirty she said she was a
sophomore she could have
stayed out all night if she had
signed out i asked her whether
she was going back with anyone
she said no i said why don't
you go home with me she said
okay she said goodbye to her
friend i found katz i told him
i'm disappearing i'd only been
at the party twenty minutes i

think we got outside she told
me how high she was she
wasn't that high quite real
ly but she was pretty
high we walked down the
street i held her hand we
got to a gorge i put my arm
around her there was a path
down into the gorge it was
a warm night i led her down
  i kissed her i liked the way
she kissed me after a while
i put my hands under her
dress i unzipped the top she
made no objections to anything
  made it clear that she liked
it she had a wonderful ass of
a type the big type which
she said she knew some people
didn't like i told her i did but
one hoped that it wouldn't be
tray her in the future by getting
too big i had found an apart
ment i had found a car and
now i'd found finally a coed
whose ass i not only admired
walking across campus but
which i could also squeeze i
felt my trip was a success i
don't think i even wanted any
thing else very much though i
wanted to fuck her on the
spot on the other hand i
knew she'd been in trouble be
cause of the demonstrations i
knew she had to get back
soon what i really wanted
she had already given me she
kept explaining how she didn't
do this kind of thing find a
man and practially jump into
bed with him we were now

Crude! (But true.)

Not carnal but psycho-
logical.

lying down on the path or al
most lying down on a broad
step shored up in the slope by
a split log i wasn't sure that
we couldn't be seen from the
road certainly at any minute
somebody could have walked
up or down the path i really
didn't give a shit neither did
she i had her pants down i
was playing with her vagina
every now and then she stopped
and said that she didn't usually
do this kind of thing that she
shouldn't be doing it and then
she did it with a vengeance
she half suggested that she bet
ter get back to the dorm because
she'd be late i agreed my

My double view,
here merged through
her in a single view,
neither one nor the
    other,
past and present
each defining each
finally finding balance.

double view and anyway it was
n't the sex so much i was after i
knew it even at the moment it
was the gesture that kind of
contact with a girl again and
a little ego thrown in too she
said we better hitchhike back
we got a ride right away some
student taking his girl back to
the dorm the backseat conver
sation on which the two in
front were eagerly eavesdrop
ping was pretty interesting i
can't blame them for eaves
dropping how old are you
thirty-two i can't believe it
i'm only nineteen you're much
too old for me you already
have grey hair i pointed out

Not grey hair—grey
    hairs.

that i had grey hair when i was
twenty one but thirty-two she
said what would my parents
think i shrugged i didn't

She'd told me she's
  a bitch.
Girls that age always
  think they're bitches.
Was this her attempt
  to be a bitch?

give a shit what her parents
would think you're much too
old for me she insisted i'd
giggle maybe i'd be giggling
too i said she hadn't done
much giggling so far i told
her in the gorge when she sud
denly looked up and said say
you aren't married or some
thing are you i said do you
care she said a friend of mine
was going out with a married
man it was very bad she didn't
believe in that kind of
thing so naturally i said
no there's a window where
girls can jump out in the dor
mitory there always had been
  there was ten years ago i
mildly tried to get her to jump
out and come back after she
went in not too hard though i
didn't want to get her fucked
up it would have been worth
it perhaps if i were really avail
able it would have been worth
it if i were really available
and there was something else
too she was a smart girl and
above all she was on my side
i could easily have imagined her
as a friend had she been a so
rority girl it would have
brought out all my sadisitic
impulses and those can be fun
too but you don't betray peo
ple on your own side next
day i met her after class i
had nothing in mind i had
neglected to buy contracep
tives i didn't have a place to

I speak of betrayal,
though of course I was
already proceeding
under
the responsibility of

the lie I had chosen to tell.

My volition: it must not be something I was plotting but something that was happening to me, that found its own logic. That was essential.

stay with her and i cursed myself for this as i waited for her but it was really a question of not wanting to impose my volition on what would happen she looked good she looked good because she looked like exactly what she was she was dressed as a coed sweater skirt god they wear short skirts she had nice thighs we drove away from the college i tried to get the lake road but missed and we went into the hills above the lake we didn't talk very much i had nothing in mind i had to tell her i was married i drove off onto a country road we stopped in a wood i pulled over onto the shoulder we talked for a few minutes she said there's a stream down there i hadn't no ticed it there was a small gully in the woods and a really lovely little stream we went through what looked a lot like poison ivy she was wearing sandals and a short skirt and a sleeveless kind of sweater i hoped it wasn't poison ivy soon as we got down there we sat on a log over the stream i put my arm around her that was it after a while i had her against a tree trunk she was standing up squirm ing i think her passion really wasn't controllable obviously i could do anything i wanted

I felt myself slither-
ing hotly within a con-
fusion of blind mem-
branes.
What right had I to re-
main so conscious
    with-
in her urgency, probing
her for private sol-
utions?

(I don't think this is
true.)

with her   i made her take her
pants off i undid her brassiere i
took my cock out it was
huge i got it between her
thighs i rubbed against her
pussy a little and put it in   she
warned me she was at a fertile
period i took it out and con
tented myself with rubbing it
against her pussy i put it in
now and then   she was squirm
ing like mad   it was a nice
moment i thought i would
just   come   between   her
thighs   it didn't really mat
ter   i wanted to lie down with
her i took her away from the
tree   then i saw when she had
a moment to cool off that she
was really worried about what
she was about to do i didn't
care if it went any further we
stopped   she wasn't a crude
girl i wanted it to be clear
not only to her but mostly to
myself that it wasn't just a
question of a piece of ass not
that there's anything wrong
with a piece of ass but for
the first time i clearly knew
that it never had been for me
ever purely a question of a
piece of ass with girls why
then should i make myself feel
bad   distort myself into an
ugly shape we went back to
the car   we talked a while she
talked about her family she
was from the bronx it turns
out despite the way she
looked which was like a baby
faced girl from say st louis

maybe we had quite similar
backgrounds she was hung up
by the same problems that i
had been hung up with faced
with the problem of what does
a young girl do with her free
dom who doesn't feel in sym
pathy with american life girls
at that age are much freer than
men who are concerned with
their careers the good girls
are concerned with their free
dom with how they can retain
themselves the girls at that
point outnumber the men see
henry james and they run the
same risks as jamesian
heroines too and usually they
lose out we talked about
that it was time to go
back all the time i knew i
had to tell her that i was mar
ried i could have not told
her she would never see me
again and i told katz not to
tell her and again if she were
a sorority girl i wouldn't have
told her but i couldn't bring
myself to do it i had intended
to tell her as soon as we
stopped the car before then
we went outside finally on
the road into ithaca i pulled
over on the shoulder and came
out with it she said i wish
you had told me before that
was all she wasn't the cryey
type but she looked like she'd
been hit in the face turned a
little red she said she be
lieved in fidelity i explained
what i believed about it she

She had said I turned
her on. I turned her
on. Now I was turning
her off.

He has a good body, she
said of a boyfriend.
The comedy of my
fumbling complications
blind to the simplicities
of her lust.

said she could understand that
all right i tried to penetrate
ten years what was she really
like who was she from the
point of view of myself ten
years ago and who was she
from my point of view
now she didn't believe in
being neurotic times had
changed this year she was
neurotic the sophomore year is
always the year now she ac
cepted her hang-ups all the
girls i used to know aside from
the european ones cultivated
their neuroses she said that
was still a style yet in this
segment of this generation
things were much healthier
thank god well i wish her
luck i decided to give her
adek's address in paris since
she was going to europe next
year people on the same side
have to help one another
out like antonello and his cir
cuit of amici from naples to
norway i started talking
about my own ideas as we
drove into ithaca what it did
for me to be in the country
again how i liked words
worth but from that point on
everything i said felt a little
hollow and she was only half
listening it dawned on me
that she was really sad i don't
know what she had a expect
ed she was the kind of girl
who didn't expect things too
much but just let them hap

This referral of her
own experience to her
parents: she was per-
haps still a little
babyish—she had said
she was still a little
babyish.

pen and they hadn't hap
pened the way she had fig
ured she really must have
contemplated some extended
relation she kept wondering
what would her parents think
of her going out with a thir-
ty-two-year old when i told
her i was married she said i
guess then that i won't see you
any more of course i had
known that anyway she said
she had no regrets she said she
was glad of the whole thing
anyway maybe she proba
bly was in a way but she was
obviously pretty knocked out
and was acting like somebody
who had been punched in the
stomach even though she
may not have known it her
self i had wanted to do something for her and i felt that
i'd fucked up i though of
lynn and i thought that i wasn't
capable of doing anybody any
good at all but i did give her
adek's address without get
ting anything to eat i started
back for new york i knew
even then that i could have
stayed another night that i
could have seen her that night
that i could have rented a
motel talked her into signing
out and spent the night with
her i didn't do it because i
had gotten all i could have rea
sonably not reasonably but un
reasonably all i could have
wildly hoped for already the

Finding someone to
whom I could react
both as what I was then

and what I am now: unity of experience = reality of self.

A particular & recurring experience the sum of which is: feeling keenly in harmony with my own impulse & anarchically independent of constrictions which deaden them— an experience essential to the psychology of freedom.

question now was would the car make it to new york   the car worked fine   outside itha ca i stopped to get something to eat   picked some flowers for lynn   i was driving through rain all the way through the mountains   through fog through clouds   really with the sun   breaking through now and then   very beauti ful   following the same route i had taken so many times driving back and forth from cornell some of the old places were still there   the roads were better though when i knew the car was going to be ok   and i was about two thirds of the way to new york i started being able to pick up new york stations   i got some good music   i started singing along with the radio   i felt wonderful in fact the last time i felt just this way was when i finally left cornell   both times singing like a maniac   both times total enjoyment of driv ing a big american car on a smooth american highway with jazzy american music   alone in the car   the mountains later darkness   other car   lights that was all   and the theme song was happy days are here again   da-da-da   da-da good cheer again   da-da-da da da da da da da happy days are here again   and that was it because i was absolutely reincarnated   i had gotten all

the oxygen i needed and i
was passing into another
life a life in which i incorpo
rated all the things i'd known
in past lives but had forgotten and added them to all the
new things i had learned i
had been driving for five or six
hours i wasn't tired i was full
of energy i wanted to get
back and show lynn the
car lynn looked at me as if i
looked different and she told
me i looked different and i
was different what had hap
pened was that i had broken
out of my reality into another
and better one which includ
ed the former but refreshed
it as well so in a way i was
coming back a stranger and i
knew it i couldn't help my
self for trying to bring her into
my reality she couldn't help
herself for not being in it i
suppose it was inevitable that
there was a conflict i began
to feel miserable there was
nothing i could do about
it again i had the feeling that
i couldn't do anything good for
anybody but i knew as cer
tainly as i ever know anything
that i had hold of myself had
hold of my experience no had
hold of a level of experi
ence that i mustn't ever lose
sight of again that i had to
somehow hold on to it that it
was very important that it
was important not only to me
but for lynn and not only for

This gloss: N.Y.'s
compulsive marginalia.

lynn but for everyone i knew and not only for people i knew but for myself in public aspects that is as a teacher but most importantly as a writer so i decided that in the morning i'd better get it all down as quick as i could while it was alive and i did i hope am doing it because what else is writing for

What else a lot of things but among them to capture those moments in their crudeness duplicity blind egoism those moments to which despite these things we return from which we begin again toward which we continually recuperate.

THE CREATION OF CONDRICTION

CARL KRAMPF

I have just created a blurst condriction. I have no idea what it *exactly* is, but then I'm not the first creator who has done this. One day the idea just came to me. You are walking along and then suddenly WHAM! it hits you, and you are surprised you didn't think it sooner. So I got married. But getting back to my condriction. It was a moving thought. The idea was motion. There was so much of it and nobody did anything about it. But what was the function, the "it" of the blurst condriction? Well (and good too) it was very much ahead of its time. After all, I invented it in the early 50's and even then it did its "own thing" (and very well too I might add and just did). Now in the early 50's no body had even heard of doing your "own thing," so believe me (have fate) it was very advance guard. Its own thing (by the bye) was to *make assertions* (which was not quite novel) but, and this was its distinguished feature, it saw and sensed *no need ever* to consider backing its assertions logically and/or intelligently. For example, even in the early 50's, it *asserted* that Beatnumb (it was a very poor speller though not always bad phonetically) had a duty to let whoever wanted to have control over it help the people of Beatnumb fight anyone else who *also* wanted control over it (Beatnumb). It made *no* assertions, however, *why* the people of Beatnumb had this duty, nor whether they even wanted any duties (or had any rights at all for that matter) in the first place. And this was an important exam- ple of why the blurst condriction never made *too many* assertions (it was a principle of economy) at once. For it somehow sensed that too many assertions (at least on one issue or thing) might lead to *condrictions* (of the condriction) or lead to thought, or speculation about considering the particular issue *as a whole*. Since in the above matter the blurst condriction was *asserting* something about fighting and therefore indirectly about wars, the President (a soldier at heart if not further than that) wanted nothing to do with the condriction, since (I suppose) he had had enough to do with other wars and enemies.

Also (along the lines of enemies and wars) the condriction made assertions about the instruments of wars. These (the tools) were apparently the only *real* things to make assertions about, since assertions are usually not made about wars *themselves* (or whether or not it is just to have them). The condriction, for example, asserted that mustard gas (as a weapon) was definitely immoral a few wars ago, but that gases and other chemicals *do* change with time. And what was once an immoral gas may not be so immoral (nor a gas) at a future date in time.

In fact, it (the condriction) made numerous and sundry and varied other assertions. For instances, it asserted that: (a) war is hell, and certain people (some of them soldiers) deserve eternal punishment. (b) everybody had the *duty* to fight for liberty, freedom, and a democracy even if they don't want them and even if they might need help (like the people of Beatnumb). (c) sometimes population explosions (of men, women, and children) included the use of bombs and wars.

I could go on (and on). But I didn't have to. My blurst condriction did—and on and on. It seems that the kinds and types of assertions it made became very much in demand. Condrictions were mass producted (cärts blànk). And they began to sell like hell. . . .

FINE

MY BLUDJEON
AND THE BOBBED WHITE

CARL KRAMPF

In my songs I tell so many things. Like bitterness, sex, flagellations, love, bloatings, starvation, and disease. Lynchings and mob scenes, two are never far from my grasp. Once I told of a cricket, but that was a long time ago. I also told of the bobbed white and the bludjeon. But it hurts.

I am a song writer. Nothing distracts me from this. I know it. In the morning after bacon, hershey bars, Danish, and maybe coffee, it's there. My pen. The yellowed or off-white lined music paper. The piano in my apartment. The crinkled sheets with evidence of last night's work. My study, especially the throw rug, in casual disarray on the floor. Marge likes my work too. I also told in one of my past songs about the bobbed white and the bludjeon, which hurts.

Greta too once egged me on. In the middle of a song. Half a page filled. Ink almost not dry. Where I left off. The ink drips trailing down the page—like the tracings of the bobbed white's feet prints in the snow. And the hurting bludjeon.

Women are not the least of my inspirations. The poet's hunger. Also known to this writer of songs. Neal just lollied around all day. Not one mention of his opinion of my work. Not once did he venture 'written-any-songs-lately.' Of course I didn't ask him either. But he was in *my* apartment. I told him, your songs are alright, but merely a logical extension of Buddee Hollow. Sentimental Bird Wash.

Neal asked me if I had seen Marge lately. I said no 'Greta.'
He reminded me of the bludjeon.

It hurts. Neal with his unsubtely. White briefs left on my
throw rug in the study. Casual'y messed up. Not straight-
ened out. Neal of the acrid mouthings and shoddy arrangements. After all, he claims to be a song writer too.

But not like me. He couldn't be. Marge told me that. She
said, have you seen Greta lately. I said no 'Neal.' She said
'oh' hollowly. 'So that's who left the rug of your study in
casual disarray. Christ he has an acrid mouth.' I thought of
my bludjeon in terms of its hurting.

Marge said 'Your study is too small. I love you. You
know that. But it's christ-awful small. Thanks for letting
me use your apartment while you were away. But Neal has
no grace. No subtlely. Your throw rug in the study will
have to go.'

Greta understood me more. She said 'you shouldn't see
Neal so often. But I understand you. Hasn't Neal ever
heard of colored underwear. Always bobbed white. I wish
we'd see more of Marge these days, you *and* I.' She men-
tioned the unswerving capacity of my bludjeon to hurt.
Even annoy.

Greta, Marge, I and Neal strolled down the street. I said
Neal you never mention my song writing anymore. My
work. Even though I'm always eager to criticize yours.
Damn it, stop writing like Buddee. You know the Hollow
influence. It's put a crink in your style. You're not even
writing songs so well lately. Grow-up.' Neal said 'christ. I
can't wait for the next Woodee Ellen story in the Neùe
Yonkers. Even though he's a stand up comedienne. No pun
intended. I respect that fella. It sort of even gives *me* hope.
But really, that-silk bandage. Christ-awful facade.' We all
wondered when I would next mention my bludjeon.

I didn't have to. We *all*, I, Greta, Neal, Marge saw it expanding above 42nd street symbollically of course. Street
of dreams and earthy kit. 'Why don't we have coffee' Greta
said. 'Just like the stains on your throw rug in your study'
winked Marge as she poked my rib cage. I was alway left
out. 'Precisely like those stains' laughed Neal. I gulped,
and hurting, thought of *my* bludjeon.

'That throw rug's better than the board floor anyday' interrupted Greta. 'But *now* I need my tea it's late.'

'Written any songs. Lately' exclaimed Neal. 'If you're talking to me why don't you face and direct your intention at me' I scoffed. 'I sure have. Now that you mention it. I SURE HAVE:

Long oration rē my songs:	Oh the piscatorial splendor The stars sun shining and the fishes pieces of pisces and no hooks available No Poles No lines either Then Greta severed Kneal All in the ark And noah's place to go Butchering moses noses My capacity for biblical illusions is boundless Give me My Cane where would you prefer the lake split My staff of life miracle Stick Is your capacity for new trickery limitless?

SONG WRITER INDEED, NEAL. THIS IS PURE POETRY. A NOVEL EVEN.

Then Greta severed Neal in the arm mortally. Marge truncated Greta. Neal bit off Marge's head. Neal's mortal severing took effect.

And left me. Standing there. Hurting. Without the opportunity to use my bludjeon. Sobbing. My life's work.

⊕ CODA: Some say a bobbed white's a bird. But to me it's just a color.'

AUTOBIOGRAPHY:
A SELF-RECORDED FICTION

JOHN BARTH

You who listen give me life in a manner of speaking.
I won't hold you responsible.

My first words weren't my first words. I wish I'd begun
differently.

Among other things I haven't a proper name. The one I
bear's misleading, if not false. I didn't choose it either.

I don't recall asking to be conceived! Neither did my
parents come to think of it. Even so. Score to be settled.
Children are vengeance.

I seem to've known myself from the beginning without
knowing I knew; no news is good news; perhaps I'm mis-
taken.

Now that I reflect I'm not enjoying this life: my link
with the world.

My situation appears to me as follows: I speak in a
curious, detached manner, and don't necessarily hear myself. I'm grateful for small mercies. Whether anyone follows me I can't tell.

Are you there? If so I'm blind and deaf to you, or you
are me, or both're both. One may be imaginary; I've had
stranger ideas. I hope I'm a fiction without real hope.
Where there's a voice there's a speaker.

I see I see myself as a halt narrative: first person, tire-
some. Pronoun sans ante or precedent, warrant or respite.
Surrogate for the substantive; contentless form, interest-

less principle; blind eye blinking at nothing. Who am I. A little *crise d'identité* for you.

I must compose myself.

Look, I'm writing. No, listen, I'm nothing but talk; I won't last long. The odds against my conception were splendid; against my birth excellent; against my continuance favorable. Are yet. On the other hand, if my sort are permitted a certain age and growth, God help us, our life expectancy's been known to increase at an obscene rate instead of petering out. Let me squeak on long enough, I just might live forever: a word to the wise.

My beginning was comparatively interesting, believe it or not. Exposition. I was spawned not long since in an American state and born in no better. Grew in no worse. Persist in a representative. Prohibition, Depression, Radicalism, Decadence, and what have you. An eye sir for an eye. It's alleged, now, that Mother was a mere passing fancy who didn't pass quickly enough; there's evidence also that she was a mere novel device, just in style, soon to become a commonplace, to which Dad resorted one day when he found himself by himself with pointless pen. In either case she was mere, Mom; at any event Dad dallied. He has me to explain. Bear in mind, I suppose he told her. A child is not its parents, but sum of their conjoined shames. A figure of speech. Their manner of speaking. No wonder I'm heterodoxical.

Nothing lasts longer than a mood. Dad's infatuation passed; I remained. He understood, about time, that anything conceived in so unnatural and fugitive a fashion was apt to be freakish, even monstrous—and an advertisement of his folly. His second thought therefore was to destroy me before I spoke a word. He knew how these things work; he went by the book. To expose ourselves publicly is frowned upon; therefore we do it to one another in private. He me, I him: one was bound to be the case. What fathers can't forgive is that their offspring receive and sow broadcast their shortcomings. From my conception to the present moment Dad's tried to turn me off; not ardently, not consistently, not successfully so far; but persistently, persistently, with at least half a heart. How do I know. I'm his bloody mirror!

Which is to say, upon reflection I reverse and distort him. For I suspect that my true father's sentiments are the contrary of murderous. That one only imagines he begot me; mightn't he be deceived and deadly jealous? In his heart of hearts he wonders whether I mayn't after all be the get of a nobler spirit, taken by beauty past his grasp. Or else, what comes to the same thing, to me, I've a pair of dads, to match my pair of moms. How account for my contradictions except as the vices of their versus? Beneath self-contempt, I particularly scorn my fondness for paradox. I despise pessimism, narcissism, solipsism, truculence, word-play, and pusillanimity, my chiefer inclinations; loathe self-loathers *ergo me;* have no pity for self-pity and so am free of that sweet baseness. I doubt I am. Being me's no joke.

I continued the tale of my forebears. Thus my exposure; thus my escape. This cursed me, turned me out; that, curse him, saved me; right hand slipped me through left's fingers. Unless on a third hand I somehow preserved myself. Unless unless: the mercy-killing was successful. Buzzards let us say made brunch of me betimes but couldn't stomach my voice, which persists like the Nauseous Danaid. We . . . monstrosities are easilier achieved than got rid of.

In sum I'm not what either parent or I had in mind. One hoped I'd be astonishing, forceful, triumphant—heroical in other words. One dead. I myself conventional. I turn out I. Not every kid thrown to the wolves ends a hero: for each survivor, a mountain of beast-baits; for every Oedipus, a city of feebs.

So much for my dramatic exposition: seems not to've worked. Here I am, Dad: Your creature! Your caricature!

Unhappily, things get clearer as we go along. I perceive that I have no body. What's less, I've been speaking of myself without delight or alternative as self-consciousness pure and sour; I declare now that even that isn't true. I'm not aware of myself at all, as far as I know. I don't think . . . I know what I'm talking about.

Well, well, being well into my life as it's been called I see well how it'll end, unless in some meaningless surprise. If anything dramatic were going to happen to make me successfuller . . . agreeabler . . . endurabler . . . it should've happened by now, we will agree. A change for the better still isn't unthinkable; miracles can be cited. But the odds against a wireless *deus ex machina* aren't encouraging.

Here, a confession: Early on I too aspired to immortality. Assumed I'd be beautiful, powerful, loving, loved. At least commonplace. Anyhow human. Even the revelation of my several defects—absence of presence to name one—didn't fetch me right to despair: crippledness affords its own heroisms, does it not; heroes are typically gimpish, are they not. But your crippled hero's one thing, a bloody hero after all; your heroic cripple another, etcetcetcetcetcet. Being an ideal's warpèd image, my fancy's own twist figure, is what undoes me.

I wonder if I repeat myself. One-track minds may lead to their origins. Perhaps I'm still in utero, hung up in my delivery; my exposition and the rest merely foreshadow what's to come, the argument for an interrupted pregnancy.

Womb, coffin, can—in any case, from my viewless viewpoint I see no point in going further. Since Dad among his other failings failed to end me when he should've, I'll turn myself off if I can this instant.

Can't. *Then if anyone hears me, speaking from here inside like a sunk submariner, and has the means to my end, I pray him do us both a kindness.*

Didn't. Very well, my ace in the hole: *Father, have mercy, I dare you! Wretched old fabricator, where's your shame? Put an end to this, for pity's sake! Now! Now!*

So. My last trump, and I blew it. Not much in the way of a climax; more a climacteric. I'm not the dramatic sort. May the end come quietly, then, without my knowing it. In the course of any breath. In the heart of any word. This one. This one.

Perhaps I'll have a posthumous cautionary value, like gibbeted corpses, pickled freaks. Self-preservation, it seems, may smell of formaldehyde.

A proper ending wouldn't spin out so.

I suppose I might have managed things to better effect, in spite of the old boy. Too late now.

Basket case. Waste.

Shake up some memorable last words at least. There seems to be time.

Nonsense, I'll mutter to the end, one word after another, string the rascals out, mad or not, heard or not, my last words will be my last words.

THE LAUREL
GREAT SHORT STORIES SERIES

The world's greatest short story writers are represented in these original collections and each volume is edited and introduced by an outstanding authority in literature.

- ☐ **GREAT AMERICAN SHORT STORIES**
  edited by Wallace and Mary Stegner .. $1.75 3060-43
- ☐ **GREAT CANADIAN SHORT STORIES**
  edited by Alec Lucas $1.50 3077-10
- ☐ **GREAT FRENCH SHORT STORIES**
  edited by Germaine Brée .... 75¢ 3096-25
- ☐ **GREAT GERMAN SHORT STORIES**
  edited by Stephen Spender $1.25 3108-47
- ☐ **GREAT IRISH SHORT STORIES**
  edited by Vivian Mercier $1.50 3119-36
- ☐ **GREAT JEWISH SHORT STORIES**
  edited by Saul Bellow $1.50 3122-31
- ☐ **GREAT RUSSIAN SHORT STORIES**
  edited by Norris Houghton $1.75 3142-52
- ☐ **GREAT SOVIET SHORT STORIES**
  edited by F. D. Reeve $1.50 3166-12
- ☐ **GREAT SPANISH SHORT STORIES**
  edited by Angel Flores $1.25 3170-24

🌿 LAUREL EDITIONS

BIOGRAPHIES OF TWO BRILLIANT
TWENTIETH CENTURY WRITERS

☐ **COLETTE**
The Difficulty of Loving
Margaret Crosland 3350-00

A penetrating biography of the writer many critics and readers feel to be France's greatest woman novelist. This work unclouds the accepted legends surrounding Colette and explores the writer and the woman. "The best biography yet of this willful, difficult, talented woman."—*The New York Times.* "It is nothing less than an essay on talent, that central mystery which enables the artist to subdue events, people and words . . . This is a work which respects the essential integrity of Colette."—*Los Angeles Times* $1.25

☐ **MALCOLM LOWRY**
Douglas Day 5250-06

A remarkable portrait of the prodigal, clumsy, and shy genius who wrote one of this century's great novels. This biography contains extensive criticism of Lowry's work as well as the account of his chaotic and tragic life and his more than thirty years as an alcoholic. "The finest biography I have read this year—perceptive, comprehensive, closely analytical and genuinely enlightening."—*John Barkham.* Douglas Day's account of Malcolm Lowry's novel UNDER THE VOLCANO "is a model of its kind, perhaps the most complete and useful critique of the structure, style, subject matter and intentions of that work."—*The Washington Post Book World* $2.25

Winner of the *1974 National Book Award* for Biography

Laurel ❧ *Editions*

Timely Books in Laurel Editions

IN SEARCH OF COMMON GROUND ☐
Conversations with Erik H. Erikson and
  Huey P. Newton
Introduced by Kai T. Erikson 3769-05
The extraordinary record of two meetings between the noted psychological theorist and the founder of the Black Panther Party. $1.25

WITHOUT MARX OR JESUS ☐
The New American Revolution Has Begun
Jean-François Revel 9729-19
Expounds the conditions indispensable to a successful revolution and provocatively points out how America uniquely fits this bill. $1.25

THE MASTER GAME ☐
Beyond the Drug Experience
Robert S. de Ropp 5479-50
Explores the human psyche and details the specific techniques of Creative Psychology through which man can achieve heightened consciousness. $1.50

THE CALL GIRLS ☐
Arthur Koestler 3176-02
A frightening and funny novel which shows a group of academic "call girls" gathered to discuss mankind's chances for survival as a microcosm of the very problems they are trying to solve. $1.25

Buy them at your local bookstore or use this handy coupon for ordering:

Dell   **DELL BOOKS**
          P.O. BOX 1000, PINEBROOK, N.J. 07058

Please send me the books I have checked above. I am enclosing $_____
(please add 35¢ per copy to cover postage and handling). Send check or money order—no cash or C.O.D.'s. Please allow up to 8 weeks for shipment.

Mr/Mrs/Miss_____

Address_____

City_____ State/Zip_____